PRICKETT'S WELL

Who the Body is?

E D I S O N   T   W I L L I A M S

Published by Wilbur Investments Ltd
Old Mill House
Clermont
St. James
Barbados BB23024

This book is a work of fiction.
The events, characters, names and incidents described are products of the author's imagination. Any resemblance to persons alive or dead is coincidental. The names and locations of actual places mentioned in this book are there only for effect, with no intention from the author to link them to real events

Prickett's Well

What mystery pervades a well!
That water lives so far
A *neighbor* from another world
Residing in a jar.

Emily Dickinson

"I wonder what we would find If we search-lit every well in Barbados."

Detective Sergeant AD Crick

PREAMBLE

Prickett's Plantation, St. Lucy, Barbados

They started harvesting the sugar-cane crop late that year. It was the end of March and, in spite of three months of intermittent unseasonal rainfall, the ground was still hard and dry. Light grey puffs of scattered clouds drifted slowly over the island that morning but without any real threat of rain. On the contrary, the morning was already heating up, the clouds offering only occasional respite from the near-equatorial sun.

Benjamin McCarthy drove the dull-red mechanical cane-harvester between the fields of tall, ripe sugar-cane along the rocky cart-road, one of a network of similar roads across the island's agricultural lands, originally designed for carts drawn by horse, oxen or donkey but still called cart-roads. Straight ahead at some distance, the land rose gently to a rocky, sour grass mound with a single flamboyant tree at its summit. McCarthy and his friends had flown kites there when they were youngsters. He turned the harvester to the left when he reached the four-cross intersection, drove to the far end and waited for the receiver truck to come alongside. Soon, the commingled sounds of hydraulic motors, elevators, blowers, cleaning fans, and choppers biting into the stalks of the tall, sweet grass shut out the cawing of black birds and white cattle egrets. The birds swooped around the machines, keeping sharp eyes out for pickings from the freshly disturbed earth and ignoring the cane-cutting cacophony completely. Cut stalks of sugar-cane flew into the first of the two caged trays of the accompanying tractor-drawn contraption. The sweet smell of sugar-cane permeated the air. A dust cloud churned in the wake of the machines.

Up and down, up and down, the machines travelled, stripping the field of its produce. Soon the first tractor trailer departed for the sugar factory and was replaced by a second, with young Joe Padmore at the wheel. McCarthy slowed the harvester as he approached the middle of the cane-field, looking out for the familiar four-foot high coral stone surround at the top of the well there. He stopped his machine a couple of feet in front of the stonework. He unscrewed the cap of the silver flask next to him, put the flask to his head and downed some of the cold mauby it contained. From a brown paper bag, he extracted a cheese cutter, bit a chunk and chewed it slowly. Finished his morning snack, he tidied up and prepared to resume his work.

He might have missed the shoe as he was about to back away, but "It called me," he said later. Older Bajans talk about this kind of instinct as if it were a separate being talking to them, what they termed *a mind*. "A mind tell me to do this," they would say, and one had to be very careful about ignoring or overruling what *a mind* told you to do. McCarthy's mind told him, "This don't look right. What the hell would a woman's shoe be doing in the middle of a cane-ground, next to a well?" He applied the handbrake and let the harvester idle. He eased his portly frame out of the driver's cabin, jumped to the ground and approached the shoe. Just then something else caught his attention, about eighteen inches away to the right: a bit of gold chain protruded from under the cane-trash. He reached down and gingerly pulled it to him. A gold bracelet with heart-shaped jewels emerged from under the trash. McCarthy stared at the bracelet then looked at the shoe, a stern, quizzical look on his face. In spite of the dust and dirt, the bracelet looked like something of value.

"Joe. Joe. Joseph," he yelled at the tractor driver. "Cumma...come here, boy."

Joe understood the unmistakable sound of urgency in McCarthy's voice. He dismounted and moved quickly in the direction of the older man.

"Looka' this." McCarthy held the bejewelled bracelet up to the young man's eyes then turned and picked up the shoe. It was a stylish, deep-red shoe with red studs all over and a spike for a heel. "And looka' this."

Joseph tilted his head to a side and studied the objects in McCarthy's hands.

"Look, Cinderella gone long time, so let we pelt the shoe in the well and see how much a cash-for-gold man would pay for the chain," said Joseph with a long steupse, the air sucked through his clenched teeth making a loud noise.

McCarthy stared at the young man, a scowl on his round, fleshy face. "Joseph Padmore, what kind of idiot you is? What you think these doing in the middle of a cane-field next to a well? You think they drop out of a airplane?"

The dismissive look on Joseph's face transformed to one of concern. "You mean…?"

"Yes. Call the police."

"Jesus Christ, McCarthy."

Joseph tugged a cell phone from his pocket, punched in 211 and asked to be put through to Greenfield Police Station. He handed the phone to McCarthy, then walked briskly over to the side of the well and peered in.

"This is Greenfield Police Station?" asked McCarthy as soon as the phones connected.

Station Sergeant Derwen "Woodie" Griffith took a bit of convincing about the need to drop everything and head down to Prickett's Plantation. "A woman's shoe and a chain in a cane-field could be the result of different scenarios. An upset man coulda tossed the shoe and chain into the cane-field."

True, McCarthy agreed, the old cart-roads, when they were shielded by ten- to twelve-foot high ripe sugar-cane plants, provided excellent concealment and were favourite parking spots for lovers, but sometimes, also, people who preyed on lovers.

"Not this far, Sergeant. We in the middle of the cane-ground right next to a well."

McCarthy joined Joe at the well. The two men peered into the dark depth, gave their eyes time to adjust, but could see nothing and after a few minutes they retreated, put off by the dank earthy smell that rose to greet them.

About forty minutes later, a white police SUV rocked its way across the uneven ground and came to a stop near the two men and their machines. The SUV had wide vertical swathes of blue and yellow reflective paint on its sides along with a written promise to *SERVE, PROTECT AND REASSURE*. The two officers exchanged greetings with the two men.

"I only come myself because it is you, you know," said the burly sergeant to McCarthy. McCarthy held out the shoe and the bracelet. The sergeant took the bracelet, raised it to eye level and let out a sharp whistle. "I ain't no expert, but this got to cost some money."

He took the shoe and passed both items to the constable. "Put them in a bag," he said.

The constable reached out, took the items, turned them over in her hands and studied them. "This shoe ain't no cheap shoe, either. See this red sole? This is a Christian Louboutin. And if these are real diamonds on the ankle bracelet, whew.... She ain't wear this shoe in here, though. This spike heel ain't got on no dirt, just dust." The constable strolled over to the SUV, still studying the objects in her hand.

The group walked over to the circle of coral stone at the top of the well, torch lights in the hands of the police officers. Light flooded the two hundred feet of the well. Four pairs of eyes peered after the beams of the two Maglite LED search-lights.

"I see something," a voice said.

"Me, too," said another.

"We could be looking at a animal down there... but this shoe and bracelet.... I think I should call Superintendent Thomas," said Station Sergeant Griffith.

A second police SUV arrived, this time from Crab Hill, and a larger circle of heads peered into the well.

"This could be another Cane-field Murder," one of the new officers said.

"No way. Different MO," said the sergeant.

The speculative discussion continued. There was a gradual drift of people to the site as news trickled out about the police presence in the cane-field. Station Sergeant Griffith ordered the site cordoned off. Two of the officers cut stalks of sugar-cane and stuck them in the ground on the shorn section of the cane-field to mark out a perimeter. They fetched yellow tape from their vehicle and wrapped it around the well and the cane stalks.

A Land Rover drove up. A man with a ruddy complexion, collar-length sandy hair protruding under a wide-brimmed straw hat, and wearing a khaki shirt and long khaki pants, got out. Sergeant Griffith recognised him as George Skeete, the manager of Prickett's Plantation.

"Wha' gine on here?"

The Station Sergeant brought him up to date. When he finished, George Skeete asked, "These men can get back to work now?"

Station Sergeant Griffith nodded and said, "I know how to find them when I want them."

McCarthy and Joe slowly moved their machines to the other end of the cane- field. It was a rectangular field, the well almost dead centre. The men turned the machines around at the far end and started to mow down sugar-cane in the direction of the well, stopping each time as near to the well as possible. The drivers positioned their vehicles near to the well during their lunch break, taking in the scene and repeating the story of their discovery over and over, enjoying a few moments of fame, until they resumed their duties. The receiver trucks went and came and finally the well head was the only solitary thing standing in the cane-field. Sergeant Griffith told his men to expand the cordon of yellow tape to create a square, with the well at the centre.

"We only got one report of a missing woman right now, but expensive chain and shoes don't fit that profile," said Sergeant Griffith to the group of policemen.

The spectators' sad, expectant faces betrayed their anticipation of the worst. They spoke in low tones and as if they already knew exactly what had happened: that a body was in the well; that it was a woman's body and that she had been put there by a man.

Over the last forty years, there had been about a dozen unsolved murders of women in Barbados. A number of the victims were found in cane-fields. These particular unsolved cases became known as The Cane-field Murders.

Theories abounded among the spectators. "This time she won't *gi'* he none and he choke she and pelt she in de well."

"Or, you know, some men can't *tek* a horn."

"How you know is a man? They got so much wickers 'bout here now."

"These people want *hinging*."

"They don't *hing* nobody 'bout here no more. Is all manslaughter, nowadays."

There had been, in recent years, about two dozen murders annually in Barbados; or rather about two dozen people unlawfully killed, since most charged with murder in recent times eventually had the charge reduced to manslaughter. This was apparently because of government's failure to make the necessary legislative change to existing law, which mandated an obligatory death sentence for murder and, because of this, ran afoul of international agreements signed by the government. The two dozen annual deaths were on the low end of the scale for the Caribbean. In Jamaica, The Dominican Republic and Trinidad, two dozen would be one to two weeks' work for the criminal fraternity there. Killings in Barbados used to be the result of domestic or other personal disputes or rum-fuelled arguments. This had changed, noted the spectators, in recent times with the popularity of illegal drugs and the accompanying baggage of guns, gangs and the gangster culture.

A short elderly man began to speak, and the few spectators drew closer to him. He spoke with authority and in that very distinguished Bajan accent that socio-linguists would describe as acrolectal. It was as if he was in a classroom.

"You see, Barbados has arrived at a peculiar definition of murder. The prosecution must prove that the perpetrator not only killed the victim but that he intended to kill the victim. And since the victim can't speak, courts only have the word of the accused, or rather the words of his attorney. An accused shooter may now successfully argue that he intended to wound the victim; but because of his poor aim or the bullet deflecting off a bone or the victim shifting in the direction of the bullet or some other spurious claim, that is the reason the victim died. But our situation may also have something to do with the gaggle of international do-gooders who turn up on our doorstep, or our virtual doorstep, protesting capital punishment for murderers and threatening boycotts or some other form of international censure. Or it may be that the defence lawyers are so much better than the prosecutors. Whatever the reason, capital punishment has not been carried out in Barbados in over thirty years in spite of the fact that it is still law. But it is not simply the fact that murder is now manslaughter, it is the weak sentencing that lets killers out to kill again. Recently, there was the case of a man who killed a woman. It was the second woman he killed. He spent four years in jail for the first. I am not a supporter of capital punishment, but our lawmakers have failed us. The safety of the public is now secondary to the rights of the criminal. Something is wrong with our judicial system."

"Mr. Haynes, you so right. The law all for the criminals, now. They letting out murderers on bail, now, to come and terrorise witnesses and victims' family. But God blin' them, if any one o' them do anything to one o' mine, I ain't want no court, I going manslaughter he." Josiah King gestured emphatically with a pointing finger, waving as he spoke. People around him laughed and he continued, "I laughing, but I ain't mekkin' no sport. Don't think because my name is Joe King that I am joking."

The small crowd and the police officers chuckled. They ignored Josiah's mild profanity. Beseeching God to blind someone was a favourite expression of many Bajans. And some in the crowd had heard Joe King's joke about his name before. He often tacked it on at the end of his usual dogmatic outbursts.

Sergeant Griffith called out, "Mr. King, I must caution you that such a statement in front of so many witnesses could come back to haunt you."

"But Griff, I ain't say that I would murder he, I only say that I would *manslaughter* he. And let muh tell you something, I will get one of them guilty lawyers to represent *muh*." Josiah King's pure basilect delivery added to the humour.

Griff laughed. They all knew Sergeant Griffith well. He was from Date Tree Hill on the eastern side of St. Lucy. An old-fashioned community policeman, he had been at the Greenfield Police Station for many years and was known for settling quarrels without having to resort to an arrest. He was a young corporal when that rank was discontinued by the RBPF, automatically promoting him to sergeant. He was now near to retirement and would most likely be the last Station Sergeant of the Greenfield Police Station. The station was now earmarked for permanent closure. Greenfield was a peaceful place. Located on a hill between Mt. View and Josey Hill, it offered a wide vista of the St. Lucy Lowlands, with its fields of sugar- cane, sweet potatoes, yams, eddoes, poultry farms and scattered villages.

"But Joe, what is a guilty lawyer?" someone asked.

"You ain't know wha' is a guilty lawyer? One o' them that you call when you guilty. You ain't need no big-shot lawyer if you innocent. A idiot lawyer could get off a innocent man."

It now seemed that people wanted to be amused in spite of the possible gravity of the situation. But the mood changed again when a van, with the name Lady Birds Funeral Home written on its sides, rocked its way slowly across the cane-ground followed by an open-back Barbados Fire Service Land Rover. Two men emerged from the Land Rover, one in his dark blue Fire Service uniform and the other wearing a black t-shirt and blue jeans.

Two women in white overalls exited the funeral home van. Some of the police officers joined them at the vehicles and helped to lug equipment over to the well: a wet suit, a tank, breathing apparatus, a helmet with torch, goggles, gloves, camera, a tripod, and a body bag from the funeral home vehicle.

The descent into the well was the task of fire officer Rohan Stewart, a stringy forty something-year-old with the musculature of a fitness fanatic. There were approximately four thousand wells in the 166 square miles of Barbados, dating from a time when sugar plantations and some homes mined their own water. They were now mostly disused, since water from the mains reached all parts of the island.

A second BFS vehicle arrived with four fire officers. They joined in discussion with Rohan Stewart and the other fire officer. Two of the fire officers set the tripod on top the well. Rohan Stewart stripped off his jeans and stepped into a wet suit while another fireman gathered ropes, and made a connection to the hawser on the winch at the back of the jeep, then pulled the other end to the top of the well and handed it over to the men who had set up the tripod. Rohan Stewart stepped into a harness and clipped it to connectors attached to the rope. Two fire officers secured the tank on his back and he pulled on goggles and a mask. He was ready for the descent into the well.

Flashes from Rohan Stewart's camera travelled upward like bottled lightning to the watching policemen at the top of the well. The clicking sounds of the camera shutter bounced upward off the dank walls and echoed like distant cracks of thunder.

Nearly an hour later, the hawser holding the sling that supported Rohan Stewart at the bottom of the well jerked sideways three times, the prearranged signal for his extraction. One of the firemen went over to the back of the Land Rover and pressed a button. The motor of the winch on the back of the Land Rover whined as it slowly wound the wire upwards.

More cars inched their way down the cart-road and more people tramped across the cane-ground. The crowd pressed closer to the yellow tape. Sergeant Griffith yelled out, "Get back. Wunnuh get back, right now." He directed the other officers to spread out to the edges of the cordoned-off area.

The gathering waited in quiet expectation, contemplation. A sweating Rohan Stewart climbed over the top of the well and removed his mask and goggles. He stood unsteadily and held on to the stonework. Sergeant

Griffith helped one of the firemen remove the tank from his back. Another fireman passed Rohan Stewart a bottled drink, which he immediately put to his lips. He stamped his feet on the ground repeatedly to bring back the circulation to them after dangling for nearly an hour. He then leaned close to the sergeant and spoke quietly into his ear.

Sergeant Griffith's eyes widened, his jaw dropped, his head turned sharply to face the BFS diver. "What you telling me at all, man?" Sergeant Griffith's head swivelled in the direction of the zipped body bag now hovering under the tripod at the top of the well. He went over and unzipped it about two feet. He and the firemen peered into the bag. The other policemen approached. The crowd pressed. The body bag was swiftly rezipped by the firemen.

"Guh back, guh back," yelled Sergeant Griffith as the crowd threatened to breach the cordon.

The two attendants from Lady Birds Funeral Home moved in to take the body bag from the firemen. Police officers accompanied them under an alley of craned necks. The jostling crowd backed away to permit passage of the funeral van. Lady Birds' attendants closed the door to their vehicle and stood by to await the arrival of the "doctor woman" to perform what was clearly biologically unnecessary but, procedurally, the correct task of certifying the death. The crowd advanced on Sergeant Griffith and Rohan Stewart.

"Who the body is?" a voice called out.

A wry smile showed briefly on the teacher's face.

"They wouldn't even let we get a peep," said another voice.

Sergeant Griffith was on his cell phone. "...Yes, Superintendent, human skeleton recovered. It has red hair."

The crowd hummed. Someone asked, "It is a white woman?" The question spread through the group of onlookers like fire through canes. Frenzied phone activity erupted. The smart ones photoed, videoed and messaged, the not so smart ones pressed against the sides of fast-talking faces.

CHAPTER 1

When Detective Sergeant A D Crick read the urgent text message from Senior Superintendent Thomas, he turned his vehicle around and headed for the Holetown Police Station. He had already heard about the discovery of the body on his car radio and from colleagues. The message from his superintendent was not a surprise. Crick had been on the trail of a suspect concerning a robbery in Sandy Lane: not the grand hotel but its annex, that original set of exclusive luxury villa developments which, dotted around golf greens, occupied the rest of what was formerly the Sandy Lane sugar plantation. But murder always took precedence over robbery. He drove slowly out of the blocks of low-income terraced houses past a group of young men hunched on makeshift seating at the side of the road. He looked at them and they glared at him, each knowing the other. He had arrested two of them before. He knew that to them he was an enforcer for a power structure that they rejected and one they considered rejected them. To Crick, some of them had succumbed to a way of thinking that sanctioned a range of illegal activities, breaking and entering, armed robbery, dope dealing, you name it. They were from the same place as he, but had chosen a different path, one that put them and him on a collision course from time to time. His younger brother, Marcus, the sociologist, said they were the natural outcome of a well-intentioned but not well-thought-out bit of social engineering. The intention was to provide housing for those unable to provide for themselves; the result was the creation of separate, inorganic communities of the poor and already socially isolated, a perfect recruitment ground for criminal gangs. They had simply built houses and left the building of communities to groups of disadvantaged persons, who needed more than a place to rest their heads. Crick didn't accept Jerome's explanation. As far as he was concerned, the people he pursued and arrested didn't give a shite. After all, not everyone who grew up in a government housing scheme turned to crime as a way of life, and the law-abiding majority lived in fear of this criminal-minded minority. That was why each time they victimised someone on his patch, he chased them down, and it was, "me and them."

He turned right just before Holders, the site of the famous annual Holder's Festival, and took the new, sinuous road through the Sandy Lane golf course leading to Bennett's Road. At the T-junction he turned left and rolled down the hill past palatial million-dollar homes on large lots that rarely seemed to exhibit any signs of life. Perhaps all human activity there took place behind the ornate stonework facades. At the bottom of the hill, he took a right turn onto Highway One, which used to be known as "de low road" by folks three miles uphill in that rural district of Orange Hill, St. James, an old community surrounded by sugar-cane plantations, where Crick was born. He drove past the smartened-up mini strip mall on the right, anchored on one end by Cave Shepherd's duty-free store and on the other by a CIBC First Caribbean Bank. It was the beginning of the Sunset Crest village, with its pre-cast concrete villas and apartments, shops and restaurants. He drove past the medical centre on his right and the decaying hoardings of stalled condo developments to his left. Since there had been no construction behind the wooden hoardings, he always wondered why they hadn't been removed to afford a view of the beach and Caribbean Sea, the asset that might just help their projects get off the ground again. But what did he know? He was only a small-island boy. A little further on, he slowed as he approached the hotel, bank and restaurant complex then turned left, opposite the West Coast Shopping Mall and just before the monument commemorating the British claim to this island once known as Ichirouganaim by its original Amerindian inhabitants. The Holetown civic complex car park was almost full. The complex housed post office, magistrate's court, a Barbados Revenue Authority office, a public library and the Holetown Police Station. The buildings had been renovated fairly recently but, apart from the arched entrance to the police station, no attempt had been made to retain its historical architectural features. The result was a non-descript two-storey building with white plastic windows, painted in a colour that reminded Crick of an old cricket sight-screen's duck-egg blue, which some would describe as paipsey, or insipid.

Holetown was a two-street town. There was a First Street and a Second Street, both located toward the northern end of a four-hundred-meter strip of main road and opposite the upscale Lime Grove shopping mall and the ancient Methodist church. Marcus once told Crick that this was an interesting juxtaposition of God and mammon. Holetown was a little town that had been through an evolution in the last fifty years. It had earned the designation of a town by virtue of being home to regional civic facilities, and it had been the seat of local government up to the early Sixties, when the system was scrapped and all political power transferred to Barbados' national parliament in Bridgetown.

According to Gerald, Crick's father, Holetown used to be home to quite a cross-section of Barbadian society. There were lower-, lower-middle- and middle-upper-income families who lived there, in chattel houses or stone bungalows or more imposing "upstairs" houses. Gerald told him that the Carews, the Simmonses and the Hutsons, prominent Holetown Bajans, once lived there. Now, none of the original inhabitants remained, having taken advantage of the commercial expansion of the little town by leasing or selling their properties to businesses. So, Holetown now bustled with restaurants, bars, shops, malls, banks and much of what Barbadians would find in a larger town, and it had spawned its own suburbs in Sunset Crest, Jamestown Park and Sunset Ridge, all located in what were once sugar-cane fields. Holetown's special place in the history of Barbados, Crick reflected, apart from being the only town in the universe named for a hole, was that in 1627 it was the landing site of the first British settlers to the island—an island already named by previously passing Portuguese sailors who, according to one story, thought the hanging roots of the bearded fig trees along the beaches resembled bearded men,

Barbados in Portuguese. Another story claims they actually saw bearded men, men whose identity remains the subject of speculation.

Crick, still fit at forty-five and fairly athletic looking, sauntered in to the station and greeted the two seated desk officers and a standing sergeant. "You got a big one, Sergeant Crick," one of the female officers on the desk said, shaking her head gently from side to side.

He made his way to the office of Senior Superintendent Cetshwayo Thomas, better known as Chet by his friends and The Chief by his subordinates. He was the Senior Investigation Officer of the Northern Division of the Royal Barbados Police Force in Holetown. The SIO put out a large hand in an invitation for the sergeant to take a seat. He got straight to the point.

"Our first problem is identification. We haven't got a clue who she is, Sergeant. There is no report of a missing white woman. Carrion insects have taken their toll, so the body is badly decomposed, and her skull is very badly damaged. We'll have to wait until they bring in a forensic pathologist to ascertain the cause of death and that could take a couple of weeks. It's an odd case."

"Any idea at all how long she been dead, sir?"

"That is a good question, Sergeant. I am told that she probably died sometime in the last six months, but we will have a more precise dating in due course."

The short, powerfully built superintendent, in his short-sleeved, open-necked, silver-buttoned light khaki suit, cut an impressive figure sitting behind his old wooden desk. He must have had some official duty that morning as he was normally dressed in civvies, or undressed, as Bajans would say. "You understand that if she is a tourist, you are going to have the international press here looking over our shoulders and printing whatever they like."

"Or whatever they *don't* like, sir. Remember the disappearance of the American girl, Natalie Holloway, in Aruba some years ago."

"That is exactly what I am talking about, Sergeant. I have already had instructions to treat this investigation as a top priority."

"But sir, I am not so sure that our victim is a tourist. From what I have heard, the state of decomposition says that she has been down in that well for some time but there is no missing person's report. A schoolgirl shacks up with a boyfriend for one night and we are inundated with calls from her family. In my opinion, this is more likely to be a spouse or partner murder, where the killer is in a position to provide a reasonable-sounding excuse for the victim's absence. That is why, in my opinion, there is no missing person's report. Remember 'Millie Gone to Brazil'? My gut feeling is that she is either local or a resident expat."

"Millie down in the well. Interesting, Sergeant." The SIO nodded. There was the flicker of a smile on his face. It was not an unkind face, an orb of a completely shaven brown head with highlights of bushy black eyebrows and a thick moustache.

The early twentieth century was a period of massive immigration for Barbadians, mostly to Panama to work on canal construction, but also to other places, including what became known as Barbados Town, Porto Velho, in Brazil, to help build the railroad there. The unfortunate Millie of the popular folk song, sung even by children in school choirs and choral groups, had been murdered by her paramour, James Bailey, who explained her absence by telling neighbours, "Millie gone to Brazil." Nobody, least of all the police, believed his explanation, for the simple reason that women either accompanied or followed their spouses to Brazil—they never preceded them. Eventually, Millie's bound and mutilated body was found in a well. The story became part of local lore and history. James Bailey was charged with her murder, convicted and hanged in 1917.

The smile faded from Superintendent Thomas' face and was replaced by an earnest look. He leaned forward as he spoke. "I have requested Detective Constable Lashley from Bridgetown, to work on this case with you. I have heard really good things about her...I have met her and am very impressed."

Crick raised his eyebrows and looked at the SIO, saying nothing for a moment, but thinking, why the ass he want to give me some little schoolgirl on this case? We already have Mason from Greenfield and it is his immediate jurisdiction. And we can also call on Moore from Crab Hill, next door, or Simmons from Speightstown. These guys know the area and the criminals up there. But when he spoke his tone was even.

"She is a promising youngster, sir, but, no disrespect...I don't think we need her, and if we did need someone, I would prefer a more experienced detective. Did you hear how that young Princess Royal College girl vomited all over the place when she saw her first murder victim, the woman that the man stabbed-up in Nelson Street?" asked Crick.

"I know. I heard about it. How the image of the bloodied victim touched her. But I also heard how it motivated her. She became obsessed with the case, and she found the killer. But you know what really impressed the boys at Bridgetown about her? They tell me that she is always thinking and she makes you think, too," said the SIO, wagging a finger in Crick's direction.

"Sir, PRC girls and boys don't normally end up in the police force. They become doctors or lawyers or accountants or teachers or professionals in some area revered by the general population of Barbados."

Princess Royal College was one of Barbados' "elite" secondary schools. Its pupils were creamed off at around eleven years old by virtue of having excelled at a national common entrance examination, which influenced, if not quite determined, the future of many primary school students. The exam was part of the legacy of the island's colonial education system. It had long since been abandoned in England.

"Sergeant Crick, the Shondette Lashleys of this world *are* the future of the Royal Barbados Police Force. She is the youngest detective in the history of the force. The world has changed and policing in Barbados has to change with it otherwise the criminals will run rings around us. For a number of years, our policymakers have been trying to raise the quality of our senior officers. First, they wanted to recruit suitable candidates for officer training school, but this, you will remember, was very firmly rejected by the Police Association, which insisted that senior officers had to come through the ranks. The second strategy was to encourage policemen already in service to pursue tertiary education. Allowances were made for suitable breaks from work to fit in with university schedules. I am one of the beneficiaries of this strategy. You should have taken advantage of this. You have the ability." The SIO's voice rose as he spoke the last few words and his tone suggested annoyance to Crick. Crick did not respond.

As far as Crick was concerned, when he left Northridge Secondary School he was finished with all that academic stuff. In Orange Hill, he grew up hearing about policemen like Cecil Thompson and Barney Lynch. And when he later read the private detective stories of Raymond Chandler and Mickey Spillane, his mind was made up. Becoming a policeman would permit him to follow his mother's repeated boyhood advice: "Always be on the side of righteousness." He liked his work; putting bad people behind bars gave him a kind of satisfaction that was to him unimaginable from any other type of work. But he would be the first to admit that he lacked the kind of political ambition the SIO had and he liked to lime with his friends whenever he could. While he was happy chasing crooks and murderers, he didn't particularly like sitting behind a desk. Paperwork just wasn't his thing. He had already decided that he would retire from the RBPF and become a private detective as soon as he qualified for a pension, rather than continue to work under people who were now his juniors.

The SIO continued, "But there is another strategy I will share with you. And that is to quietly but actively convince bright young minds that there is a future for them in a modern Barbados Police Force. It is an unpublished policy, but I am sure you and others are aware of it. The Police Association can't possibly oppose it, even though it has made some of the rank and file of the membership uneasy. They fear that it will hamper their promotional opportunities; they will very likely be superseded by younger, less experienced but better educated officers. Recruits like DC Lashley are ideal for the force. You know she just missed out on a scholarship to university. She couldn't afford the new fees. Her stepfather wanted to support her but had suffered a mild stroke and was off work for a while during her last year at PRC. She told me that she had been attracted to law enforcement from an early age. She always admired the prosecutors on television dramas and felt that they devoted their lives to righting wrongs.

They were on the side of those who had been victimised. She wants to be a prosecutor. Combining a stint in the RBPF with university seems to her ideal preparation in the meantime."

Crick knew DC Lashley was a done deal.

"I have nothing against this young girl, sir. I will work with her. Who knows? I might even learn something from her." There was no mistaking the hint of sarcasm in his voice. "Now, to get back to the case. It may take a couple of weeks before a forensic pathologist gets here, but I would like to start working on some theories right away."

"What are these theories, Sergeant Crick?" the SIO asked, raising his eyebrows.

Crick sat back in his chair and looked at the SIO, a man two years his junior. He was itching for a smoke but couldn't ask the superintendent to break the law in his own office, so he controlled the urge. He shrugged his shoulders and sat back in his chair. "Well, as I said, I think she may be local or resident. We could start by finding information on a redhead whose partner claims she has left the island. There are not that many redheads in Barbados. It's already on the radio and will be in tomorrow's newspapers. That's bound to bring in some leads. I think we could wrap this one up in short time."

"Sergeant, we have not had any success in arresting the man who was responsible for The Cane-field Murders. Then there was a little girl who disappeared from Eagle Hall, vanished without a trace. Our small size should be an advantage in solving crimes of murder, and our inability to solve these cases is a stain on this police force. We must solve this crime.... Have you considered that this could be an attempted copycat of The Cane-field Murderer?"

"Well, I don't think so, but I suppose it can't be entirely ruled out. First of all, there is a long gap, more than twenty years, between the last Cane-field Murder and the discovery of this body. Then the little we know so far of this victim does not fit the profile of the other Cane-field victims. From what I hear, the jewellery and shoe are an indication that this victim was expensively dressed. She was well off or the companion of someone well off; I imagine she was dressed for a party or some other fancy event.... The Cane-field victims went looking for jobs. They responded to recruitment ads. None of them ended up in a well and not one was white."

"You are right...but our lack of success with those murders still haunts this force. I think of the women often. I am very doubtful about the local angle...an expat is a distinct possibility."

The conversation continued for the next half an hour. Crick kept thinking about DC Lashley. He reminded himself that his agreement to partner with her was not required; it was a done deal. He didn't mind having a woman on the case; he was more concerned about her experience, or rather lack of experience, no matter how clever she was supposed to be. But since Moore and Mason from Crab Hill and Greenfield could assist, both of whom had more experience than DC Lashley, he felt comfortable enough.

The SIO stood as Crick prepared to leave. Crick was about three inches taller than the superintendent, who would have just made the five-foot-eight minimum height requirement for male admission to the RBPF at the time he joined the force. They shook hands and Crick felt the power of those banana-sized fingers of this short, square, tank of a man.

Crick turned, pushed the door open, exited the room and headed out of the station, immediately welcoming the contrast between the fresh warmth of the air outside and the chilly cool of the air-conditioned office. He was dressed casually, in low-cut running shoes, light brown pants and a matching loose-fitting polo shirt, worn outside to cover his holstered Glock. He put on his Ray Bans, lit a cigarette, and strolled toward the beach. The smell of his tobacco mixed with the kitchen exhaust from the Surfside Beach Bar combined to blot out the scents of the sea. Tanya and Natalie came to mind. He quickly cast aside those thoughts; instead he focused on the scene in front of him and the reggae music coming from Surfside, over to his right. Straight ahead, a dozen small boats lolled in the calm, blue-green waters of the Caribbean Sea. A rather large yacht slid slowly across the horizon, heading north. Tourists mingled on the beach in the burning sun. A beach vendor sat outside her tented shop waiting for someone to come and buy from her selection of multi-coloured wraps and assorted crafts. The leaves of coconut, casuarina and manchineel trees barely moved in the nearly still air. A group of young men sitting on and around a picnic table chattered away in loud voices interspersed with much laughter. Crick knew them all. Tourists sitting at freshly painted picnic tables shaded by umbrellas just outside the restaurant talked and laughed. A woman was dead, but the world went on as normal. "In the midst of life, there is death," his mother used to say.

"Wha' going on, Crick?" Someone from the picnic table called out.

Crick looked in the direction of the voice and saw a young man with a smirk on his face. He walked over to him and the other fellows.

"You hear 'bout the redhead lady they find in the well in St. Lucy?" Crick asked.

They had, and Crick listened to their theories. "She mussee did down there for a hundred years or more" was the consensus, but he knew differently and told them so. They seemed shocked.

"We will help you, Crick, 'cause you never harass we, like some other cops," the smirker said with as serious a face as he could manage.

Crick lit yet another cigarette and said, "I got to go now, fellers." He turned and walked back toward the station, stopping under an almond tree to finish his cigarette. His thoughts turned to the young female detective. He had heard that she was smart, very ambitious, and was using the RBPF as a stepping stone to a career as a prosecutor, and the SIO had now confirmed this. Well, Crick would soon see what she was made of. He dropped his cigarette butt, ground it into the shallow sand with the sole of his shoe, left the shade of the almond tree and headed back into the station.

"You had a call from a Bobby Lewis," said the constable on the desk, handing him a slip of paper as he passed.

Crick sat at his desk and scribbled on a notepad. He wrote a list of names to call, then he picked up the slip of paper with the number for Bobby Lewis. Crick wasn't surprised that Bobby would try to contact him. Bobby had always shown a more than keen interest in police matters. They met through cricket. In their first encounter, Police against Pickwick, Crick knocked Bobby's centre stump flying with a first ball yorker and goaded him as he made his way back to the pavilion. In the second innings, Bobby scored a defiant ninety-four runs. Mutual respect between sporting adversaries turned into a sort of casual friendship. They didn't visit each other's homes but, as spectators, they often shared drinks at cricket games and sometimes after games. And Bobby would often give Crick a call to see if he could wheedle out any information on a reported crime. Bobby took a close, curious interest in such matters and often had some alternative theory. Crick found him entertaining. Although he was now quite comfortably off, Bobby was the grandson of poor white folks from the eastern parish of St. John, that minority within a minority in Barbados, who migrated to Christ Church when his grandfather was offered employment with a Bridgetown merchant. Bobby was a popular sportsman; he had also played field hockey and football. Sport and his work in insurance put him in touch with virtually every community in Barbados, most importantly to Crick, here, the white community. If there was a local or resident white woman with red hair who had mysteriously disappeared, there was a good chance that Bobby would know, or know someone who would know. Bobby might just have something for me, he thought before dialling the number on the slip of paper. "You have reached...." Crick left a message, including his cell-phone number, for Bobby.

Next on his list was Rohan Stewart. Crick wanted to be sure that Fire Officer Stewart had brought up every scrap of relevant material he found at the bottom of that well and to discuss the other man's observations. Then he called Burgess at Immigration to ask him to check for female visitors who had overstayed. "I don't think she is a visitor but can't rule it out," he said to Burgess. Crick knew Burgess well and even though a formal request from SIO Thomas would go to the Chief Immigration Officer, he also knew that in this small island so much happened through relationships. He also called Station Sergeant Griffith at Greenfield. Finally, he reached out to Detective Constable Shondette Lashley. "I want you to work with me on this case. SIO Thomas is working on the approval for the transfer. He doesn't anticipate any problems." He hadn't planned what to say, but he was comfortable with the deliberately deceptive implication that it was his idea to bring her on board. It was the kind of thing SIO Thomas himself might have done. It was not the first time that he had found himself imitating Thomas' style. Crick understood you became a leader only when you had followers.

Lashley didn't hesitate. "I would definitely like to work on this case." Her obvious enthusiasm was exactly what Crick expected. He knew this case suited her ambition and, not to be discounted, empathy with the female victim. Crick had heard about Lashley from a couple of Bridgetown detectives. It was apparent to them that detective work was not simply a job to her; bringing wrongdoers to justice was important and Crick liked that. But those guys in town had said that she could be difficult.

The SIO popped his head around the corner and said, "DC Lashley is on immediate secondment to the Northern Division. Make contact, pick her up and get going."

CHAPTER 2

The slender, lean-looking young woman, wearing black jeans and white running shoes to match her top and bag, her eyes hidden behind a pair of big round dark glasses, jumped into the white Suzuki Vitara and flashed Sergeant Crick a big smile. She had a high forehead, a longish neck, and an inch of shiny, tightly curled hair. It was a strong face.

"How you, Detective Lashley?" asked Crick.

"What is the white population of Barbados, Sergeant?" she asked as she settled into her seat, removed the bag from her shoulder and placed it between her feet.

"Questions, questions, questions. They tell me you are always asking questions. But you didn't reply to mine. So I guess you're good.... About fifteen thousand people. Why?"

"I am fine," she said, flashing that smile again. Then: "You are wrong." She said this with a frown and levelling a corrective finger. "According to the CIA's report, white Bajans are three-point-two percent of the population, and we are only about two hundred ninety thousand people. Your estimate is way off."

"Now hold on a minute. You asked me what was the white population of Barbados, not the white *Bajan* population. We got expats from all over the world living here now."

"You are on thin ice, Sergeant...."

"And listen to me, don't pay any attention to that CIA information. The CIA is using American standards of whiteness, not Bajan standards. They are very different. In America, you are white if all your known ancestors are white. But in Barbados, you may be white with a black grandmother or grandfather or even one black parent. Basically, if your skin is fair enough and your hair straight or even naturally relaxed (with curls), you are white in Barbados. White is not a simple matter of colour or ancestry, here, it is a cultural matter. Some East Indians, fair-skinned ones, are considered white in Barbados, you know. I wonder where they put the mixed population. That would be interesting."

"Two-point-six percent."

"Two-point-six percent?! They must be joking. Those are definitely American standards. But what do they mean by *mixed*, anyway? I mean, given our plantation history, I wouldn't like to try to put a number on the amount of black Bajans with at least one white ancestor or the number of white Bajans with at least one black ancestor. In two generations, people can change race, you know. It has happened throughout our history."

"Actually, you can't change your race, but your descendants can belong to a different ethnic group," said DC Lashley.

Crick steupsed. "You know exactly what I mean," he said then added, "but you can change your race, if you change country."

"*No, you can't.* You can change your racial identity or classification, which is cultural or political. But that is different from changing your race. And actually," she spoke quickly, "there is only one race, the human race."

A series of pings sounded from the bag between Lashley's feet. She reached in, extracted an iPhone and started massaging the screen.

Crick just looked at her and shook his head. I got a right smart-ass, here, he thought to himself. Then he thought that he wasn't being fair. In fact, her careful use of language reminded him of the Doc. His thoughts turned to the Doc, as he was called. Every school had a memorable teacher. Teachers became great when they, and their teachings, lived on in the memories of their students. D.R. Haynes was one of those teachers. He was deputy-head and taught History at Northridge Secondary. He didn't teach just the prescribed text. He had a wider agenda as a teacher. "History, if taught right, explains. It explains the world; it explains the peoples of the world. It tells us who we are and how we came to be what and where we are. It grounds us. But history is a dangerous subject. It arouses passions. It is not a kind subject. There are people in this world still trying to settle thousand-year-old scores related to some historic ancestral conflict. We must learn to use history but not to let history use us."

The Doc used to say that one could write an entire book on the subject of colour in the history of Barbados; the colour of people, that is. Crisscrossed genes of four hundred years of miscegenation, largely but not exclusively the result of an unbridled variation on what the French called *le droit du seigneur* (and you could trust the French to have a name for it), had produced a potpourri of looks in Barbados. You might encounter someone with two black parents and typical Afric features but fair-skinned. Or you might see someone with dark skin but reddish hair, or freckles, or light wavy hair, or blue eyes or what Bajans call cat eyes. These atavistic variants were even more intricate in the larger Caribbean territories of Guyana, Trinidad and Jamaica, where the admixture of ethnicities was greater. In those territories, it was not unusual to meet a person with recognisable characteristics of African, Indian, Asian and European features. And such a person may be considered black or white, depending on her shade of skin, when visiting Barbados. The Caribbean had been called the world's first experiment in globalisation. One of its by-products was this abundant evidence of genetic drift, this ethnic mélange, which was both celebrated and cursed. It may be celebrated by some, proud of the physical traits of unknown ancestors, but traits that gave them special status and greater self-confidence within their societies; cursed by others who had come to believe that their *Africanness* was inextricably linked to underachievement and a lower status within their community.

Lashley put away her iPhone and said, "Sergeant, the CIA's information comes from Barbados' census, so it is about who *we* say we are, not who they say we are."

"Wow. I thought they were doing their own counting from one of their NSA satellites." Crick laughed then continued. "Times are changing. I feel that sixty years ago we woulda said different. Some people who now classify themselves as black would have previously called themselves mixed."

"Maybe, one day, none of this will matter."

"Maybe, just maybe," said Crick, "but that's a big maybe. Let me ask you a question. If you see a Northern Ireland Catholic and a Protestant walking down the road, would you know which was which, or a Sunni and a Shiite, or a Serb and a Croat, or a Hutu and a Tutsi?"

"No, I wouldn't. I take your point. I really don't understand why our differences are such a cause of friction and worse in this world."

"History, girl, history...the answer is always in their history," commented Crick, trying his best to imitate Doc Haynes' elocution.

"So this Jane Doe, you think she is local or foreign?" asked Lashley.

"She is not Jane Doe, she is Millie."

"Millie?" Lashley asked, turning to Crick with a quizzical frown.

"Millie down in the well...oh Laawd, poor Millie," said Crick, tapping his fingers slowly and rhythmically on the steering wheel while reciting the second line of the folk song.

Lashley snickered. "You know something, Sergeant, how interesting you should give it a sad tone. I have never heard it like that before. It is such an up-tempo song; you wouldn't think it is about someone's death. This says something about our culture. That song mocks Millie's death."

"Not really. That would not have been the intention of the song. You would never have heard about Millie if it wasn't such a popular song. But we can debate that another time. Let us talk about this case."

"If I remember correctly, the original Millie was slashed with a razor and dumped in a well. And we sing and laugh at it? What does that say about us?" said Lashley, ignoring Crick's directive.

"They found her killer; our job is to find this one. So let's focus, Constable."

Lashley frowned, fumed silently, then said, "Well, there aren't a lot of red-heads in Barbados, so if she is local, we should identify her soon enough and then we will find the bastard who put her in the well. One thing for sure, the killer is local, somebody who knew where to find a well in the middle of a cane-field in St. Lucy, the most remote part of Barbados...presumably behind God's back."

Barbados was shaped like a leg of lamb and St. Lucy was the small end, its handle by which it could be gripped by a fist. Crick knew that if you shook St. Lucy, the whole island wobbled. It was the most northern of the eleven parishes, the beginning or the end depending from which direction you approached. It was the only one of the eleven named after a female saint and the second least populated parish of Barbados. Caressed, splashed and bashed by water on three sides, it was practically a peninsula, almost a world unto itself.

"Yes, the killer is her partner or sibling or father, someone who can explain her absence to friends and family," said Crick.

The Suzuki Vitara glided around the James A. Tudor Roundabout by the old Globe cinema, straightened up on Martindale's Road and headed for the Queen Elizabeth Hospital.

In the QEH morgue, they looked at the skeletal remains and the red hair that slid out from the cold drawer. They were drawn to the damage to its skull.

"She get some good blows to she head. She head mash up," said the mortuary attendant.

"Yes. Someone smashed this poor girl's head in," said Lashley, a gloomy expression on her face.

"And she was probably banged around on the way to the bottom of the well. She would have hit the bottom at high speed," said Crick. "We'll have to wait for the pathologist's report."

They both remained silent and thoughtful for a few moments until Crick nodded toward the door.

As they drove out of the hospital's car park, Lashley said, "It upsets me. To see someone, particularly a young person, a young woman, whose life has been ripped away like that. It's a part of my job I may never get used to."

"Believe me, you'll get used to it," replied Crick.

"We need to catch this bastard, Sergeant Crick."

When Lashley was not responding to the pings from her iPhone, she and Crick continued talking about the case as they drove north toward St. Lucy. They recognised this case was different. The victim had been dead for some time, yet no one had ever reported her missing. This was an unknown scenario in Barbados, new territory for this island of small communities where the concept of an unknown person didn't really exist. And the location of the body was puzzling. She hadn't just washed up on the shore. She was placed where someone thought she would never be found. But who was that someone? Only a local would know his way to that well. If she was a single visitor, she would not have checked out of her accommodation, and this would have given rise to a report. It was this that informed Crick's thinking that she was a local or resident expatriate with a partner who could excuse her absence. Once they knew who the victim was, who her family, friends and associates were, they would find her killer.

They were halfway up to St. Lucy on Highway 2A, just past Lancaster, when Crick's cell phone rang. He passed it to Lashley. "Here, you answer it."

"Bobby who?...Yes, he is here but he is driving. Can I say something to him?

... He wants to talk to you."

Crick pulled the SUV onto the shoulder of the road.

"Yes, Bobby.... Later this evening would be fine.... You sound worried.... Eight o'clock at Allman's Sports Bar works for me...see you there."

Crick clicked off and said to Lashley, "A bit strange. Bobby doesn't think he has a lead, but there is something he thinks he should tell me. You will be off duty by then. Do you want to come with me?"

"Sure," said Lashley.

"You'll be off the clock, understand?"

"That's fine with me. How well do you know this Bobby fellow?"

"I know him pretty good. He is a great talker and I a good listener when I need to be, so we complement each other. He is quite a complex fellow. He likes to think he knows the inside story on every event. I am not sure who will benefit more from our meeting. He spends more time on his smartphone than you, thinks he knows everything. He reads a lot but only whatever will reaffirm his own beliefs. He is a Fox News watcher who believes that Barack Obama was born in Indonesia. But he is a true-true Bajan who probably couldn't live anywhere else in the world."

"A real live birther right here in Barbados," said Lashley.

"Yep. And we'll probably meet some more before this case is solved."

The countryside opened up as they travelled further north. Once past Mile-and-a-Quarter, the communities grew noticeably smaller and there were more open spaces, former sugar-cane-fields now covered in wild grasses. Crick always liked the countryside. He grew up in Orange Hill, St. James, just below Apes Hill, and went to secondary school in the north. He knew the north. Most likely that was an additional reason the SIO wanted him on this case and hadn't just left it to the single detective at Greenfield Police Station. They reached the well around 3:30 in the afternoon. The forensics team was still there. A rather huge lighting system straddled the top of the well, its powerful lights turned off, its job done. Lashley recognised the broad back of her cousin Olivia. Olivia was a distant cousin in reality, but family was family. Olivia wasn't in charge of the forensic detail, but Lashley went up and tapped her on the shoulder. "Hi, cuz, what you got for us?"

"Hey, Shonnie. Hi, Sergeant Crick. I am afraid I don't have any good news for you. We found some condoms in various states of decay on the side of the cart- road but can't say at this stage whether they may be related to this case. We may be able to get some DNA from the inside of the shoe. The first responders permitted the harvesters to continue up and down this field, cutting canes and rolling over possible, potential evidence. It is evident that a number of vehicles used these cart-roads. I understand that this is a park-out area. We are assuming he approached the well from its nearest position to the cart-road, which is the side opposite to where they tell us the shoe and bracelet were found, that he threw her head first, and the shoe and ankle bracelet flew off when her leg hit the other side of the well."

Olivia heaved an imaginary body off her right shoulder to demonstrate as she spoke.

"After the throw, he would have turned and gone back to his vehicle, so we have a sense of where on that cart-road the vehicle stopped. There are oil stains in that area, but clearly from more than one vehicle and differently aged. I doubt we'll get fingerprints off the shoe or jewellery, but we'll try. Her other shoe was not in the well, nor has it been recovered. It may have come off in the car or at the original crime scene. As I said, our first responders apparently weren't initially sure that this was a crime and didn't immediately treat it as such. That man over there was only concerned, at the time, with getting his men back to work." She pointed to an old man in khaki pants and shirt and wide-brimmed hat. He was in the company of two women, one older with white-streaked hair and a young blond girl. "He's George Skeete, the plantation manager. He turned up a short time ago. I believe that this is his third visit here today. His second visit was after the body was brought up and he had taken a fresh interest in the case. He wanted to know what he could do to help because he knows this area like the back of his hand. The two women brought those flowers and placed them at the side of the well. The young girl has been in tears. They say they have no idea who the victim might be."

Crick and Lashley observed the trio by the well then Olivia continued, "She has been down there a little while. We scraped the top of the well for possible DNA of the perpetrator. But I doubt that time and the weather have left us anything. We took a lot of pictures of the well, but I am not sure how much help you will get from us on this case at this stage. Obviously, this is the secondary crime scene. It would be most unusual for women wearing expensive shoes and jewellery to be parking out in a cart-road for sex. As of now, we have no idea where the primary crime scene is."

Crick turned to Lashley. "It looks like we are going to have to solve this the old-fashioned way. We have to find someone willing to talk."

"I am going to have a word with the young girl," said Lashley.

Lashley strolled over to the trio by the well, extended a hand and introduced herself to the two females. The older woman cast curious eyes over Lashley, up and down. The young girl was busy texting. She stopped pressing on her smartphone and looked up at Lashley. Her eyes were still moist, her make-up a little smudged.

"How old do you think she was?" the young girl asked.

"It's too early to tell."

"Do you think she has been down there for a long time, for years, maybe?"

"After the forensic pathologist gets here, we will learn all that information. Do you know of a redhead girl or woman who supposedly left the island but has not been heard from for any length of time?"

"No...and none of my friends know of anyone." Her phone buzzed. She turned her wrist and glanced at the screen then dropped her wrist again.

"I didn't get your name," said Lashley.

"It's Samantha. They call me Sam."

"Sam, you seem really upset about this. Is there something you should be sharing with us?"

The young girl fixed a studious stare on Lashley's face then gritted her teeth, shook her head from side to side, and tears ran down her cheeks.

"Sam, I want you to take my number and contact me if you hear anything or remember anything."

Lashley returned to Crick and Olivia and shared her concern about the distressed young girl. "I wonder if she is hiding something from us."

"I doubt she would come here if that was so. Just a case of victim empathy, I think. This affects everybody," said Crick.

"I understand. I already had a message from Meghan, an old school friend studying in Canada, asking about the victim. Meghan claimed me as a cousin our first day at PRC because we had the same last name. We have been friends ever since," said Lashley. She looked back at Samantha—Sam—by the well, still crying into her smartphone. "It doesn't take long these days for news like this to spread."

CHAPTER 3

It wasn't far from the crime scene to Greenfield Police Station, just along Highway 1C and then along winding, potholed roads to a point between Mt. View and Josey Hill. No one today remembered why a police station had been placed in that location more than a hundred years before. It was obviously thought needed at the time. Rural police stations were often located high on a hill, from where the police could spot trouble in the days before telephones existed. So perhaps it was because Greenfield's elevated position gave it a view of the St. Lucy lowlands. But now modern communication and transportation had made it redundant. Like the defunct station at Bissex in St. Joseph, it had outlived its purpose and would suffer the same fate.

"This is like foreign country to me. I remember going to the Animal Flower Cave once on a school trip. But apart from that I've never been to St. Lucy," said Lashley. "I spent my early years in Bridgetown until my mother married my stepfather and we moved to Christ Church."

"I went to school in St. Peter. I know St. Lucy pretty well. You know that there are four towns in St. Lucy?"

"I only knew of four in the whole island. Bridgetown, Oistins, Holetown and Speightstown, and none of those is in St. Lucy. But I used to see Connell Town on the front of buses and always wondered about this fifth town that we weren't taught about."

"Well, in St. Lucy, whoever gave names to places favoured hyperbole, so they have four so-called towns of their own. In addition to Connell Town, there is Moon Town, Swampy Town and Avis Town. The namers also liked exotic-sounding names, as you will discover. "

Greenfield Police Station looked as old as it was: a long, low building with peeled paint that might have been cream at some time. Station Sergeant Derwen Griffith greeted Crick and Lashley in his office. He remained standing as he spoke. He was tall, broad shouldered, a bit heavy around the waist, a powerful-looking figure of a man. He knew Crick. He had taught him how to shoot. Sergeant Griffith's greatest contribution to the Royal Barbados Police Force was his prize-winning marksmanship and his teaching of this skill to young officers. He didn't invite the two officers to sit. He introduced Lashley to Detective Mason. "He will be working wid you on this case."

He turned to Mason. "We looking for a man who know this area good, a man who could find dat well in de middle of a cane-field in de dark," the station sergeant said.

"It need not have been in the dark. This could have been done any time of day. I suspect that it was done while there was some sunlight, early morning or late evening," replied Crick. "The main road back there is not a busy road. There are canes on either side of the road, so once he was not followed he was safe, and once he turned the corner at the four-cross of the cart-road he would be invisible to the world. A vehicle going in and out of that cart-road would not necessarily arouse suspicion, even if it was seen. Once we have information on when she died, your station should try to find out if anyone remembers seeing a vehicle heading down there around that time, anything strange...."

"We know. We just waiting for information. But in de meantime we looking at persons in dis area who we tink could do something like dis," said the station sergeant.

"He is unlikely to be from around here. No, he wouldn't leave a body on his own doorstep. He chose to dump the body there. Don't forget that once the canes are cut the top of the well is visible to passers-by for many months every year," said Crick. "Someone in the area would know that. Anyone from anywhere could be attracted to it."

"If I may say something," said Lashley, asking a permission that she really did not need, it seemed to Crick.

The three men turned toward her.

"An intelligent killer would not put the body on his own doorstep. But what if the killer is unstable or not too smart and simply sought to put the body in a familiar place, a place where he was convinced it would never be found? We should consider that. So a possible suspect in your area would likely be someone with some history of mental illness or someone really challenged."

"You mean a idiot," said Sergeant Griffith.

"I mean what I said. Another thing, Station Sergeant Griffith, did you take any photos of the people who gathered at the scene today, the spectators?"

"No, but I know a lot o' dem. De ones I don't know would just have been people passing who stopped to see what was happening," replied the Station Sergeant. He then turned to Crick and said, "Your old teacher, Doc, was there."

"Really? I will give him a call. I am sure he will have something of value to tell us. That man don't miss much."

"Sergeant, I think we should try to identify all the people who were there today. See if any of the persons you know took pictures on their cell phones. Someone in the crowd could be a person of interest," said Lashley.

"I'll get my team to work on it," said Sergeant Griffith.

They said their goodbyes.

"See you at the briefing at Holetown tomorrow morning," said Crick to Mason.

As soon as they got in the car, Lashley said, "I real hungry."

"Let's go back to Prickett's and see if we can pick up some local gossip. There is a rum-shop there with some good ham cutters. Do you eat ham, or are you one of them vegans?" said Crick, flicking a cigarette out of a pack.

"Ah, Sergeant, I would appreciate it if you refrained from smoking while I am in the car."

"I want to give up on this damned habit anyway," he said, slipping the pack back into his pocket. He then opened the car door, stepped out, walked a few feet away and lit his cigarette. He smoked half the cigarette and threw away the end.

"You were asking if I was vegan?" said Lashley when he returned to the car. "No, sir. I eat everything...have to have my pudding and souse most Saturdays. My favourite TV programmes growing up were on the Nature channel. I accepted long ago that some animals were put on this earth as food for other animals."

The village of Prickett's was made up of mostly chattel houses strung out along either side of a narrow, nearly straight road downhill from Prickett's great house. The village used to be called Prickett's Tenantry until the Barbadian government enacted legislation to facilitate the purchase of plantation tenantry spots of land by long-term occupants at a fixed low cost per square foot. Older folk still called it the tenantry. It had a bygone feel about it, as if modern Barbados had entirely passed it by.

Crick slowed to a stop in the middle of the village then backed into the space in front of Bennie Greaves' ancient Toyota Corolla station wagon at the side of the wooden shop with Banks beer logos plastered all over it. He and Lashley walked up the three wide stone steps and entered the nearest of the three shop doors. Over to the left, around the short side of an L-shaped counter, they saw four men sharing a bottle of white rum. One after the other, they poured shots into small glasses, threw back their heads and tossed the rum down their throats, their faces gurning in that familiar contortion of habitual rum drinkers. They topped up their glasses with water from a small pitcher and swigged that down. One man in a blue shirt swayed constantly. Lashley wondered to Crick how long he had been at it. There was a doorway near to the men that led into a back room from where he and Lashley could hear excited voices and the slamming of dominoes.

At the back of the bar, there was a central doorway leading into the back room with shelves on either side filled with rows of various spirits and packets of snacks. At one end of the bar, there was a glass-fronted upright beer cooler.

This time, or *dis time*, depending on one's socialisation, was how Bajans often expressed speculative opinion on events. But it was said with a degree of certainty, to sound as if it was fact. It could only be exceeded by an emphatic *it got to be*, which was also a statement of opinion. Crick smiled at the *dis times* and *it got to bes* coming from the back of Bennie Greaves' rum-shop.

"Rum-drinkers always seem to know more than anyone else," said Crick.

"Are you speaking for yourself, Sergeant?" Without waiting for an answer, Lashley continued: "Perhaps one day some academic will produce a thesis on the relationship between the consumption of rum and the promotion of knowledge." She laughed a gentle mocking laugh.

Crick looked at her and shook his head. She laughed again, louder and less self-conscious.

The rum-shop was busy for that time of the day. High-pitched discussion abated as news of the presence of the two officers filtered into the back room. The slamming of dominoes paused. A couple of men hailed Crick as he stood at the counter. "What's up, Crick?"..."Wha' happenin', AD?"..."I ain't see you in a long time, man." Crick waved and shouted out names. "Francis, Derek, what's happening?"

Lashley had leaned toward Crick, as if to whisper something to him, when a slightly built short man emerged from the back of the shop with a half-filled glass of white liquid in his hand. He called out, "Artifus Demetrius Crick. Only murder would bring you to these parts. You are pure bad news. But you look good, though."

Lashley bent over, laughing, a hand over her mouth. She straightened up and looked at Crick. "Artifus Demetrius? I was about to ask. My God, what were your parents thinking? No wonder you—and just about everyone else—call yourself AD."

"Herbert Nathaniel Broomes, you ain't change at all," replied Crick, ignoring Constable Lashley.

"What you want me to change for?"

"Well, for a start, you might buy an old school friend a drink."

Broomes laughed. "It is you who hasn't changed. I know what you want. But what about your young lady, what would you like, dear?"

"Do they have bottled water?" asked Lashley.

"They have pipe water, and I can put it in a bottle for you," said Broomes, mock serious. He followed up with a short guffaw.

"Oh. I'll have a Sprite or ginger ale, then."

Broomes walked over to a table on the far side of the bar and rested his glass.

Lolita Greaves appeared behind the counter. The sound of bones scraping wood, coming from the far corner of the back room, signalled the start of a new domino game. Mrs. Greaves looked over the ornate frame of her glasses at Crick. There was a pencil sticking out of her hair over her right ear.

"And what can I do you for, young Crick?"

"A couple of your famous ham-cutters, please."

Mrs. Greaves looked behind her at the remnants of a shoulder of baked ham on an old, large, oval platter, sitting on the bottom shelf of a wood-framed glass cabinet. There was a bit more than enough for two ham-cutters. She turned, extracted the platter, and picked up a long knife. She sliced two salt breads in half, lengthwise, and then proceeded to carve ham off the bone. She poured Bajan pepper sauce over the thick slices of ham she placed in the first salt bread, prompting Lashley to put up a hand and quickly say, "No pepper sauce for me, please."

The detectives made their way to the table with Broome's glass. Broomes followed. As soon as they sat, a figure, a man with a shaven head and moustache, then a second, then a third, the swaying man, began to approach their table.

"They are looking for news. Someone with information would come alone," said Crick softly.

"Skipper, dey know who de woman that get kill is yet?" one man asked in a typically lilting St. Lucy accent.

Crick chuckled, turned to Lashley and asked, "You hear the accent?" The variations in accents in such a small island were a source of amusement to many.

"Yes," said Lashley. "And back in Bridgetown, I still laugh inside when someone says that they bought some nats in de bas stand."

"Well, you are going to be hearing a lot of the St. Phillip accent from Detective Mason," said Crick. "You know, Phillipeans pronounce their parish's name as *Sen Phillop* and speak with what linguists call an '*open-mouth*' accent. But in St. Lucy, it is all down to undulation, that sing-song pattern. No other parish in Barbados has that accent."

A throat cleared loudly. "Dis time, she is some *wutless* tourist dat some man pick up in a night-club. We see some of dem on de beach down the west side wearing *nextkin* to nothing, and all over the beach bums like if dey in a bedroom," the swaying man in the blue shirt sang out.

"It sounds to me like you are blaming this woman for her own death," said Lashley.

The men turned frowning faces toward DC Lashley. They were silent for a moment. They looked at Crick then back at Lashley. They did not ask, "Who she?" but Crick understood that was what was going through their minds. So must have Lashley.

"Fellows, meet Detective Constable Shondette Lashley. She is a rising star in the Force. Now, which of you got something for us?"

The first man to approach them, the one with the shaven head and moustache, glanced around the room. "If we hear *anyting*, you can be sure we will call and ask for you. But we don't feel nobody 'bout here do this."

"Well, we want to hear who did it, not who didn't. You can also speak to Detective Lashley if you can't get hold of me."

The men turned away and rejoined their friends, perhaps a bit disappointed in themselves that they had no news to share.

"It's all everybody's been talking about all day," said Broomes. "They feel she is a tourist. That would be bad news for tourism. And it would put you fellows under the microscope."

"We are always under the microscope nowadays. We work hard to catch criminals. The job is getting more dangerous all the time. We do our part, but the defence lawyers are slick and we have a problem with the sentencing a lot of the time. The criminals have all the rights and there is not enough consideration for the victims."

"You sound like our old teacher Dalton Roosevelt Haynes— the Doc. Do you read his letters to the newspapers or hear him on the call-ins?" said Broomes.

"Of course, I read his letters. I heard he was at the scene this morning. I am so sorry I missed him. His eightieth birthday is coming up in July. Some of the old scholars are planning a get-together for him. Maybe we'll get you to do one of your famous impersonations of the Doc."

"I enjoyed his classes. Such a good teacher and a nice man. Great sense of humour. Very old-fashioned and conservative in his personal tastes but quite radical in his views on history and politics."

"Best teacher I ever had," said Crick.

"Yes, he was. He was the teacher we talked about outside of school, with our friends, our brothers and sisters, even with our parents."

"Yes, man. My parents blamed him when I started to question some of their beliefs, accused him of filling up our heads with a lot of foolishness," said Crick.

"He called the first three hundred years of Barbados' history 'those brutal years of plutocracy.' He said Barbados, like the other Caribbean islands, was 'built on an amoral foundation.' He said the only people with any sense of morality in those early years could be found among the captive peoples, the indentured servants and the slaves. But the Doc gave credit to the reformers, here and elsewhere, who helped make the region into what it is now. We are still a work in progress," said Broomes.

They talked about some of their old schoolmates. Lashley laughed quietly at the stories and some of the nicknames. But when they started to talk about a fellow they called Nuffada Nicholls, she stopped them.

"Wait, wait, wait. You actually called someone Nuffada to his face?"

"Well, yes, up until his growth spurt. Then he became one big fellow and he started bodybuilding. His real name is Nevada Nicholls. But to this day no one knows who his father is, not even he *murr*," said Broomes, laughing hard with Crick.

But Lashley wasn't laughing. "That is cruel," she said, staring at Broomes. They looked at her and she continued: "This fellow had a *murr*, not a mother? I am sorry, but you are being very offensive. "

"Jesus, woman, you take offence too easily," said Crick.

"Ah, she has a point about Nuffada," said Broomes. "Nicknames can be quite cruel, you know. There used to be a one-armed man in Bridgetown, a great cricket fan, and the only name I knew him by was Oneie. And it is the name he answered to. But we are just having a bit of fun, so lighten up. Uh beg yuh."

"Whatever happened to —Nuff—to Mr. Nicholls?" asked Lashley.

"Oh, he became a policeman," replied Crick. "He used to be my partner at one time. He was quite a character. He emigrated. Went to live in the US."

"Didn't he leave under a bit of a cloud?" asked Broomes.

"Yes. He resigned after he was accused of beating up a suspect. He claimed it was self-defence, that the man had attacked him. The man denied it, said that he recognised Nuffada, and when he called out his name Nuffada hit him. He didn't remember anything after that. Nuffada claimed the man had attacked him, that they fought and his injuries were the result of the fight. But it wasn't the first time that Nuffada had been accused of beating up a suspect. Another time, he and another policeman arrested a wanted man. On their way to the station, Nuffada told the driver to stop the car. He turned to the arrested man and told him to get out and run. The man didn't move at first. Nuffada shouted at him, 'Get out and run, you idiot.' The man got out and ran and so did Nuffada, who was a very good track athlete at school. Nuffada caught him, threw him to the ground and started playing football with his torso until the other policeman caught up with them and put a stop to it. They then filed a report that the man had escaped custody and was injured during recapture. Nuffada resigned under some pressure and emigrated. I hear he is a security guard in New York, now."

"I hope you appreciate that this man's violent behaviour was most likely a response to the treatment he received from people like you because he did not know his father. Something for which he should never have been blamed," said Lashley.

"Foolishness," said Crick. "I know a fellow who used to be called Double Ugly. His name was shortened to Doubles, and he never beat a soul. People still call him Doubles, and he is one of the nicest people you could ever know. Intelligent, funny and just plain nice."

"But there was a total difference in their upbringing," pointed out Broomes. "Nuffada was raised by a semi-literate mother who had six children, and none of the others looked anything like Nuffada. Doubles had two great parents. We are good friends, grew up in the same village. Women used to say that if they ever got married, they would like their marriage to be like that of Doubles' parents."

Lashley was shaking her head. "I am sorry, but cruelty should never be funny."

"Nuffada was one hell of a policeman, though. He was my partner at one time. But I managed to wangle a switch. You see, he could not control his temper.... We still talk about him in the Force. He was obsessive. If he was on our case, he would be hiding out near the entrance to the cart-road part of every night for the next week to see what cars would be going in there. The case would take over his life," said Crick.

"Sergeant, why don't we organise a camera by the entrance to the cart-road?" said Lashley.

"Interesting idea, but we'll have to see about that. We'll talk about it some more in the car." Crick turned back to Broomes. "But how come you are here today?"

Lashley gave Crick a look. Crick understood the look. He understood that she understood that he was changing the subject, and she wasn't too pleased about it.

"Three months ago, I took early retirement. It's an option after twenty-five years with the bank. I am still getting used to having all this time on my hands, so I occasionally pop down to see my auntie and to chat with the fellows. I still play a good hand of dominoes or hearts."

Crick bit into his ham-cutter and took a swig of his rum and coke. What will I do when I retire? Maybe do some cricket coaching with youngsters. He returned to the present and thought of how his old school friend's banking and rum-shop connections might be of assistance with the investigation.

"Broomsie, write down my number. Give me a call any time you hear anything interesting."

"Well, you know that if I hear anything, I'll let you know. But here, take my number as well."

Crick and Lashley made it to the vehicle without anyone approaching them. This rum-shop crowd knew nothing, at least not yet. Rumshops were favourite haunts for some detectives. Crick was a subscriber to the view that alcohol-loosened tongues wagged easier than sober ones. That was partly his rationale for frequenting such establishments. He had solved many a case by keeping his ear close to the ground—or to the barrel. The new technology was amazing indeed, but not many cases in Barbados were solved just by the use of technology. The solutions to cases normally started with information gleaned from witnesses or persons who heard from witnesses.

"I don't like your friend Broomes," said Lashley as they moved off.

"What? Why?" asked Crick, glancing at her.

"He treats people with contempt. He looks down on people because of their perceived status. I am sure he is only one generation away from having parents as poor as Mr. Nicholls'. But I guess some people very quickly forget where they came from, or don't want to know."

"You are overreacting to a bit of humour. Lighten up, girl."

"I don't care if he is your friend. People like that disgust me."

"You know, there are some real things in this world to be disgusted about, and Herbie Broomes is not one of them. If you are looking for things to be disgusted about, I could give you a list, from the many cases I have dealt with over the years."

"Actually, I'd prefer to hear some more about this old teacher of yours. What made him so memorable?"

Crick's focus alternated between her and the road a few times before deciding to let the Herbie Broomes matter rest. There was something eating away at Lashley. With someone like her, he thought, there would be another time.

"The Doc was one of those teachers you never forget," he said evenly. "In his class, we talked about everything. He was the first teacher to tell me not to believe everything I read in a book. The first time he walked into our class, he said, 'I am your History teacher,' and then asked us, 'What does history mean to you?' We started spouting about dates and events from the Olive Blossom to the World Wars to Emancipation. He listened then told us that there are some things we ought to know about history. We should always remember that recorded history bore the perspective of the narrator, and that history was not just dates, events or battles. It was about people, not just kings, queens and warlords, but ordinary people, the way they lived, the choices they made or were able to make within the context of their existence. 'History,' he said, 'will help you to understand your place in the world, how you came to be where you are and who you are. But the most important thing about history is the lessons. Lessons which, if learned, can help us to avoid the repetition of old mistakes.' Perhaps the most important lesson the Doc preached was that people can change the world. The changes in Barbados in his lifetime were so incredible that he warned us we may find some events in our own history hard to believe."

"You were lucky to have such a teacher."

"You right 'bout that. You know, when he first came back from university, he taught at your school, but some parents complained about him and eventually he was 'promoted' to deputy-head of my school."

"What was the nature of the complaints?"

"I hear they said that he did not stick to the curriculum, he engaged in a lot of discussion about current affairs. Once he substituted for an absent reverend and offered a different, a secular, explanation for one of the miracles in the Bible. There was also an answer he gave to a white student who asked if it was fair to be blaming white people today for something that happened long before they were born. He replied that it was not fair at all then added, 'But you must understand that when you inherit an asset, you also inherit the liabilities that go with it.'"

"If they have that birthday celebration for him, I would like to come. Do you think that would be OK? I like talking with old people and he sounds particularly interesting."

"I am sure that will be alright. I intend to call him as soon as I get back to the station because he was at the well this morning. And I have to go to see him soon. Why you don't come with me?"

They dropped off the police vehicle at Holetown. Crick smoked a cigarette as soon as he got out of his car and, once inside the station, telephoned the Doc. Doc knew about half the people who were at the scene that morning, but he had more questions than answers. He thought that the police would be under a lot of pressure to solve the case because of its possible damage to the island's image.

Crick drove out of the station with Lashley at his side and headed to Bridgetown so that she could retrieve her car. They intended to go their separate ways, Lashley to Christ Church and Crick to St. Thomas, after meeting up with Bobby Lewis.

"I had a chat with the Doc just now. He was very interested in the case because he thought that the body must have been down there for a great many years and that there was no connection with the shoe and jewellery. He was surprised to hear that his time line was very wrong."

"I really want to meet this man," said Lashley.

Crick dropped her off at the Bridgetown station and they proceeded towards Christ Church in convoy. During the drive, Crick kept thinking that everything he had heard about Lashley's personality was true; the edginess, taking offense at the slightest opportunity. At least he didn't have to live with her. In all things, give thanks, his mother would say. His dead father would have cussed her upside down, drunk or sober.

CHAPTER 4

Robert Stephenson Lewis' voice floated from the right side of Allman Sports Bar. He stood and waved at Crick and Lashley. They headed in his direction. Crick introduced Lashley, and Bobby smiled a big nervous smile as he shook hands with them. Crick, observing the way Bobby kept glancing at her, surmised that Lashley had aroused his curiosity.

"What can I get you to drink?" Bobby asked.

Crick opted for a rum and water and Lashley for bottled water. Bobby was already halfway through a beer. He was still wearing a tie, a green and cream one matching his cream long-sleeved shirt. His thinning brown hair was combed backwards over an emerging bald spot.

"How is that granddaughter of yours, Tessa?"

"Tassa, not Tessa, man. She is fine. She keeps me entertained. She can't spell to save her life, but that doesn't stop her from writing. She likes writing. And how are Christine and the boys?"

"They good, man. How about something to eat?" Bobby asked.

Crick and Lashley both declined. Instead, Crick took another swig of his drink and shook his glass. The ice swirled and clinked.

"What you got for me, Bobby?"

Bobby scratched at his chin, his eyes shifted from Crick to Lashley and back. "I am not sure if there is anything here. But I know a fellow who used to come to the club and play a little cricket. He liked the game, but he was not really that good. He don't come to the club no more. But I hear that he frequented nightclubs and had been seen with a certain young girl recently. He is a well-known surfer, makes jewellery for a living. I understand he is very creative. Girls like him. He is a bit of a playboy. But this particular young girl he was supposed to be dating is twenty years old. She come from a good family. He is in his mid-thirties."

Crick leaned over toward Bobby. "Who's the girl, Bobby?"

"Her mother is a high white, and both her parents were very upset about the situation."

"What is a high white?" interrupted Lashley.

"You never hear 'bout a high white before? They are the whites who always had money, and power, 'bout this place. Now listen, I am not accusing him."

"So why you want to talk to us, Bobby?" said Crick.

Bobby smoothed the hair over his balding spot. "The girl, Rebecca, disappeared about three months ago. I understand she had a big row with her parents and decided to leave home. She left the island, and apparently this fellow was supposed to be joining her, but he is still here."

"Do you know where she went?"

Bobby looked at Lashley as if he was trying to read her thoughts before answering. "No, but he told somebody that she went to Canada."

"Well, if she is in Canada, that shouldn't be too difficult to verify. But why are you suspicious?" asked Crick.

"AD, the person who told me knows this man *good* and knows when he is lying. He was uncomfortable talking to his friend about the girl. So the friend told him that he was holding back something. He denied it, tried to laugh it off, but the friend knew he was lying."

"Who is this man and how can I get in touch with him?"

"You got to know the man, AD. It's Frankie Odell. You must have played cricket against him."

"I don't remember him. Obviously, he didn't make an impression on the cricket field." Crick laughed.

Bobby gave directions to Frankie Odell's home and added, "He's in the book. The phone number is in his name."

"Tell me something, Bobby," Lashley said. "Who are Rebecca's parents, and did your friend tell you what made Rebecca's parents so upset—apart from the age and class difference?"

"Ahm...she is Tom Hill's daughter...."

Lashley and Crick stared at Bobby Lewis.

"Wait, you trying to tell me that Tom Hill daughter disappear and no alarm been raised?" said Crick.

"She left home last year and don't speak to the parents. She and Frankie were living in an apartment, but since she disappeared he move back home. They, particularly the mother, had a problem with Frankie. Rebecca is a natural-born rebel. Her parents sent her to boarding school in England, but she was expelled at fourteen years old and had to finish school back here. They managed to put her in her old school and then she went to the Community College. She likes to party and likes boys like Frankie, boys with a bit of an edge to them."

"Tell me a bit more about Frankie," said Lashley.

"My father family come from St. John, but they left down there a long time ago. My father wanted to make something of himself. My father know Frankie's parents. I don't know him all that well, but one of our club members is a good friend of his. Frankie dropped out of secondary school and started to be an apprentice mechanic. He liked cars but hated being dirty all the time. A friend then got him a job as an apprentice jeweller in town. When he saw how much people would pay for jewellery, he found his calling and discovered he had a talent for it. He eventually developed his own niche, left the shop in town, and operates from his garage at home. He combines natural woods with gold and silver and any old metal that he can shape and polish up. It's pretty jewellery. He sells to stores or at festivals and sometimes in high season in hotels on vendors' days. Some people journey all the way to St. John to buy from him, especially if they want something custom-made. He spends his spare time surfing and I understand...." Bobby paused, looked around and lowered his voice when he continued, "He used to sell a little ganja on the side, but he don't worry with that since the jewellery business took off. He is a free spirit, the kind that some women are attracted to."

"Where did Rebecca go to school in Barbados? Would you know any of her other friends?" asked Lashley.

"I don't really know her friends, there is a bit of an age gap between us, but she went to school at St. Felicitas."

As soon as they walked out of the bar, Lashley said, "I wonder what Frankie did to him."

"What do you mean?"

"I mean, what would motivate him to go the police with such flimsy evidence? I think your friend is strange, or this Frankie has done something to him. The daughter of a prominent family disappears and we hear nothing about it? Very strange."

"Well, you discover a lot o' strange things when you investigate a murder. The parents may have killed her. It is not unheard of."

"We should speak to Rebecca's parents."

Crick thought they should speak to Frankie first. He intended to discuss it with the SIO at tomorrow morning's briefing and leave that decision up to him. He felt that the superintendent may prefer to make the call to Rebecca's parents himself, if he thought it necessary, or he may even choose to deflect it upwards. Lashley was young indeed. She didn't seem to understand how this kind of thing was handled, how power was dealt with in this society.

"We'll speak to this Frankie fellow first," said Crick.

"Tell me something. If this was just plain Tom Hill, with no *high white* wife, would you put off talking to him about his missing daughter, Sergeant?" Lashley looked over at Crick. The challenge was in her eyes as well as her voice.

The challenge took Crick by surprise. He considered the question to be insolent but curbed his instinctive response. She understood more about their island's power dynamics than he had assumed. He locked smouldering eyes with Lashley and calmly said, "We don't know if his daughter is actually missing. So here is what we do. We investigate. We contact Horse Hill Station. The officers there must know Frankie pretty good. See what we can find out about him. Then we pay him a visit after tomorrow morning's briefing. We question him and take it from there. Right now, he is only a person of interest. Tomorrow, he may either be eliminated or considered a suspect. We also find out who her friends are and speak to them. You notice that I have ignored your question. That is because it ain't worthy of a reply. Now, you got any other bright ideas to discuss?"

"Sergeant, I am not trying to be rude. One thing you will find out about me is that I always speak my mind."

"Young lady, speaking your mind ain't always a virtue, and sometimes it is a distraction, especially in a little place like Barbados. There is a lot you have to learn. See you tomorrow morning. Good night."

Crick tugged at his cigarette packet and marched toward his car. From his rear view mirror, he saw Lashley watching him before she walked to her car. He picked up his phone.

CHAPTER 5

Shondette Lashley pushed the unlocked door and called out, "I'm home." Her mum and dad were in front the television. She went over to the sofa, where her mum was lying, her head on a pillow and feet in dad's lap. She kissed them both.   "I am famished," she declared.

"Tell me something new," replied her mother with a laugh. "You know where to find your dinner."

Two bright-eyed little girls in pyjamas, but very much awake, rushed into the room and hugged Lashley.

A maternal voice of sweetness laced with authority sang out from the sofa. "Back to bed, now. Your sister's had a long day."

Ten minutes later, an herbaceous aroma wafted into the living room as Lashley re-entered with a bowl of beef soup with dumplings, sweet potato, breadfruit, carrots and beets. She dragged the tray table over to the chair next to her mum and dad and sat heavily. "This is just what I need."

"We saw the story on the news about the body in St. Lucy," said her dad, "and figured you were working on it when we got your text that you would be late. Are you on that case?"

Lashley sipped a spoonful of soup, exhaled audibly and said, "It's not in my division. What made you think I would be investigating?"

"I don't really know. I just put two and two together. You working late and the news about the dead woman," he replied with a shrug.

"Who you working with on the case?" asked her mum.

"Sergeant Artifus Demetrius Crick. We have no real clues yet, but we may, just may, have a useful lead. This soup is real good, mum," said

Lashley, adroitly changing subject. She tried never to talk too much about her work at home. Home was where she escaped the horrors of her job, where she wanted to shut out memories of criminals and their victims.

"Thank your dad, he cooked it."

"Thank you, dad. I should've known," said Lashley, giving him a smile.

Gladstone Lashley was really her stepfather. He had come into her life when she was eight years old and four years after her biological father, Branston Downes, the man who lived with them, had been arrested for inflicting a serious beating on her mother. It wasn't the first beating, but this time the policeman responded differently. Instead of the usual mini-lecture to her father, he handcuffed him, took him down to the station, and charged him with assault and battery. But her mother refused to press charges and the charges were dropped. That did not end Branston's hostility and abuse, until one day a little girl went to the police station and asked for the policeman who helped her mother. She told him that she was afraid that her father was going to kill her mother. The policeman with two others found Branston and spoke with him. Branston left the island.

Her mother said she didn't want another man in her life. Two years later, she met and repeatedly rebuffed Gladstone Lashley, a cook at a luxury resort at the time. He now worked as a private chef at a west coast villa. But he wouldn't go away; he became the family's best friend and then her mother's husband. He spent the years they were together trying to compensate for Branston's behaviour, trying to be an ideal husband, and it worked. They had two children of their own. The experience transformed her mother. Lashley came to adore her stepfather. She changed her surname to his. The bar had been reset and raised for Lashley's consideration of a husband if and whenever that should be.

Lashley finished her soup. "I am going to see what the girls are up to then hit the shower and do some homework."

She pushed the door to her sisters' bedroom and crept in. "Ha! I caught you. Facebook, huh? Shouldn't you two be asleep?"

The girls giggled and took turns hugging their big sister.

41

"We heard about the woman with the red hair. Are you looking for the person who killed her, Shonnie?" asked Pamalla. She was the younger sister, and always full of questions about why people did what they did.

"Yes, but I want you two in bed right now. I have to prepare for a criminology exam."

The older sister, Kelly, put a hand on the mouse and clicked a few times until the screen faded. The girls wished their big sister goodnight and went reluctantly to bed. Lashley turned the lights off as she exited the room.

The full blast from the shower rained tepid water over Lashley. She liked it like that: just enough warmth to take the chill off and as powerful as possible. She closed her eyes, didn't like what she saw, and opened them again. The skeletal vision with red hair disappeared, but thoughts of the lady in Prickett's well remained. For her, she wasn't Millie. She couldn't be Millie. Millie belonged to that damned song she couldn't sing with the rest of her class at school.

Millie down in the well
Oh Lawd, poor Millie
Wid de wire wrap round she waist
And de razor cut up she face
Wid de wire wrap round she waist
And de razor cut up she face

Everybody laughed as they sang that song except her. Millie could have been her mother, if it wasn't for that policeman, perhaps. The song should have been a dirge; instead, people danced and laughed as they sang it. "What does that say about us?" she asked herself. For Lashley, the woman in the well was the redhead head lady. But who was she? She doubted very much that she was local. A resident expat? Possibly. They needed to ID her. Facial reconstruction would make matters easier, but the damage to her head would present some challenges.

She towelled herself dry and went toward her bed, still sombre. She reflected on a day spent with a man some said would never make it past sergeant because of his drinking and a certain disrespect for authority—with, apparently, the exception of his current boss, Superintendent Thomas. He was also reputed to be something of a womaniser. She could understand why some women would be attracted to his impish smile, his broad shoulders and narrow waist, but he was not her type.... Why did she think that? After all, she still wasn't sure what her type was. At least she knew what it wasn't. But maybe there was more to Crick than met the eye. Everyone talked about how many cases he had solved, how many criminals he had locked up.

Lashley settled on her bed next to her laptop. She looked at the books on her bookshelf, in the corner to the left of the bed. She had been reading two books. One was Anthony Harriot's *Police and Crime Control in Jamaica–Problems of Reforming Ex-colonial Constabularies*. She opted for Richard Rhodes' *Why They Kill*. It was not a required text but had been recommended by Dr. Bridgeman, her course tutor. She removed the bookmark and started reading from where she had left off. But she couldn't concentrate; too many thoughts and images of the bones and battered head of the redhead lady. Eventually, she drifted off to sleep.

She awoke next morning to the sound of trees romping in the wind and the familiar buzz of a mad-bull. A standard addition to kites on the island, it consisted of a loose paper attachment that vibrated in the wind. Kite makers varied the design to produce different sound effects, from the raucous mad bull to the melodic singing angel. Lashley looked out of the window and saw trees bowing and dancing then springing back upright for a few moments' rest, waiting for a fresh gust to dance again. She searched for the kite flyers and saw two young boys on the ridge that ran behind their house, taking advantage of the high winds before heading off to school. Theirs were the first kites she had heard for the season.

It was a cool, blustery morning. Further east, there was a cluster of clouds, dark and heavy. They could be in for some rain. Or maybe the winds would blow the clouds away. She reached for her iPhone.

CHAPTER 6

AD Crick sat in his Nissan Sentra and pressed some numbers on his cell phone. His older son, Darren, answered. Crick was happy to hear Darren, and Darren seemed happy to hear him. They talked about school and football. His little brother, Damian, was already in bed, and anyway he still wasn't speaking with Crick. "Mom's not home," Darren said without being asked. Crick wondered where she was but didn't want to trouble his son.

"Let her know that I called. I will call her tomorrow. Goodnight, Dar."

Crick and his wife were separated. Natalie had always complained about his irregular hours. She didn't accept that his work always demanded such lengths of time away from home. Then a very good friend of Natalie's had phoned to tell her that a friend had told her, "AD got another woman." Natalie confronted Crick. He flatly denied it. "I ain't got no woman, I got friends."

Crick told the other woman about the phone call. Two nights later, he was at home in bed talking with Natalie when the phone rang. Natalie answered and listened for a while then spoke. "Who the hell are you?" she asked. "My husband is in bed next to me, get lost." Natalie hung up and turned to Crick. "Some people have nothing better to do than to try to create mischief. Can you imagine some woman just called to say that you were in Black Rock at a woman's house? Unbelievable."

"Unbelievable," Crick repeated and followed up with a steupse.

Natalie dismissed the call but next day spoke to her friend about it. "Imagine my husband next to me and some foolish idiot calling me to tell me he at some woman house. We got too many mischief-makers in Barbados. They see you living good and want to break that up."

The friend agreed with Natalie but apparently was so confident of her source that she rechecked. She got back to Natalie, this time with a name, Tanya, and an address. Natalie, at first doubtful, decided to seek out the woman. She approached her outside her apartment when she arrived from work. Tanya tried to deny the relationship but Natalie suddenly thought that she recognised her voice. "It was *you* who called my house two evenings ago–wasn't it?"

Tanya broke into tears. "We are in love–"

"How dare you?" Natalie shouted, calling Tanya a beast and a whore. If not for the intervention of one of Tanya's neighbours, it could have escalated into a full bassa-bassa. The women, both physically strong, shared not only the same man but the same taste for confrontation. Other neighbours appeared at windows and doors as Natalie walked away cursing.

Crick rushed home as soon as he received Tanya's call about the incident. Natalie attacked him. She flew at him, repeatedly banging her fists into his chest. She cussed him with words he had never heard her use before. "Get the fuck out of this house. Go to your whore. You promised you would never do this shite again."

"I can't leave my boys," said Crick.

"Either you go or I am going. And, either way, *my* two boys are staying with me."

She emphasised this as if to say the boys were no longer his and that he had betrayed them as well.

"OK...OK. Maybe we should have a cooling off period—"

"A cooling off period? You want a cooling off period? As far as I am concerned, you can go and drown yourself in the Arctic."

Crick knew there was nothing he could say at that point to change Natalie's mind. She was never much of a compromiser. He moved out. But he didn't move in with his lover. Instead, he was now a lodger with his first child, his daughter, Joycelyn, from a relationship prior to his marriage.

Crick eased out of the car park and made his way to the ABC highway, studying his situation. The redhead lady, Bobby's story, the foreign press, the potential impact of the case on tourism, his new partner (*damn lil' girl, thinks she knows everything*), all these ran through his mind.

He drove up Rendezvous Hill and joined the ABC highway, heading west. He took the third exit at the first Warrens roundabout and went up through Jackson and Welchman Hall to his daughter's home in Sturges. He turned into the driveway at No. 6 Bougainvillea Terrace, slowed to a stop. He pulled up his handbrake, lit a cigarette and remained in the car, in the dark. He thought some more about the day's events and about the other case he had been working on, the Sandy Lane robbery, which had been handed over to DC Johnson. Then his thoughts turned again to Tanya.

They had met by chance about three years ago. He was still in the Bridgetown division at the time. She managed a little store not far from Central Police Station. There was a robbery at the store and he went to investigate. She was quite shaken up and he did his best to put her at ease. He popped back into the store the following week to see how she was doing and she was appreciative, thanked him for his concern. She came to the police station two weeks later to identify a suspect and they met again. Later he visited her at the store to let her know when the hearing was scheduled. Her presence was not required at that time but there was a distinct probability that, in spite of his prior record, the accused would make bail if he pleaded not guilty and she would then be needed at the trial. He noticed that she was meticulous about her appearance and possessed a natural smile, not the coached smile of many store personnel. From their first meeting he found her attractive but she showed no sign that the attraction was mutual.

The robber was freed on bail and Crick visited again to advise her that she should be cautious. He gave her his mobile number and said, "If you ever see him anywhere near the shop, call me right away." From time to time, he found himself popping into the store at off-peak times without any real need to buy anything. It was as if he was drawn there by some force like that of a divining rod to water. She was always professional yet warm, friendly, and seemed genuinely happy to see him. He would always buy something, trying not to show interest in her. He wondered if her friendliness was simply gratitude for finding the man who had robbed and threatened her with a cutlass or just her nature. But in time their chats became more personal. A simple "How was your weekend?" would produce a detailed response and an exchange of information. She learned that he was married with two boys in their early teens, liked cricket and calypso. He learned that she had a boyfriend, no kids, liked movies and sports, played hockey at school and, after school, for the Empire Cub near where she grew up in Bank Hall. Then one day, about a year after the robbery, she volunteered that she and her boyfriend had broken up over the previous weekend. It was mentioned casually. She seemed rather philosophical about it, neither hurt nor sad. "It wasn't working out anyway," she said, shrugging, then added, "and I am not interested in any man right now." Had she said that for his benefit?

Then, one Saturday they ran into each other at a cricket match at the Empire ground. Empire was playing against Police. There was an awkward, simultaneous, "What a coincidence," followed by laughter. She was dressed sportily, shorts and tank top, and Crick was very taken with her appearance. He now saw what those elegant, loose-fitting clothes she wore at work were hiding. Thoughts of nibbling on that provocative botsy flashed across his mind. *Behave*, he told himself.

"How do you stay in such good shape?" he asked in as innocent a tone as he could manage.

"I live outside the city, just off Dayrell's Road. I walk to and from work every day, if it isn't raining, and I still play hockey. But it's also in my genes. You should see my mom: sixty-three and still petite as ever."

They sat together. She surprised him with her knowledge of cricket, particularly her incisive criticism of her side's field setting. In this out-of-work place, riotously supporting her team, she was like another person, sparkling, and witty. Crick felt drawn to her and for once thought the feeling might be mutual. Before they parted he offered to buy her lunch sometime. She thought that would be nice. The one lunch was followed by others, but only occasionally. They were short affairs, the lunches.

They became friends. They had similar taste in movies. She liked detective stories. He did, too, but only the really good ones, good enough that he couldn't find any flaws. They decided to take in a movie at the drive-in one evening. It was a romantic comedy. They laughed a lot. When they returned to Dayrell's Road, she asked to be put off on the main road at the corner of the gap where she lived; she would walk the short distance to her apartment. They kissed on the cheek. He sat in his car, watched until she disappeared and wondered what the evening was all about. Days after she said, "Let's not do the cinema again." She declined to say why when asked. AD felt then that she was feeling what he was feeling and that she was overriding her emotions. He respected her for this. And he was unsure of taking their friendship into the lovers' zone. He was a husband and a father and also he didn't think of her as a bit on the side, an outside woman, a chossel. This was different. He was afraid of an unhappy outcome. They had become such good friends; he wanted to do nothing that would possibly harm their relationship. They talked on the phone nearly every day. She used to laugh and say to him, "If only you were single...." Then, without warning one day, she said to him, "I have a movie you would like. We could watch it at my apartment." He had never been inside her apartment before. He took the invitation as an indication that she had overcome her reservations about taking their relationship to a different level, and he was right. They did not get to see the end of the movie. There was much giggling and laughter and about halfway into the movie Crick put an arm around her shoulder and drew her close. She looked at him, raised her lips to his in a long kiss. Soon clothes were shed and she rode him right there on the rug in the centre of the room. She came loud, collapsed onto his chest and said, "I wanted to do this for the longest time."

After that night, he kept going back, his "working late" or "night out with the boys" became more frequent.

Now, he had to end the relationship if he was ever to save his marriage. He was convinced that he was in love with two women at the same time. Could a man love more than one woman? As far as he was concerned, he was in no doubt on the answer to that question. Marcus, his younger brother and confidant, said, "Definitely yes." Marcus taught Sociology at Cave Hill. Crick was certain that he was experiencing what his brother had described as concurrent love. "In the world of our African ancestors, Natalie and Tanya would both be your wives." Crick convinced himself that he wasn't having an affair; he had two wives. Marcus went on to say that many Afro-Caribbeans actually still practiced polygamy, but with their families spread out, not in one compound as in much of Africa, and with the disadvantage that only the first wife was recognised by the law. "Just think of our grandfather. He had children from four different women. Relocation and legislation do not and cannot automatically remove centuries of cultural practice."

"Pay no attention to your brother. Sociologists can rationalise anything," his sister Ertha, the eldest sibling, warned him. Ertha had been particularly scathing in her criticism of Crick's behaviour, arguing that he didn't care enough about his children and he was a typical wutless Bajan man. He rejected her say on his children but was not unmindful of her remarks and started to consider that the best thing for him to do was to try to uncomplicate his life. That would mean giving up Tanya. He felt he loved both women but had a greater sense of responsibility to Natalie, the mother of his two boys. He had broken up with the mother of his first child. They were both young at the time; he didn't want to lose this one. He was going to beg, do whatever it took, to get Natalie back. He began to question his feelings for Tanya. Was what he felt for her really love or was he in some kind of a midlife crisis, flattered by the attention of a younger woman? And what did a woman, fifteen years his junior, really want from him? Was she really in love with him? She knew he was married. In the week after they first made love, he tried to end the relationship. "This is not right for you," he told her. "You deserve to have a man of your own and I can't be that. You should find someone else." She said she couldn't, that it wouldn't be fair to that person because she would always love him, as she had for more than two years.

Crick lit another cigarette, inhaled deeply then slowly blew smoke out the car window.

The light on the corner outside of the house came on. The front door opened and he saw his daughter's outline in the doorway. She stepped onto the veranda. "Aren't you coming inside, Dad? How many more cigarettes you need to smoke?" she asked.

Crick got out of his car. "I was trying to finish work before I stepped through your doors."

"Good idea," said Joycelyn.

"How's Tassa?"

"Asleep. I had to send her to her room early. She defied me again. She is headstrong like all the Cricks. She pinned a note on her door. You have to see this."

They walked down the corridor past the spare room and stopped in front of Tassa's room. Written in red crayon on a sheet of paper and stuck on the door, the notice said, "**DO NOT ENTER OR YOU WILL BE MINST MEET!!!**"

Muted laughter echoed through the corridor. Crick opened the door. He quietly entered, studied the sleeping figure for a moment, then bent down and gently kissed the forehead of his first grandchild.

He backed slowly out of the room. He looked at Joycelyn. "Where is Gary?"

"Watching TV."

"Will you be home in time for dinner tomorrow night?" Joycelyn asked. "Mum is coming over."

"Ahm...I ain't sure...we'll see."

He and Joycelyn were very close. So much so that when Natalie ordered him out of home, he had no qualms about asking if he could stay with her, Gary and Tassa. She said yes immediately. Living with a granddaughter had added a new joy to his life, too.

Crick headed down the corridor. He was tired and restless, but he wanted to shout out Gary. He made an effort to develop a relationship with the man, who was twelve years older than Joycelyn and on his second marriage. Gary clearly adored Joycelyn, but Crick sensed that he was not really keen about having his father-in-law as part of the package.

CHAPTER 7

The Royal Barbados Police Force was divided into three divisions: the Central Division in Bridgetown, the capital city; the Southern Division at Oistins in Christ Church; and the Northern Division at Holetown in St. James. The Chief had summoned Crick and his team for a special briefing. The Chief headed up the Northern Division CID, which oversaw detective investigations in the five most northerly parishes, St. James, St. Thomas, St. Andrew, St. Peter and St. Lucy,

Thomas focused his attention on Sergeant Crick. "I called in your entire team this morning because I want to make sure that each one of you understands the importance of solving this case quickly. The commissioner was on me about it this morning, and I know he has heard from the Minister of Tourism as well as the Prime Minister. Sergeant, if this woman you call Millie is a tourist, all hell will break loose. We have no missing person's report to match her. They say she has been down in that well awhile. Someone somewhere must have missed her."

Crick cleared his throat and spoke up. "By tomorrow, we hope to have some information from Immigration on females who had overstayed. But this morning, right after the meeting, I'll be following up a local lead." He took out his notebook and read. "I received information that a Barbadian girl, a redhead, may be missing. She left home, or her parents kicked her out, and subsequently, it is alleged, she went off to Canada. Her name is Rebecca Hill. I have already been in touch with Immigration to see if there is a record of her departure."

"Hill, Hill." SIO Thomas put a hand to his face, rubbing the right side of his jaw with the back of his fingers. "She isn't *the* Thomas Hill's daughter, is she?"

"Yes, sir, she is."

"Christ, you mekking sport, right? Something isn't right here, Sergeant. There is no way that his daughter would be missing and an alarm hasn't been raised. That would be more than strange.... The white community would not have waited for the police to investigate; they would have been out hunting for her themselves. I am going to speak to the commissioner about this. He has had some dealings with Mr. Hill." The superintendent wrote quickly in his diary.

"Hold on the commissioner for the time being, sir. We are visiting a person of interest right after this meeting. We need a greater reason to believe that it may be Rebecca Hill before possibly unnecessarily upsetting her family."

Crick reported on the meeting with Bobby Lewis. The SIO again expressed scepticism that Thomas Hill's daughter could be missing and her parents not have done anything about it. Crick explained that she was, according to his source, estranged from her parents.

"I don't think this is a very promising lead, but of course you must follow up on it," said SIO Thomas. "Even if she has ceased communicating with her parents, she must have some old school friends who have maintained contact with her."

"DC Lashley is looking into that, sir," said Crick. "We are also considering that there might be a drug connection here. The woman in the well could have come in with a drug shipment, then something went wrong, she ended up dead and the local connections disposed of the body. There would be no record of entry."

"Very interesting theory, Detective," said SIO Thomas, "but she was dressed for a party, not like she just got off a drug boat."

"It was just a thought.... The drug boat may have been her means of transportation, but she may well have been living here, undocumented, for all we know."

This started the discussion on other alternate theories until the SIO brought it to an end. "Some of these theories may become avenues to pursue when we unearth leads, leads that will produce evidence. Right now I am pushing to see how soon we can get a forensic pathologist here so we can begin to identify the victim. Our first challenge is to find out who she is."

"Until then, sir, I am working on the premise that as redheads are fairly uncommon here, people remember them. Our task is difficult but not impossible. From this morning, Moore and Mason will be interviewing hotel staff, beach vendors and water sports personnel about any recent redhead sightings," Crick said.

———

Crick had decided against calling ahead to set up his meeting with Frankie Odell. Like Lashley and SIO Thomas, he didn't put much value on what he had heard, but a thought did cross his mind that this Frankie, who had spent a lot of time on beaches, might have connections with people who could help identify the victim. Or if involved, he could also be capable of disposing of the deceased's jewellery, her earrings, her necklace, watch if she was wearing one, even her handbag, as none of these things was recovered with the body.

Right after the briefing with SIO Thomas, Lashley joined Crick and they drove east to St. John, through light intermittent rain. The road was a continuous, gradual rise from Holetown until they reached the eastern hills.

Crick's cell phone chimed shortly after they got on the way. Lashley moved to pick up the device from the centre console and Crick said, "I'll take that." She watched his face relax with a trace of a smile as he spoke. "I'll call you back" was all he said. He clicked off and looked straight ahead, his face serious now.

Brisk winds buffeted the unmarked police Suzuki van as they progressed toward Horse Hill. There was a noticeable drop in the temperature.

They turned in to the Horse Hill civic complex named for Eric Holder, the American Attorney- General whose father came from this area. Barbados was proud of its émigré descendants who had achieved in the outside world, even if they had contributed little to the island's actual progress.

The officers at Horse Hill knew Frankie Odell as a cool fellow, with no history of violence. "We catch him speeding a couple of times when he used to drive the little Mitsubishi Colt with the big engine in it," said the Horse Hill station sergeant, "but nothing else. It wouldn't surprise me if he still smoked a little herb, even though he cut off he dreadlocks now… but murder? Nah, man. That would surprise me. But I been around long enough to know that you never know."

Crick followed Bobby's directions to the green and yellow house with a gallery opposite a bus stop halfway down the hill and next to a rum-shop. Two women were seated in the gallery. He and Lashley exchanged greetings with them as they pulled up and introduced themselves to them once out of the car.

"We would like to have a word with Franklyn. He home?" asked Crick.

"What the police want with my boy?" the younger of the women asked with a look of suspicion.

"We just want to ask him some questions about a friend of his," said Crick.

"Well, he ain't here," responded the older lady.

"Where might we find him?" asked Lashley.

Rhoda Odell, the younger of the two, shrugged and spread out her hands, palms upward, her head leaned to a side, forehead creased, lips pursed. She eyed the two detectives nervously. "Officer, I live in this part of St. John all my life, just like my parents and grandparents. My family never had any trouble with the police. Frankie is a good boy, but he didn't want to work the land like his father and grandfather. He had made his mind up from a young age. He used to say, *'No fork and hoe for me*. I ain't no red-leg.' Yes, that's the word he used. He called his own parents what many in Barbados called us behind our backs and sometimes to our faces. And I hated it—I hated him for saying it. But Frankie is a good boy."

Crick looked at Rhoda Odell. Beads of perspiration had formed on her forehead, her hair was untidy. He looked around at the peeling paint of the house and felt a degree of empathy for her. Crick also saw defiance in Rhoda Odell's face. Despite her words of defence, she was probably imagining the worst, wondering, "What the France that boy gone and do now? Hope he ain't get caught up in no more drugs." Crick studied her. Her grey-streaked black hair reached halfway down her back. Even though she was overweight, he imagined that she would not have been unattractive as a young woman. He saw some similarity with the photo his sister Ertha kept of a pious-looking old lady in a long white dress buttoned at the neck that reached down to her shoes, their great-grandmother. As a boy, he used to think that same look of defiance on her face was distrust of the camera, but as he grew older he saw it for the strength and determination of a Scottish descendant of indentured servants who married a black blacksmith in 1890 Barbados and bore nine children.

"Mrs. Odell, Frankie ain't in no trouble. But he might be able to help us get in touch with one of his friends. I am sure he would be happy to help us," said Crick in the most reassuring tone he could manage.

Mrs. Odell visibly relaxed. She looked at her companion, who briefly raised her eyebrows and gently nodded.

"Frankie left here early this morning with a surfboard on the jeep. He must be gone down to the Soup Bowl."

Crick thanked her. Bathsheba's Soup Bowl was the main surfing arena in Barbados, the location of the sport's major local events, and a regular practice ground. He motioned to Lashley it was time to go.

"What if Frankie *is* in trouble? Will you come back and talk to his mother?" asked Lashley on their way to the car.

"No, not at all…. I would send you."

Lashley stopped and stared at Crick's back as he approached the car. "You know I would come, too," she said.

"Well, if you coming, come," replied Crick.

"I am serious, you know."

"Me, too."

Lashley shook her head, sighed, and resumed walking toward the vehicle, refusing to engage further with Crick in his bit of Bajan badinage.

They drove down the winding road, taking in the panorama of rolling hills covered with tropical flora dominated by tall coconut palms, and casuarinas commonly called mile-trees because of their height, all set against a backdrop of the expansive churning blue-green waters of the Atlantic Ocean. Scattered rooftops seemed out of place in what might have been a sanctuary. They turned left at the crossroad and weaved their way slowly along the bumpy winding potholed road toward Bathsheba.

"Sergeant, your friend Bobby. His surname, Lewis, is a Welsh name. I thought these people were Irish and Scottish."

"If you don't know the answer to that, I wouldn't. You been to school since me. Maybe his mother simply married someone called Lewis. Wasn't Henry Morgan a Welshman, and wasn't he indentured here before going to Jamaica? I live in Welchman Hall, and there is a plantation called Morgan-Lewis. And don't forget T.T. Lewis. There must have been Welshmen who became indentured servants as well. We just don't hear much about them. I'll have to ask the Doc."

"Some of these people weren't really criminals, you know. Their crime was being poor and uneducated, society's unfortunates. They lived in a time when poor people could be taken advantage of at will, could be thrown in jail on the flimsiest of excuses," said Lashley.

"That's true. And after conviction, it could be off to the colonies. These people were victims of a class system as poisonous and cruel as the racist structural beginnings of our society. Our system was an extension of the British class system, the addition of a lower rung. But indentured servants had an important advantage: they could eventually merge with the establishment."

Lashley's smartphone pinged and she reached into her bag and started to finger the screen. Crick's thoughts drifted back to his schooldays and Doc Haynes' discussions on the white population of Barbados. Most of the current whites were descendants of English, Scottish and Irish peoples who were contracted as indentured servants or press-ganged, which became known as *Barbadosed*. The Irish were Catholic captives of Cromwell's war and had been infamously given the options of "the sword or Barbados." Indentured servants were virtual slaves, the Doc told them, but their period of indenture had an expiration date, after which they were discards left to scrunt for a living. Their lives were not much better than that of the slave population. Over time, many of their jobs were taken over by the free labour of the African slaves, first the field work and then the craft skills and housework.

But poor-white people represented a problem for the colonial-era authorities in Barbados and were subjected to much abuse by the high whites, those by then wealthy and politically powerful plantation owners and Bridgetown merchants who blamed their victims for their fate, portraying them as ignorant, worthless, lazy scoundrels and, in the case of the Irish, rebellious as well. But a white underclass was simply an embarrassment to the powers-that-were; it represented a stark contradiction to their projection of white as superior. So Barbados' authorities tried to export them. They shopped around the region for a solution to their poor-white problem. The problem was finding another island willing to take them. They had only limited success. Eventually, deals were made with the authorities in St. Vincent and Grenada, but the uptake was not as great as the Barbadian authorities had hoped, in spite of the offer of inducements in the form of plots of land of their own. Most of the so-called red-legs chose to remain in Barbados, so a new and much more attractive solution was put in place for them: educational reform. Secondary schools were created for poor-whites in an effort to provide them with the tools for improving their living standards and social status. The aim was to incorporate them into the white establishment. It worked. Those with the luck, skills and talents for upward mobility benefitted from this reform. Most then migrated to the southern parishes of Christ Church and St. Michael, near to the commercial centre of Bridgetown and the prospect of new forms of employment, and new lives as white people in a colonial setting. The strategy succeeded to the extent that over time their descendants merged into the white establishment and eventually became the majority of that group, the word "poor" no longer linked with their ethnic identity. With the improvement in their standard of living came mass forgiveness of their former exploiters, erasure of that part of their history from their collective cultural memory, fierce protection of their new status along with gravitation to their former owners' brand of conservative politics. The Doc said it was an example of Stockholm syndrome, long before such a term existed. He had to explain to them that this described the condition whereby, over time, captives identified with their captors. "And this was not exclusive to the poor-whites," he reminded them. "Some upwardly mobile coloured people went down the same route, too."

Some other poor-whites intermarried, their descendants blending into the black population, and others, an ever diminishing group, simply remained poor and white, like the family of Frankie Odell.

"Odell is obviously an Irish name," said Lashley, as she put away her smartphone.

"Did you know that Irish indentured servants often joined up with slaves in efforts to overthrow the plantocracy?" asked Crick.

"No, not at all. I stopped History in third form. But you know, my mother's uncle who lived in England for many years told us how friendly Irish people were to him. He described it as a kind of...mutual empathy, the result of, at one time, having a common enemy."

"That's interesting," said Crick. "But even if you had continued History, you may never have heard the things the Doc taught us. He was not a sticker to script. He taught what he called *meaningful* history."

When they reached, they only saw three surfers at the Soup Bowl. Frankie Odell was not among them and none of the surfers had seen him for the morning.

"We'll ask the boys on Horse Hill and Belleplaine to look out for him," said Crick.

"I hope we can get an early day today. I don't want to miss my capoeira session," said Lashley.

"Capoeira?" Crick asked in a loud voice then continued, "How come you chose a Brazilian martial art?"

"I used to do judo, and I danced at school. When I first saw a demonstration of capoeira, I just loved the movements. There aren't many of us. But we are gaining new members all the time."

"Are you any good?"

"Ah, I am full of tricks. That's why they call me Mandi, short for *mandingueira*, a clever fighter." She looked at Crick and smiled the broadest of smiles. Her smile dramatically altered her features; it removed that hard, untrusting edge to her, thought Crick.

"Let's try the police canteen for a late lunch and then swing by Culloden Road to see if they have anything for us," he said.

They were at the bottom of Horse Hill when Crick's cell phone rang, a different tone to the previous time. DC Lashley hesitated. "Answer it," Crick said. After listening for a while, she said, "It's Burgess from Immigration. Rebecca Hill left Barbados on January 16, on West Jet, headed for Toronto. That rules out Frankie Odell."

"Not yet. Ask Burgess if she returned."

"…He doesn't know."

"Tell him to check."

Lashley did as she was told then clicked off.

"Even if Rebecca came back, we may still have cause to question this man about the deceased's jewellery, if she was wearing any. Plus I want to find out more about the connection between the rebel daughter of Thomas Hill and a St. John red-leg."

"Why do you call the man a red-leg, Sergeant? Is the term not considered derogatory?"

Crick thought about the question. "You misunderstand me. You took what I said out of context. Red-leg is how I think the Hills would see this fellow, Frankie, not how I see him."

"Do you know the Hills?"

"Lord have mercy, girl. You are something else. No wonder you never had a boyfriend."

Lashley's mouth opened wide. Crick's sideways glance caught the embers in her eyes.

"I don't know who would have said that to you, Sergeant, but understand this: my private life is off-limits—off-limits."

"Wow wow. Sorry, lady, sorry."

All conversation ceased.

CHAPTER 8

Crick's back was slapped over and over again after they walked into the police canteen in Bridgetown. Lashley was greeted with some polite smiles, some sideways glances from the blank faces of older policemen and policewomen, but warm greetings from the younger officers. Her sudden secondment to the Northern Division had served to confirm the suspicions of some that she was on a fast track to promotion and did not earn her the admiration of everyone in a society not comfortable with ambition, where "She working for promotion" was a comment of derision. After all, good things were supposed to come to those who waited. In the old days, if a person did not offend and stayed long enough, promotion was more or less assured, but the rules had changed in recent times. Promotion was now more dependent on qualifications and results. Younger officers were leapfrogging up the ranks. It was a contentious issue and one that had recently been challenged in court by officers who objected to being superseded.

The aroma of the canteen, an old-fashioned Bajan cook-shop, sharpened their appetites. Crick got the last bit of rice and beef stew, Lashley chose cou-cou and steamed kingfish with extra onions, a side of sweet potato and vegetables but not much sauce. They separated by age and gender, Crick joining three older policemen and Lashley two young female officers.

"Culloden Road may not be much help on this case. They haven't got a lot to work with, and we don't know where the murder actually took place," Crick responded to his lunch colleagues. "We got to solve this one the old-fashioned way. We have to dig until we find those who know what happened."

"The old-time fellows like Johnny Salt Bags and Barney Lynch had an advantage," one of the senior policemen around the table, a slender chap with a soldier's bearing, said. "In those days, a detective could leave Bridgetown and go to St. Lucy and nobody up there would know him. They could do undercover work. There was no television and social media in those days to display their images all over the place. The last person to do that kind of work was Lionel Manning, who we used to call Leopard.

"You ever hear 'bout the time they send Leopard to investigate a case up in St. John? He was a young detective then. A man from up there was collecting money from people all over the island for some non-existent insurance company. Leopard borrow a car, a Borgward, from a friend who was a insurance salesman, and drive into the district. He knew the car would be recognised and thought that was an advantage. He went into a rum-shop, where the suspect was known to frequent, introduce himself and had a drink with the fellows. One of the men ask him what work he does do. He say he was a insurance agent. One of the men say, 'I thought I recognise that car.' Another man joined in: 'My brother is a insurance agent, too. Who you is work for?' Leopard answer quick and confident. He say Colonial Life. The man say, 'My brother, too.' Leopard ask him, 'Who is your brother?' The man say, 'George Weekes. You know George?' Leopard say, 'If I know George? I thought I recognise you when I come in the shop. You look just like George.' Well, the man screw up he face and all the men look at Leopard real funny. The man brother was really a half-brother, son of a red man from Bailey's Plantation. He didn't look nothing like the man Leopard was talking to. There was tension in the place. Somebody say, 'He is a police.' Men start to circle round Leopard. Leopard stand up. You know, he was a man barely five-foot-eight. He say, 'Police? Don't call the police. They would arrest me.'

"'If you ain't a police, you is a crook then, one of them con men.'

"Leopard pay for he drinks and head for the door. When he reach the Borgward, one of the men from the shop was right behind him. The man say, 'Skipper, I think we could work together.'

"Leopard look the man up and down. 'I like to work by myself.'

"'Man, we could make a lot of money working together. You could work in the areas I can't go.' The man tried to do a selling job on Leopard, explained how his scheme worked. He was selling phoney life insurance policies. 'You selling life insurance to young people, it is only a problem if somebody dead.' He take Leopard to his car and show him his paperwork, the forms that he asked people to fill out. Leopard arrest him on the spot." The group laughed. The old soldier continued. "Since that time, the island get even smaller, and the communication thing too sophisticated. We have to import policemen from other islands to do undercover work, now."

The old soldier leaned over toward Crick and in a low voice asked, "How you getting on with the young girl?" He nodded in Lashley's direction. Other heads leaned in Crick's direction.

Crick answered with a question. "Tell me something. What do you know about her personal life?"

The heads leaned even closer and listened to the old soldier.

"Talk to Inspector Springer. He know the family good. When she was a little girl, he arrested her father for beating her mother. He is a friend of her step-father."

———

Lashley and her two young female colleagues were joined by a young male officer. The two female officers had just returned from making an arrest in The Orleans. "It was a family fight. But can you imagine that, after we arrived, this young fellow threatened to burst his cousin's face? I mean, we were right there and that didn't deter him. What about your case, Shondette?"

Lashley explained that they had only just started. "The identification of the victim could be a problem. In my opinion, she was not local. We have no missing person's report fitting our redhead's description. We don't yet know the location of the primary crime scene and the decomposed state of the body is another difficulty."

Questions flew from her companions. What about DNA from the perpetrator? Anything under her nails? Anything on top of the well? Was she dragged? Anything left of her clothing? Any shoe prints? What about the vehicle that brought her there? Can they identify the murder weapon? What about facial recognition?

Lashley rose, said her goodbyes and looked over at Crick. As she left her group and headed for his table, there was a tap on her shoulder. She turned and saw the smiling face of one of the female officers she had just left at the table.

"There is someone you should talk to. He is a friend. He is a blogger and a photographer. He already phoned me for information on the case for his blog. You must know him. He used to work with the *Daily Standard*, Kyle Carmichael."

Yes, I know him. He was ahead of me at school but I haven't seen him in some time. What's become of him?"

"Well, he repairs computers, but probably makes more money taking photos of the rich and famous visiting Barbados and selling them to the international media."

"Really? What is he, six-four or six-five tall? It's hard to imagine a fellow that big hiding in the bushes to take a photo of someone."

"If you have the right equipment, you don't have to hide in the bushes. It is the size of his lens that counts," she said with a giggle. "But Kyle may have a photo of your victim if she was attractive and frequented tourist beaches. When you see photos of celebrities on the beach in Barbados, in some magazine or newspaper, there is a good chance that Kyle took them. You should talk to him."

"Let me have his number and I will give him a call."

———

They drove directly to the forensic section in Culloden Road to check with Lashley's cousin Olivia Turton for any bit of useful information.

"What are you doing here, Sergeant Crick? You are too pushy, you know. Your boss called my boss already, and now you show up. You know we have to wait on the arrival of a forensic pathologist," said Olivia as soon as she saw Crick and Lashley enter the Culloden road laboratory.

"Of course I know that. But I know you would have examined the body and already have some thoughts. I only want to know whatever you can tell me so far, unofficially," said Crick.

Olivia looked from Crick to Lashley and shook her head.

"Well. We not too long finished cleaning the bones. So I can only share my macroscopic observations with you."

"Remember that I like you to talk to me in English—or Bajan," said Crick, wagging a finger.

"Well. At this stage, there is not much to tell in any language, Sergeant. I can confirm that she was female, approximately five-foot, five inches. She suffered severe injuries to her head and shoulders, several fractures, in the fall. Her neck was broken, and that would have finished her off. But there may have been contusion of the cerebrum prior to when she was thrown in the well. Her injuries are almost all consistent with her fall into the well. However, there is evidence of a head wound over her right ear which does not appear to have been a result of the fall. It is more in keeping with a blunt-force injury from the corner of a square, heavy, sharp-edged object, an ante-mortem injury. The blow was delivered either by a left hander if she was facing the person at the time or a right hander if her back was turned. That blow most likely caused some intracranial haemorrhaging. She may have died even if she wasn't dropped in the well, but she was certainly doomed the moment she was dropped. That drop finished her off, for sure. The forensic pathologist will be doing microscopic examinations. We will be able to tell you more then."

"Thanks, Olivia. It sounds like she was murdered twice," said Crick with a smirk.

Olivia laughed and shook her head. Lashley stared at Crick.

CHAPTER 9

Whenever she left a capoeira session, Lashley felt invigorated. This evening, she had had a good workout. As she walked out of the centre, bag slung over her right shoulder and water bottle in her left hand, she thought all she needed now was a shower.

The evening's session had been interesting. There was a new member, Damian Crichlow, a thirty-year-old architect who wanted to lose weight and get fit again. He said that he had been reasonably fit in his schooldays, played a bit of cricket and football and was a shot putter. After school, his fitness gradually fell apart. He had reached that point where he knew he had to do something about it.

Then the *mestre* came over to her and said, "The new guy is yours tonight." She gave the introductory talk. Capoeira was started in Brazil by African slaves who were forbidden to practice their martial arts by the Portuguese authorities who saw it as preparation for war. The word *capoeira* is simply the Portuguese spelling of the word *kapwera*, which means *fight* in the Umbundu language of Angola. The slaves, to preserve the sport without alarming their captors, added music and turned it into a dance in which the movements of the martial art were retained but not the physical contact. The characteristics were constant movement, balance, speed and deceptive power.

He listened intently throughout her talk. She started to show him basic then more complex moves. It was during this phase of her demonstration that he managed to leave his jaw in the arc of a roundhouse kick and collapsed on the floor. Lashley dropped to her knees beside him, apologising.

He was dazed but not injured. He recovered swiftly and smiled. "I think I just learned a lesson."

Lashley knew he had been hit hard, and was impressed that he responded with a smile. He smiled much, perhaps to mask his obvious shyness. He didn't say much apart from joking that he had never been kicked by a woman before. "But that may be because I only played football with boys."

"Are you a student, miss?" he asked.

"Yes, but I am also a police detective."

"For real?" he said, wide-eyed.

Later, he mumbled goodbye to her in that timid manner of his as he was leaving.

One of the other capoeiristas teased her later about him. "I swear he said, 'If I ever break the law, I wouldn't mind being arrested by her.'" Lashley thought it was a better line than "You could arrest me anytime" or "I could show you what to do with those handcuffs, baby." The latter was a bad enough line without the "baby." The baby part really irritated her. Crude was such a turn off to Lashley. At least Damian Crichlow was polite, very polite.

The little, old, blue Toyota Carat made its way home, Lashley's mind elsewhere for the entire trip. Things do happen when you least expect. Lashley had planned an evening of reading. She had visited the library after work and before her capoeira session. She had picked up a copy of *The Red Legs of Barbados* by Jill Shepherd, and Sean O'Callaghan's *To Hell or Barbados: The Ethnic Cleansing of Ireland*. But now Damian Crichlow was on her mind. She could see his smile as they were introduced, the kind and gentle eyes. She had looked deep into those eyes and felt comfortable and relaxed. But she had stifled her own smile and looked away. Somewhere in the back of her mind, her mother's warnings about men who would fool her, use her, deceive and punish her, overrode the warmth she felt looking into those eyes and focussed on the lesson.

CHAPTER 10

"Good morning, Detective. How did your capoeira go last night?" Crick asked as soon as Lashley walked into his office.

"It went well," Lashley responded after a moment's hesitation. Crick noticed a slight change in her demeanour and wondered what it was about. But she quickly recovered and asked, "And your evening?"

Crick had met up with some of his old school friends at the Fisherman's Pub in Speightstown to discuss plans for a party for the eightieth birthday of Dalton Haynes. The case of the redhead lady turned out to be the first item on the agenda and would have remained the only item had he not put his foot down. They all had theories but nothing of use.

"I understand their interest in the case. There is a certain amount of intrigue. But I had to beg them to talk about the Doc's birthday. In the meantime, they are all on the lookout for useful information. I will see if I can arrange a mutual off day so that you can come with me to see the Doc. Two other old boys are coming as well."

"I would like that," said Lashley. "By the way, how is that granddaughter of yours?"

Crick laughed. "She is something else. She joins me when I exercise at home and now wants to go running with me in the morning. She argues that she can keep up with me because she has young legs and I have old legs."

Lashley smiled, and nodded beyond Crick. "What are Moore and Mason doing here?"

"The Chief wants to see us again this morning."

Superintendent Thomas was back in plainclothes. It had been three days since the body was found.

"Police and Immigration officials fanned out across the island yesterday and knocked on eleven doors. They were looking for eleven females who had overstayed their allotted time: four Guyanese, three Jamaicans, one Vincentian, one German, one American and one British. They said they were really interested in the German, the American and British persons, but since the records indicated that the others had overstayed, it was decided to go after them as well. I had to point out to them the diverse ethnicity of the Caribbean's population and that a redhead could be from anywhere in our region. The American, two of the Guyanese and two of the Jamaicans could not be found. The persons at the addresses on their entry cards had no knowledge of them. The British girl turned out to be a Black Londoner from Tottenham staying with her ailing grandmother. The German woman was living in the hills in St. Andrew with her Rasta boyfriend. She was blond. The American's name is Brianna Davis. She had given an address in Christ Church but the Davis family at that place had never heard of her. The address on the immigration card was very precise, it didn't simply say Rockley, Christ Church, it included the street name as well as the name of the house. The Davises have no idea why someone they didn't know would give their address. She is our focus now."

"I can't believe that Immigration was ready to rule out the Guyanese or Jamaicans," said Lashley.

"Well, they were," responded Superintendent Thomas.

"I think is the American, though" said Mason. "You would get a redhead in Guyana and Jamaica, but they are not that common. That precisely wrong address is a very deliberate falsification. That is a red flag." Mason spoke in sharp bursts as if he was always in a hurry to get the words out. He would stop and start like a driver testing his brakes.

The group was silent for a moment.

"One thing for sure, we won't find her killer until we find out who she is," said Moore.

"The Davises are still on our radar. I am told that they seemed very sincere people, but you never know," said the SIO.

"Are they in the telephone directory?" asked Lashley.

"Yes, they are. Immigration checked. This would support Mason's point about a very deliberate falsification. This woman's local connection could have simply picked their address out of the phone book because their last names were a match. She could be our Jane Doe."

The SIO wrote in his diary.

"Any update on Rebecca Hill?" asked Crick.

"We have a bit of a problem there. The Canadian landing card no longer requires visitors to declare their intended address. The immigration officer has discretion on this and will only seek this information if there are grounds for doubt of purpose of visit."

"We'll just have to ask her parents or the boyfriend for contact information," said Lashley. "But I have a friend at school in Canada. They may know people in common. We may be able to get an email address or telephone number."

"Let's start with the boyfriend...and yes, go ahead and contact your friend," said the SIO.

Sir, I think we should ask the Americans for a photo of Brianna Davis and possibly familial DNA," said Lashley.

"The request for a photo is being processed. We need more reason to believe that our victim is Brianna Davis before we involve family members."

CHAPTER 11

Meeting over, Crick was on his way outside for a smoke. The constable at the desk stopped him, pointed and said, "That man waiting for you, Sergeant." Crick glanced casually at the man in the baseball cap then walked over to him. The man removed the toothpick from his mouth and spoke in a deep voice and the unmistakable accent of a man from the country. His accent was broad as the broadest cane-field. "My name is Franklyn Odell. I hear you looking for me."

He was about six-foot tall, give or take a half-inch, lean, hard and tanned. He wore a smart-looking pair of knee-length shorts with large pockets on the sides and a flower-patterned shirt unbuttoned to expose a hairy chest. A couple of inches of blond hair protruded from under his baseball cap. He removed his dark glasses and exposed grey-green eyes.

"Sorry I only now making it, skipper. I had some business to attend to, which was why you didn't find me."

"What sort of business?" said Crick, studying him.

"Jewellery. I make necklaces and stuff, any little trinket the tourists would buy. I was out gathering woods."

"Woods?"

"For a huge order I got. Earrings. Six dozen. Different stores 'cross the island—"

"You know Rebecca Hill?" Crick asked, a little more brusquely than he had intended.

For the first time since presenting himself, Frankie paused, his eyes narrowed.

"Yes." He paused again. "She bought some jewellery from me. We became friends."

"More than friends was what I heard," Crick said with a cajoling smile. Frankie smiled back, but then his face fell.

"Rebecca's in Canada now. I hear from her all the time, by text message mostly. What you want with her? I thought it was me you been looking for?"

"Is she your girlfriend?"

He took a little time to think about his response. "Well, one of them." He smiled and looked away then back at Crick and asked again, "But what the police want her for?"

"Why did she go to Canada?"

Frankie held back for a moment. "She needed a break from this little island."

"A break from you, Frankie?"

"Not from me, skipper."

"From who, then?"

Frankie tried to read Crick's face. Crick, a curious look on it, waited for Frankie's response.

Frankie said, "From that family of hers, nuh?"

"Do you know where she is staying?" asked Crick.

He gave Crick a lizard look, cocked head, sideways glance. "Ahm, no."

"Come with me," said Crick. He turned and headed toward his office. Frankie followed.

Crick offered him a chair. Frankie sat and looked puzzled. Crick propped his backside on the end of his desk, looked down and fixed his eyes on Frankie's face. Frankie's cell phone rang. He ignored it.

"The truth will set you free, my mother always used to tell me, Frankie. So when I ask you a question, I expect you to tell me the truth. If you don't tell me the truth, I will begin to wonder what you trying to hide and too besides, you ain't a very good liar, Frankie. Now, leh we start again. What or who is she running from?"

Frankie eyed Crick thoughtfully. His cell signalled it had received a message. Frankie wriggled in the chair, eased the phone out of his pocket, took a peek at it, thought for a moment, wriggled again and put the phone back. His face relaxed somewhat as he spoke.

"Man, everybody against me and Becca. My own family, even my best friend, but most of all that family of hers. They give she ghurka cause she going out with me, all of them against me. You know them is big-up people. Listen, she aunt, she mother sister, light in Becca backside one night. Tell she that them come from proper stock, people that can trace their ancestry hundreds of years back to England, important people, and I ain't nobody, I ain't even got a job. And then she up and tell Becca that I probably descend from one of the four hundred."

"Who the hell are the four hundred?"

"Well, I never hear 'bout them, and Becca didn't know either, and the aunt won't explain. But Becca ask she outside cousin, Robin Stewart, the historian."

"Wait, Robin Stewart is her cousin?" interrupted Crick.

"Not many people know that the two of them is family. Robin always know because his mother tell them from early. Becca only find out when she went to a lecture one evening at Frank Collymore Hall. Robin was lecturing about the plantation history of Barbados. She was fascinated by the lecture and went to speak to Robin after. When he realised who she was, he explain that his great-grandfather was her great-great-grandfather. She was shocked, man. She never knew she had black family. She couldn't wait to get home to talk to her parents. Her mother say it was a lot of foolishness. Her father said it was possible but didn't confirm it. He say he ain't know what he great-grandfather got up to all those years ago. But Becca believe Robin, she could see a similarity in features with her father, and he had that reddish hair. She and Robin start exchanging emails after that. She wanted to know more about poor-white people in Barbados, her father's ancestors. She was very disturbed to hear how the planters used to treat them. Robin was vex, vex when Becca tell he 'bout what she aunt said 'bout the four hundred. He tell she don't mind she stuck-up aunt, he could tell she a thing or two about some of her ancestors; she only proud of them because she know nothing about them. But it even like *he* didn't want to explain 'bout the four hundred."

Frankie paused. Crick looked at him studiously and waited for him to continue.

"Robin tell she that in Sixteen-somebody, I forget when, there was a shortage of white women in Barbados for the men that they had grabbled up from Scotland and Ireland and England and pressgang to Barbados. So you know what they do? They rounded up four hundred prostitutes from the streets and brothels of London and ship them to Barbados." He paused momentarily, measuring Crick's face for reaction. "But the women didn't all go to poor- white fellows; some planters pick out the prettiest ones and made them their wives."

Frankie looked straight at Crick with narrowed eyes and ground his teeth.

"Frankie, one of my high school teachers used to say, 'A famous writer once said, 'read history and weep.'"

"History is shite, man. I don't care where I come from. I know who I am. That is all that matter."

"Since you say you are in contact with Rebecca, would you let us have a phone number and address?"

Frankie locked eyes with Crick, then he looked away. He transferred the toothpick from his hand into his mouth and started to chew on it. "Why do you want this information?"

"Lend me your phone for a second, please?"

Frankie gave Crick the lizard look again. "But you still ain't tell me why you want to get hold of Becca."

"We want to make sure she is alright, man."

"Of course she alright. I got to call her as soon as I get outside—Wait, *blummah*...you don't think that she is *that* redhead woman...? Jesus Christ. No, man, Becca good, real good, she fine."

Frankie looked around then leaned in toward Crick and in a soft voice said, "Look I barely know you, but I feel you, man. I going tell you a secret. Rebecca is pregnant, she having our baby. She is staying with my aunt in Mississauga. The baby is going to be adopted. But she is fine. I can call her right now." He jumped up, tugged the cell phone out of his thigh pocket and hit a couple of buttons.

The door opened and the SIO's secretary, Bevaney Wood, entered. She bent over to Crick's ear and spoke softly. "Sergeant, the super wants to see you. Lashley, Moore and Mason are back in his office already. He says you can let Mr. Odell go."

Crick turned to Frankie and said, "You free to go, man. We can talk another time."

———

"We can lay off Frankie Odell, now," said Superintendent Thomas. "According to the Canadian authorities, Rebecca Hill is alive and well and kicking in Mississauga."

They expected some detail related to Rebecca Hill's disappearance but none was forthcoming from the SIO. He left it to the imagination of people whose work was deductive reasoning. The team exchanged glances. There were smirks, even muted giggles, and a subject was silently added to the post-meeting agenda.

"Well, that's the one local lead eliminated," said Detective Moore. "That leaves us with expats and tourists. Doesn't it?"

"That's right. We have to try and find the rest of the overstayed female visitors. As soon as we have their photos, we will publish them," said the SIO.

"The critical question here is how come no one misses her. What kind of person disappears and no one notices?" said Crick.

"A runaway, a prostitute, whose parents gave up looking for her a long time ago. Someone probably paid her to come here," said Mason.

"Even prostitutes have friends who will miss them," said Lashley. "If we can find out where she is from, that's a good starting point to finding out who she is, what she was doing here in Barbados, and with whom she associated."

"Whom, whom?" whispered Mason, glancing at Moore and winking, prompting a little glare from the SIO. Lashley proceeded as if she had not heard.

"There is another angle that we haven't discussed so far. She could be a Bajan who lived overseas, came back and had a family or old boyfriend squabble. Maybe a parent died and they quarrelled over an inheritance. She would not be an overstay. She would be completely off our radar."

"She would be off our radar but not off that of other relatives. We urgently need that identification and a time of death. Then we can find people who saw this redhead lady wearing those fancy red shoes and expensive ankle bracelet. I imagine that she would have been noticed. Once we identify her, the rest should fall into place. Leave the speculation to the public," said the SIO.

"Sir, I am curious about something. If everything was brought up from the well, that would mean that any other jewellery was removed before she was dumped, her earrings, watch, bracelets, rings and necklace all gone, and her handbag...."

"You are making an assumption," said Moore, "and even if you are right, we don't know what they look like."

"No, we don't," continued Lashley, "but if they were found, it might be possible to connect them to her and her murderer through DNA."

"And whoever was in possession of them would have a lot of explaining to do," said Crick.

"That jewellery would have been sold or made into nice gifts for somebody's girlfriends. We'll need some luck to find them. In the meantime, let us continue our search for sightings of redheads," said the SIO.

Outside of the office, Crick had started to press numbers on his cell phone when Lashley approached him and asked, "Will you call your friend Bobby?" Crick turned the ringing cell phone toward her quickly then put it to his ear. He waited then said, "Bobby, AD here...Rebecca Hill is fine...I would like you to keep listening...call me if you hear anything else."

―――――

Crick returned to his desk, turned on the little radio he kept in his top drawer, and listened to his favourite call-in programme. The mystery lady in the well was one of the topics of the day. There was a procession of callers to the radio station. There were two types of callers to radio stations in Barbados, and in a way they were opposites. Some enjoyed the notoriety the medium could bring, others the anonymity while getting their views aired. The absence of factual information on the case did not deter either group from putting forward their theories. "Dis time she come off a cruise ship."…"Is she really a redhead or was her hair dyed?"…"That expensive Jewellery and clothes got to tell you that she connect with some big shot. They will never solve this crime."…"They never solve Stokes or Pele, or The Cane-field Murders, so how you expect them to solve this?" Crick switched stations until he found some easy-listening music, music that permitted him to think.

Crick had come to the conclusion that the redhead lady was on the lips of people everywhere: not just in the street, the rum-shops, buses, and homes, but he was sure also in clubs, in offices and boardrooms. The police were receiving calls but no good leads. The leads will improve when we publish photos of the shoe and jewellery, he thought. Why haven't they been published already? The wheels could turn too slowly in this island. He would ask the SIO to give Culloden Road a nudge.

It was always a huge task selecting good from bad information. This was a problem for police everywhere in the world. But in small communities like Barbados, where gossip was traded from mouth to ear even faster than a dollar moved from hand to hand, the task was much more difficult. No one knew how contaminated a dollar was; it was the same with information. People would spend the dollar anyway, but information had to be vetted and weighed and sifted by police. Crick commenced writing on the small pad in front of him. He wrote the name "Millie" at the top of the page then, one under the other, the words beaches, nightclubs, restaurants, hotels, duty-free shops. He tried to map out the likely activities of the unknown redhead. He had changed his mind about his original gut reaction to the identity of Millie. He now believed she was a visitor. Then he thought about wells: I wonder what we would find if we search-lit every well in Barbados?

CHAPTER 12

DC Shondette Lashley sat at the small desk in a corner of her bedroom to the right of the louvered glass window that overlooked the tiny back garden of her home. Her iPhone buzzed and vibrated under the printed sheets of paper she had been reading. She slid the papers aside, glanced at the device and saw that it was her cousin Olivia. She gently tapped the face of the phone and asked, "What's up, cuz?" It was six days since the body had been extracted from the well.

"Hi, Shonnie. Our unofficial notes on the redhead lady will be with your boss first thing tomorrow morning. This is a preliminary report. The final official report will be done after the forensic pathologist arrives from Trinidad."

"Tell me what you know, cuz."

"The body had been down in the well for approximately thirteen weeks. We are going to try to narrow that down some more. But two hundred feet down a well in the tropics alters the rate of decomposition and our ability to be precise on time of death. My personal opinion is that the TOD is probably during the Christmas-New Year period. But that's not just a scientific opinion. It is based on what she was wearing. It seems seasonal to me, something you would wear to a Christmas or Old Year's Night party. The skull is badly damaged but my boss agrees with me that one of her injuries, on the side of the head, is not consistent with her other injuries. It is consistent with a blow to the side of her head by the corner of some kind of blunt instrument, but this blow, while serious, did not kill her. It would have knocked her unconscious, possibly even put her in a comatose state. In the opinion of the chief analyst, she may have been alive when she was tossed into the well. Her prior injury could have been serious enough to make the killer think she was already dead. The injuries to her head and body suggest that she was thrown in head first; there are no significant injuries to her lower body, apart from her right ankle, which probably accounts for the broken ankle bracelet and the red shoe. She bounced around during the fall, so it wasn't a clean straight drop, possibly a panicked or tired throw. There are fractures and broken bones to her shoulder, and her neck, as I told you, was broken."

"What about the shoe and bracelet? Any information on those?"

"Oh, yes, most definitely. But that is not in this report. The shoes are Christian Louboutin Pigalle Spikes. These shoes are not on sale in Barbados, but they can be purchased at any Christian Louboutin outlet worldwide or online for a cost of twelve hundred and ninety-five US dollars. We are trying to find out where they were purchased. The ankle bracelet is 18-carat gold, and the diamonds are real. It may be a custom-made order estimated at about five thousand US dollars, ten thousand Bajan. We are still working on the remnants of her dress and thong. There is no evidence of sexual assault. And there is one other very important thing: she was a cocaine user. Forensics sent her dental records and DNA profile to the FBI, the RCMP and Scotland Yard for a possible match to their records. The cocaine angle means we may be able to involve Interpol. Oh, and her age—she was twenty-three years old."

After thanking her cousin, Lashley sorted the papers on her desk and phoned Crick.

———

The ringing of the cell phone startled Crick. He was on his way to his daughter's after visiting Tanya and deep in thought. Tanya had been calling him regularly. He had been visiting her less often since he had been ejected from home. Tanya had been dismayed that he had not come to live with her. He wouldn't even spend the night. He blamed it on the demands of the high-profile case he was working on. His feelings about her had not changed. He still wanted to be with her, but he also wanted to be with Natalie and the boys. He was afraid that wasn't going to happen. He and Natalie were speaking again, but she still didn't want to see him. "Anything we have to discuss we can do so on the phone." They came to an agreement on the boys. He had to apologise to them and had to discuss with her whenever he wanted to see them. She made sure she wasn't there when he passed by.

He was tense with Tanya, now. It wasn't quite the same. The passion had always been the thing, but now it had flattened. Their lovemaking had become perfunctory, and her repeat, Richter-scale orgasms had dwindled to one, if they were lucky. Things had changed. He had had extra-marital affairs before but never an extra-marital relationship and never the internal conflict that this situation now produced. The relationship with Tanya had lost ardour. She suggested they go away to another island for a short holiday. He agreed but said he wouldn't go until he had wrapped up this case.

The first ring of his phone didn't register. After the second ring, he grabbed it, looked to see if it was Tanya. To his relief, it was Lashley. He relaxed and answered.

"Uh-huh...uh-huh...uh-huh...."

He slowed down as he listened to Lashley, taking it in but somewhat distracted by thoughts of Tanya.

"Thanks for sharing. I'll see you in the morning." He pushed his foot down on the accelerator and headed to Sturges.

CHAPTER 13

Crick listened to the details of the report all over again in the next morning's briefing. His mind wandered while the SIO was speaking. He tried to focus, but the women in his life were still on his mind. "I have to uncomplicate my life," he told himself. He noticed that the SIO was glancing at him from time to time. Crick shifted his gaze to Lashley while the SIO continued speaking. He noticed that Lashley cringed when the SIO talked about the body being tossed in the well or, as he said, "It look like he jest pelt she down deh so." The lapse into dialect was not unusual for the SIO. He would, for emphasis, sometimes switch from Standard English to his usual acrolect to mesolect or even basilect, or as Barbados' greatest living poet Kamau Brathwaite called it all, Nation Language. The SIO was clearly emotional as he spoke. Human brutality touched even the most well-seasoned of cops. Lashley spoke as soon as the SIO finished.

"The dental records and DNA profile will only produce a result if she is already in their system. Truth is we don't have a clue where this woman is from. If she is not in their system, we should ask for a familial or an autosomal DNA test."

"What's auto something DNA?" asked Moore.

Moore's question was aimed at Lashley but the SIO responded quickly.

"Familial DNA could identify a sibling or parent in the system. But if there is no relation in the system, you get nothing. *Autosomal* DNA would reveal her genetic ancestry, her origins. But even that may not tell us where she lived recently. What it could tell us is something about who she is. The more we know about her, the nearer we are to finding that out. Any more ideas?"

"We could also have a forensic recreation of her face done," added Lashley.

"Some good suggestions, Detective. We may do that after the pathologist has completed his work. But you do know that facial reconstruction is not an exact science. We are also trying to find out where the shoes were bought. Once we publish the photo of the shoe, the other one may turn up."

"That's got to be gone long time, Chief. It was either at the original crime scene or in the boot of the car. And whoever had it would not keep it," said Mason.

"If we do find it, we may be able to recover a fingerprint," said Crick.

"It's not just the other shoe; it's unlikely that someone would hold on to a single shoe. That's probably gone to the landfill. But her handbag and necklace, earrings and rings, those are very valuable items," said Lashley. "We talked about this before. They must have been deliberately removed for resale."

"Resale or, possibly, gifts to girlfriends," said Crick. "The big problem is that we do not know what they look like."

"Her necklace might match her ankle bracelet in some way. We can check the cash-for-gold shops. Her handbag might be a match for her shoes," said Lashley.

Detective Moore wanted to focus on the idea that the victim was a high roller. For him, she was a visitor, and the team should be looking for couples who stayed in luxury villas over the Christmas-New Year period. "You wear them kinda clothes to big parties 'round Christmas time. We should be questioning villa staff, maids, cooks, security guards and house managers about a redhead lady whose partner left on his own and claimed that she had gone ahead."

"We should also be asking them about a couple with a supplier," said Crick.

"You know they could have brought the coke in themselves," said Mason.

"That's possible, but no tourist would know how to find a well in the middle of a cane-field," said Lashley. "The cocaine is more than likely linked to her fate."

"Very good point," said the SIO. "We'll talk to the Drug Squad. They can help us with information on suspected suppliers to the rich and famous. Sergeant Crick, I'd like you to head up to Oistins. Please stay after the meeting to discuss. Constables Lashley, Moore and Mason, I would like you to check on the cash-for-gold shops. We are looking for items matching the ankle bracelet and for information on sellers in the last three months."

The team filed out except for Crick, who immediately noticed a change in the SIO's face. He'd seen that look before. It was the time when he told Crick that his lack of ambition and his wutless ways were hindering his progress, and if he wanted to make something of himself, he should do something about his behaviour.

"You were not really with us this morning, Sergeant. Is something bothering you that you did not want to share with the group?" asked the SIO.

"Not really. I am fine, sir."

"So this case has your full attention, yes?"

"Definitely, sir."

"How are things at home?"

Crick looked away and suddenly noticed the SIO's family photo on the credenza behind his desk. He immediately thought of Natalie and their two boys. But he also remarked that photo was not normally there; it had been moved from the other side of the office, opposite the Super, where it was within his view whenever he was at his desk, never behind him. Crick nodded slowly. He looked around the office for any other alterations. He saw none. The master manipulator, the man who taught him how to persuade witnesses to talk, was up to his tricks again.

"You haven't answered. Is something wrong?"

He knows, of course, Crick told himself, then said, "Things are fine, sir. I have a decision to make, but it will not interfere with my work."

"Well, if you want to talk it over, my door is open. I hope you make the right decision."

"Will that be all, sir?"

"Yes."

Crick rose and made his way out of the office. He hopped in his car and headed in the direction of Oistins. He felt he should have told Chet Thomas that his personal life was off-limits, the way Detective Lashley had told him, and then he wondered how the SIO knew about his personal crisis.

———

The RBPF Drug Squad was headquartered at the Southern Division in Oistins in the parish of Christ Church, just past the fish market and in a complex that also housed the magistrate's court, health clinic and library. Crick met there with Sergeant Branford Clarke of the Drug Squad. They had been to the Police Training School together and got on well there. And even though they never worked together after that, they had remained friends. Crick got straight to the point.

"We think there is a possibility that there could be a link between someone on your radar and the presence of cocaine we found in the body from the well. An apparent high roller and, *we are guessing*, west coast temporary resident or visitor."

"You can buy cocaine on the west coast beaches quite easily, but it is also delivered to luxury villas. We are very actively investigating the set up down there right now." He reeled off a few names of possible persons of interest. Then he said, "There is a fellow called Arman...."

"We know Arman," said Crick. "He is a water sports operator near us in Holetown and has a bar further up the coast. We are aware of the rumours but have nothing on him apart from stories from his competitors, which could be prompted by jealousy of his success. But it sounds like you fellows have been holding out on us."

"Not really.... Confidentially, we are hoping to catch an even bigger fish. We are the Drug Squad, Crick. Up until this situation, Arman was all ours. He may now be on your patch."

"Tell me something. Why don't we import policemen to be tourists on the beaches and clean up this racket?"

"Good question. We suggested it a few times but got nowhere. I don't understand it."

"We need to work closely on this case. It may be the perfect mix of drugs and murder," said Crick.

Sergeant Clarke agreed and Crick made his exit.

———

Crick picked up a fish-cutter in Oistins and started eating it on the way back to Holetown. His lunch was interrupted by a telephone call from the Holetown station. "There is a man trying to reach you. He didn't give a name but left a cell phone number." Crick took the number and called, wondering what the person wanted. It was Frankie Odell, and he wanted to meet with Crick. He did not want to talk on the phone. He was in Jackson. They agreed to meet at the Mill in Canewood, St. Thomas. Twenty-five minutes later, they sat at a table in the outdoor bar cum restaurant at the Mill and ordered two Deputies.

"I know a fellow you should be talking to," said Frankie. "I know him from when I first start up with my jewellery. He used to sell some of my stuff. We butt-up at a shop-lime last night. He hear that the police talk to me about the woman in Prickett's well. Everybody like they hear 'bout that. This fellow say he know a man that might know something about the woman. He would talk to you. He know you, but he ain't coming to no police station, and he ain't calling no police station." Frankie handed Crick a slip of paper. "You can call him on this number."

"Thanks, Frankie. I'll give him a call. How's Rebecca?"

Frankie smiled a wide smile, setting off creased lines around his eyes. He seemed to enjoy the moment before speaking. "Rebecca good, man, we had a long talk last night. You know, she wanted me to come to Canada to live. But I don't want to leave this rock. My navel-string bury here, man. This is my home. I am a Bajan. She was in shock when I tell she that the police thought she was the woman down in the well. I going up to see her soon. I going up to Canada for a bit and we have plans for when she come back."

"Sounds good. I happy for you," said Crick, "and good luck, man."

"I going need it, because it going be cat piss and pepper 'bout here when she come back. She mother and aunt going make she shite. The old man ain't happy, either, but he dealing with it different. He had a talk with me. He say she should come back home, but she mother ain't want that at all. So we will find a place. And maybe all the men that used to run she down will stop, now."

"A lot of fellows used to run her down?"

"*Eff*? *Marred* men and all. They got one fellow, I used to play a little cricket with, *marred*, got children, and he wouldn't let Becca 'lone at all, at all. He must be feel he is King Jaja. But if he don't stop when she come back, it going be me and he."

"Ah, man, you don't want to go and get yourself in trouble, now. But if you get any trouble out of this fellow, gimme a call and we will have a little word with him."

"You know the man, Crick; he used to play cricket. He is a insurance man, one Bobby Lewis."

Crick gulped and looked away. "*Be Christ*, Lashley was right," he said to himself then turned his attention back to Frankie.

"Yes, I know Bobby. If you get any trouble out of him, just call me and I will have a word.... And listen, you must invite me to the wedding."

"Wedding?" Frankie threw back his head and laughed then turned serious and smiled. "What make you think we getting married?" he asked.

Crick didn't answer, and after a moment Frankie continued:

"It going be a little thing, man, a quiet do, no big fuss. But a lot o' things happening for me right now...she is a real special girl, man. I ain't want no other woman, now."

"What kind of things happening, man?"

Frankie stroked his chin and his expression changed. He looked quite solemn when he spoke.

"I had a long, long talk with Becca old man. He call me and invite me to the office. He asked his secretary not to disturb him for the next half hour, but we talk for over a hour, and most of the time, I was listening. He was real cool, man. He lean back in his comfortable high-back leather chair, swing to he left, and raised his feet. He rested them on top of the mahogany casing which housed his waste-paper bin. He wanted to talk to me about Rebecca. She was on his mind constantly, he said. He told me that Rebecca was named after his own mother, who he loved dearly in spite of her being such a rebel. He often thought that given the status of women back in her day, his mother needed that outward show of strength, that constant bravado, that independence of spirit, to survive with any degree of integrity. And maybe it was because she was born in 1937, the year of the historic rebellion that changed Barbados, that she was the way she was. He said his own strength was more of a quiet nature, his personality the opposite of hers, more like his father's, who would not have survived his mother without that calm rationality and knowing when to say nothing as well. Like his father before him, Rebecca's was a planner; those who didn't really care for him would call him a manipulator. But everything he achieved in his life was the result of thoughtful planning. He had only ever applied for one job in his life, his first job. After that, opportunities were brought to him and he chose the right ones. Now he was one of the most successful Bajans on the island, chairman of the board of a network of companies, on a first-name basis with the prime minister and, if the rumours are true, destined to be knighted in the very near future. He is a very proud man."

Frankie sounded different, Crick noted.

"The core company had been started by his father-in-law, who, unlike him, had inherited wealth, the result of a few centuries of plantation and commercial ownerships by his forebears. He and Diane had the two children, James and my Rebecca. Rebecca was smarter than James but was always a own-way child. In so many ways, she was a throwback to his mother; she even had her mass of red hair. They had sent her off to England at thirteen years old to that expensive *public* school, but she hated it. She missed Barbados, and some of those English girls made fun of her accent and asked her if it was true that her family made their money from slavery. She lasted one year. He and Diane were devastated. They got her back into her old secondary school, St. Felicitas. But she and her mother were always at odds. The relationship seemed to be getting better but there was always some new aggravating factor. She thought her mother was pretentious and snobbish, she didn't like Rebecca's friends, and they argued all the time. He had issues with Rebecca, too. It was as if she chose boys just to upset them. At one time there was that rally driver who used to curse like the pirate his great-great- great-grandfather was, then that surfer who didn't seem like a bad fellow but really had nothing to offer. There were so many young, ambitious and successful men who would be happy to marry her, but she told him, 'They all want some of your money, Dad. Frankie Odell loves me for who I am, for what I stand for, and that is all that matters. You could disinherit me if you wish, I don't give a damn.'"

Frankie paused and looked at Crick as if he was hoping for a response. Crick obliged. "You're the man, Frankie."

"The old man said to me, 'If you are the man she loves, I need to know more about you.' He wanted to know about my plans and how he could help...but he was really concerned about the relationship between Becca and her mother. Things were bad before. All that talk about him ignoring his black family had led to some big rows. Her mother didn't like her friends—and now her pregnancy. I let him know the reason she decided to give up the baby for adoption and to do it overseas was because she didn't want to embarrass her father and mother. Her mother agreed it was the best thing but still refused to speak with her. He wanted to arrange accommodation for her, but she refused. I arrange for her to stay with my aunt Vi in Mississauga."

She was not comfortable at Aunt Vi's, but staying with her had seemed to offer the best possibility of keeping her pregnancy quiet. She did have friends in Toronto where she could have stayed, but she knew they would have shared her secret with their friends. She wasn't ashamed of her pregnancy; her overriding concern was the timing. She wasn't ready to be a mother yet and then, equally important to her, there was the desire to spare her parents any embarrassment. The pregnancy was not planned. She had, from time to time, been negligent about taking her contraceptives.

"In spite of their differences, she loved her parents, her father particularly. Her mother, she knew, had her best interests at heart, but the two of them were so different. Her mother lived in the past; her mother used to say that Barbados was a great place to live, up until about 1950. What Rebecca had learned about the history of Barbados was at odds with her mother's views. Her year in England had awoken her to the reality of Caribbean history and the source of her mother's family wealth.... Not that she wasn't aware of it before, to be honest. But her UK experience changed her perspective on the matter. It started with teasing by a couple of the girls and escalated when they left photos on her desk, downloaded from the Internet, images of slave ships, photos of drawings of Black slaves being whipped. Then they left a book on her desk called *To Hell or Barbados*. She had mixed feelings about accepting and reading the book. She didn't trust the motives of whoever left it on her desk...but it was about Barbados. She looked around the class and saw the awkward smiles of the two she thought had placed the book there. She ignored the book at first, then with a look of defiance picked it up, thumbed through it and put it aside. But she did take it back to her dorm and she did read it, in one night.

"Next day she thanked the two girls for their gift and asked what they thought of the book. They hadn't read it; they were drawn to the title and bought it for her. "Well, you should read it. You will learn a lot about your country, this England, about its history of butchery." She tried to hand it back to them, but they refused, ever so quickly, and were clearly rattled by her words. Everyone else was nice to her, but those two girls were mean week in and week out. They annoyed her until one day she had to hit one of them, and the school expel her.

"Rebecca brought the book back to Barbados with her but couldn't interest her parents in reading it, and it disappeared from their home. She accused her mother, which led to a blazing row. No one ever owned up to taking it and it was never seen again in their house. But her interest in Caribbean history and her family's had been stirred.

"I let him know that I loved his daughter, I loved my craft. I could make a living out of it and that Rebecca and me intended to get married and have a happy life together.

"He said a lot of interesting things to me. You know his father was as poor as my father. His father raise eight o' them, four boys and four girls. All went to secondary school. He work hard for his children, and Becca father is a hard- workin' man, too. He give me a lot of good advice. He tell me that he hear I am a master craftsman. He organising a shop for me, in town in the mall."

"You going up in the world, then. It sounds like he has accepted you into the family."

Crick called over the waiter and Frankie insisted on paying for the drinks. They hugged and went their separate ways. Crick was struck by the way Frankie spoke now, how he switched to more Standard English and how his life was about to change.

CHAPTER 14

Later in the afternoon, Lashley and Crick drove north toward Speightstown in a Black Toyota Auris. It was a different unmarked car to the one they had driven before.

"Is he a fan of the R & B group?" asked Lashley.

Crick gave Lashley a quizzical stare before she explained. He had never heard of the R & B group called Summa Dat even though he liked R & B music. And the only thing he knew about the Summa Dat they were about to meet was what Frankie Odell had explained to him. "The fellow was liming with the boys one day when a girl walked past and he ssssts at she. Girls normally ignored him but not this one. She stopped, turned around, look him up and down, and when he said, 'Hey, you hear me say I want summa dat?' she answer, 'You want summa dat? Why you don't go and ask you sister for summa dat, you old dog?' The boys cackle out. On her way back, the girl shouted out, 'Hey, Summa Dat.' From then, on he was Summa Dat."

Lashley didn't think she could call him Summa Dat and tried to insist on his real name. Crick had asked Frankie, but he didn't know it.

"Despite your objection to nicknames, you are aware that in Barbados sometimes you don't know a person's given name unless it is someone you went to school with or until you see the person's funeral announcement in the newspaper. The *replacement name*, then, could be that complete. The Doc used to say that given names tell you something about your parents, nicknames or replacement names tell you something about you and sometimes about your culture. Apart from the obvious and traditional nickname arising out of an incident, you may find an individual with a West African name as a replacement name. It might be the name of an ancestor or the name of where that ancestor was born. The Doc used to give us examples of people he knew. He asked us if there was anyone in our district with an African-sounding nickname. These could be examples of how cultural memories survive and resurface. I recalled that In Orange Hill there was a man known as Amonicki, another called Bonghee and another called Karalla. These were not their given names. Then in the 1994 football World Cup, there was a Nigerian player called Amunike, and recently in the news was a place called Bangui, the capital of the Central African Republic. Karala, I discovered, was the name of a town in Guinea. My father had a friend who was known as Karalla... I think that is Summa Dat ahead."

The slightly built, short man in a tracksuit bottom, white t-shirt and sneakers strolled nonchalantly along the Speightstown bypass road, occasionally glancing over his shoulder. He stuck out his thumb in that universal signal of the hitchhiker as soon as he saw the black Toyota with the darkened windows and hired-car plates approach. The car stopped, the man pulled open the rear door, slid on to the back seat and said, "Summa Dat." Crick said, "Hai," and Lashley said, "Hi." With that briefest of introductions, the car moved on.

The car stopped under the trees near the beach at the southern end of the abandoned Almond Beach Hotel. Crick kept the motor running, windows closed and air-conditioning going. The area was almost deserted. There was one other car and a couple was having a swim nearby. Crick and Lashley turned toward the man in the back seat.

"So, I hear you know Arman real good," said Crick, with heavier emphasis on *real good.*

"If I know he good, skipper? Listen, me and he went to the same funeral last month. You know the fellow that get shoot up in Christ Church? When I get in the church and settle down, I look round the other side and I see half the back of he head, because there was a big man sitting next to he and blocking off my view. But right away, I know it was Arman. I know Arman backwards. I did working the beach for years. But my good friend

Styne is he good friend from primary school days. Arman real name is Ronald Ricardo Russell."

Arman was Ronald until his first week in secondary school. Then he became R-Man, and later on Arman. Arman was originally from St. Andrew but at eleven years old went to live with his grandmother on the west coast, which used to be known as The Gold Coast, that strip of St. James famous for its attraction to wealthy holidaymakers. It was lately referred to as The Platinum Coast. Arman loved the sea down there, swimming, and beach life in general. He left secondary school at sixteen and became a beach vendor, already wise in the ways of the adult world of a hustler. Eventually, he acquired a jet ski and went into the rental business to tourists. Over time, he expanded his watercraft and operated up and down The Platinum Coast. He not long ago set up a bar called the Triple R. He had been arrested once, when he was still quite young, for possession of marijuana, but the case never went to court. At the time, he told Styne, "I take care of that, man." But his friend thought it was a boast to promote his image as someone with power, a man with connections, because that was how he saw himself from that early age. The reality was that the quantity of marijuana was small, he was young, and the station sergeant let him off with a warning.

"Look, I is a regular at the Triple R Bar. Nowadays, people from all over the world does come and ask for Arman. People staying in million-dollar villas, people in *nuff* of these west coast hotels, and even people off o' some of these luxury yachts. He is a man does go partying on some of them yachts. He used to be a beach hustler like the rest of the fellows before he hook up with Jammer."

"He is close to Jammer?" asked Crick.

"Eff?" responded Summa Dat, raising his voice.

"Who is Jammer?" asked Lashley.

"A big man in this area," said Crick, even though the question was directed at Summa Dat.

Summa Dat did not reply immediately. Instead, he studied Lashley and then he spoke.

"You ain't know 'bout Jammer yet? You *must* be new. Jammer is one of them exiles. He does lay real, real low, but he controlling a lot of stuff. It is Jammer who take Arman to the big time. Now he wearing Armani clothes. He does scratch off the 'i' off the shirts to make it look like he wearing Arman. He wearing Rolex watch and walking into nightclubs between two women. These women come from all over the world; some of them does barely talk English. He is Jammer front man for everything, the drugs, guns and the escorts, but you will never see the two o' them together. They got a limousine now, you know. Serious dope, guns and women is what Arman is about, now. The little bar is only a front."

The swimming couple walked past with barely a glance at the Toyota's darkened windows.

"Guns? Where does he keep the guns?" asked Crick.

"I don't know," said Summa Dat.

"Do you know if there is a website for the escorts?" asked Lashley.

"No."

"Back to the guns. If you had to guess, where would you say he stashes his guns?"

"One time I woulda tell you at Princess Omenana. But she and he don't go so good now since he hook up with Jammer."

"Tell me something. Why are you talking to us?" asked Lashley.

Summa Dat grunted, looked out to sea but said nothing for a while. They waited for a response. The sun had slid behind the horizon and left the day to slowly doze off to sleep. Summa Dat was now merely a silhouette in the back seat. Then he said one word.

"Jammer."

The two police officers looked at each other.

"What about Jammer?" asked Crick.

"I don't think Barbados ever see anything like he yet. This man smart and vicious, yeah? He does speak Spanish, you know. I got to tell you, that is one man I fear. That cat-eye, red-skin bastard does give me the creeps. Wunnuh got to stop Jammer. This man ain't even 'bout here five good years yet and controlling things. That is all I got to tell you."

"Come on. Tell us what you really want to tell us," said Lashley.

Summa Dat frowned, steupsed and said: "A word to the wise should be enough."

They dropped him off by the turn-off to Clinkett's, turned around and headed south, back toward Holetown.

"Wha' you think?" asked Crick as soon as Summa Dat had closed the car door.

"Might be good information, but no definite link to our case at this point. It sounds like he really has it in for this Jammer. What do you think?"

Crick tapped his nose twice. "This tells me we are on to something. First, there is the cocaine angle. We have a high-end user and a high-end supplier in the same zone, assuming that the primary crime scene is not too far from the well. We have to find out where they intersect. But two, there is the prostitution angle. Millie may have been one of the girls Summa Dat talked about, one of Arman's escorts. And finally, Summa Dat knows more than he was willing to tell us."

Lashley frowned at the mention of Millie but did not comment. Instead she suggested, "Perhaps we should have pressed Summa Dat some more."

"It wouldn't have worked. He just wanted to point us in a direction. It is up to us to find our way from here. His type don't ever want it to be thought that they are —cock-rats—snitches, in your language. But if we need to, we can have another go at him."

"Two things, Sergeant. I know what a cock-rat is. The language of the street hasn't totally changed yet, you know. Second, I am going to do an online search for Barbados' escort services, but I was wondering if your man at Immigration checked on yacht passengers. Summa Dat mentioned yachts. I seem to remember a question being raised once in Bridgetown about the processing of yacht passengers and crew."

"That is three things and a couple of good points," noted Crick. I am not sure how thorough and detailed a check is made at the seaports by Immigration officers handling yachts. I'll talk to Burgess again."

"Sergeant, what do you make of Summa Dat's motive for ratting on a friend?"

"That's simple. His real target here is as he said, Jammer, not Arman. Jammer has moved Arman away from his old friends, taken him to another level. Jammer don't associate with these other guys. He is all business. He doesn't fit with this culture. He is all Bronx. He probably thinks these small-island characters have to adjust to him, to his way of doing things. It doesn't work that way. And Jammer will find out. His underlings may be happy with the money they are making now, but you can be sure that they will always want more. They are natural schemers and will look to discover his contacts over time. If they do, they won't need him anymore. They say you don't succeed at anything in Barbados without gaining enemies. This is a greater truth in the criminal community. So you can add jealousy to Summa Dat's motive."

"We really need to take a look at this Jammer," said Lashley.

"I am sure he is on the Drug Squad's radar. But is he connected to our case? I don't know. So we have to start digging."

As they headed south away from Speightstown Crick enjoyed the Toyota Auris's smooth ride. It had come into the island as a reconditioned vehicle and was confiscated from a drug dealer by the state after his conviction. A change in colour, new "H" number plates, and it became police property, now used to catch drug dealers.

"You know what you were saying the other day about the song 'Millie Gone to Brazil.' I was speaking to Doc Haynes yesterday and asked him about it."

"How are the birthday plans coming?"

"He says he doesn't want too much fuss for his birthday, but I am sure he is going to be one happy man when he sees so many of his former students...and hears of their progress. But back to your comments on Millie. He was of the opinion that you are using current cultural standards to judge something which belongs to a different period in history. Context is very important. Song was how news was communicated before radio and before the average person could read a newspaper. Songs had to be lively and dramatic to be more easily remembered. He mentioned another song, but in that case the victim was a man."

Crick started to drum on the steering wheel. "You know this?

"Murder in de market, murder...Murder in de market, murder...
Murder in de market, murder...Betsy Thomas she kill Payne stone dead.
　　"Payne dead, Payne dead, stone dead...Payne dead, Payne dead, stone
dead...Payne dead, Payne dead, stone dead...Betsy Thomas she kill Payne
stone dead.
　　"Ah ain't kill nobody but muh husband...Ah ain't kill nobody but
muh husband...Ah ain't kill nobody but muh husband...So ah kin face de
judge independent...
　　"Payne dead, Payne dead, stone dead...."

"I never heard that song. But my question still remains. Did they really have to be happy songs?"

"But who tell you they were happy songs?"

They argued about it all the way back until Crick drove the Auris around the rear of the St. James Parish Church and let Lashley off where he had picked her up. She would walk back to the Holetown station to pick up her car. The Auris vehicle was not to be seen anywhere near a police station.

"I am heading straight off," said Lashley. "See you tomorrow."

"See yuh. Get home safe." Crick waved her goodbye and then watched as she set off at a brisk pace. He told himself that rumours of her awkward personality were exaggerated. Perhaps it had been by fellows who didn't like women standing up to them or who had difficulty with women with their own opinions.

CHAPTER 15

Crick had had a hard night. He had been up to Orange Hill for his weekly visit with his mother. Ma Crick was happy to see him. Unlike his sister, his mother had never said much about the breakup of his marriage. She had been saddened but seemingly blamed it on his genes. She told him, "You just like your grandfather. He had nuff women. Every few years somebody would turn up at our house and say that they were family to us."

"I promise you, Ma, that I ain't got no outside children."

"They find out who the woman in the well is yet?" she wanted to know. And Crick told her, "No, not yet."

"She must be a wicked woman."

"Why would you say that, Ma?" asked Crick.

"You should read your Bible. She is a Lilith....The Psalms say the wicked shall perish. Like smoke, they vanish away. You should try to live a godly life, son. Don't let wicked women lead you astray, or you, too, will vanish away."

"She is not wicked and she did not lead me astray, Ma."

"You should read your Bible, son. You want a cup o' tea?"

"I could do with a rum, Ma."

"You know you ain't going find none of the devil water in here."

"Not since Pa died, you mean."

Crick hugged his mother. "You know I just giving you a hard time, Ma. Right? I will have a cup of tea with you."

They talked some more. She was unhappy with the changes she saw in the village. "A lot of new people come in. The young people smoking nuff dope and fighting dogs and walking 'bout with guns. This used to be a peaceful place. But me, I leaving everything to the Lord. He never fail me yet, son."

He hugged her again before departing for Gambie's rum-shop.

The boys in the shop were real happy to see him and he was happy to see them. He forgot his personal problems and his mother's dire warning as he knocked back some Mount Gay Black and listened to the drinkers expound on all manner of current affairs national and international in-between plying him with questions about the case. There were more experts in rum-shops than in any other establishment of learning on earth. Crick heard many theories about the redhead lady's killer; none that he hadn't thought of himself or already heard. At some point they put on Gorg's 2014 Crop Over hit, "I Got My Rum," and the entire crowd joined in a raucous rendition of the song. Crick somehow thought that the lyrics "My woman left me...she tek de TV...she tek de stereo...but I got my rum" were a snide reference by his rummy friends to his situation, even though it was he who had been kicked out. He let it slide and joined in the song. Before long, he was the lead singer and the chorus was mixed with much laughter.

He left Gambie's a bit bleary eyed, but the old Nissan drove him home to Sturges. He had to meet his team next morning at Holetown station.

CHAPTER 16

Detective Barry Mason, recently transferred from the southern to the northern division, asked in that open-mouthed St. Philip accent of his, "Sergeant. Tell me summore 'bout Jammer." Words tumbled out of Mason's mouth as if he was in a hurry to get rid of them. The team was still getting used to his stop-start manner of speaking.

"Let Moore tell you. He born and raised in Speightstown and know Jammer personally."

"His real name is Jamar Bentham," said Moore, straightening up in his chair. "He was born in St. Lucy, on the eastern side, up near to Cuckold Point. He lived with his mother and grandmother until he was four or five then he, an older sister and his mother joined his stepfather in the States. He returned to Barbados five years ago at forty-one years old. It is rumoured that he put up the monies for the water sports equipment at that new hotel in St. Lucy, Apple Bay. The concessionaire is his cousin, a Speightstown man. The Speightstown police believe that his cousin would not have had the start-up capital. So they think that Jammer bought the equipment and is leasing it to his cousin. They have no evidence of this as these are no paper arrangements but are still very binding as you would know. There are a couple of speedboats, jet skis, wave runners, sailboats, and a glass-bottom. Actually, that glass-bottom boat predates the hotel and is the property of the cousin. Everything else belongs to Jammer, we believe. His grandmother died some years ago. When he returned, he at first resided with an aunt in Pie Corner. He has been a model citizen here on the face of it. He lives a quiet life in a rented bungalow in St. Lucy. He seems to host a succession of women at his home. The neighbours can't say a bad thing about him. But there are all sorts of rumours. We go to the same gym in Speightstown."

"Jammer is what the fellows call an exile. We have a file on him, courtesy of the New York authorities," said SIO Thomas. "He lived in New York most of his life. After he graduated from high school, he went to work in a bank as a teller in Manhattan. At some time, he made friends with a customer who ran an extremely successful nightclub. Apparently Jammer was attracted by the size, of the customer's bank account. The nightclub became Jammer's favourite hangout and he developed a friendship with its proprietor. Jammer then started working for him, evenings and weekends as a delivery man. The customer was involved in crime, selling guns, drugs, and women. Then one morning, Jammer fell victim to New York's stop and frisk laws when exiting a nightclub with a loaded weapon on him. A subsequent search of his apartment revealed two more guns and a level of luxury not supportable by his salary as a bank teller. He served about eight years in prison before being released and repatriated to Barbados."

"And he has never been in any trouble with the law here?" asked Lashley.

"No, nothing at all," said the SIO.

"His sentence seems a bit long for a first offence, though," said Mason.

SIO Thomas took up the response. "One of his weapons had been used in a robbery some time before, possibly before it came into his hands. That was enough to link him to organised crime. But we have reason to believe that he still has strong connections with his gang back in New York. Apparently, they never gave each other up. Since his return to Barbados, we have seen a huge increase in the amount of cocaine in the north of the island."

SIO Thomas reflected before continuing. "Since the 1980s, more than a thousand criminals have been repatriated to Barbados from the USA. Most of them were minor offenders but a small number were hardcore. Like Jammer, they were Barbadian-born and had gone or been taken to the States when young. Unlike Jammer, some had no close relatives in the island and soon after their return here, developed an association with the local criminal community, their new family."

Crick took over. "The boys at the Drug Squad suspect that Jammer is importing cocaine from Colombia, through Venezuela, Guyana and Trinidad. Some of it stays here but most of it ends up in America, taken by mules. The mules take two cases, one with personal effects and the other with concealed dope. The suitcase with the dope never makes it to the conveyor belt in the arrivals hall at the other end. Jammer has baggage handler connections at the airports who transfer the baggage tag to an identical suitcase with some clothing and other personal items in it. That is the case that ends up on the conveyor belt and is picked up by the mule, who clears customs with two clean cases. The bag with the dope makes its way out of the airport through the baggage handlers' network. The Drug Squad fellows believe Jammer has brought a level of sophistication to the drug trade in the north of the island. But they have nothing to charge him with right now. He is never anywhere near the dope. He has a Barbadian passport and visits other islands from time to time to set up deals. Jammer is the top exile in Barbados right now."

"You remember the Dead Bolt Man, so called because of his particular expertise with unlocking dead bolts? He was an exile. The man who murdered the two people in Salters, he was an exile. Some exiles speak Spanish, probably through a close association with Puerto Ricans and nationals from the Dominican Republic in New York. This language ability has facilitated linkages with South American crime cartels," added Crick.

"Barbados became a transit point for cocaine, part of a triangle involving Colombia and the USA (New York and Miami). The drugs went north; cash and guns came south. Often the triangle expanded to a quadrilateral, inclusive of Trinidad," said the SIO

"How might he be connected to the redhead lady?" asked Lashley.

Crick spoke again: "Coke. Nearly all the coke north of Holetown is his. If she bought it on the beach or had it delivered to her hotel or villa, it would have originated with the same wholesaler. A foot soldier would have sold it to her. That might explain her connection to someone who knew where to dump her body. But we don't really know at this point. We are fishing. Sir, I would like Detective Lashley to make contact with that aunt of Jammer's and pay her a visit. Let's see what else we can find out about the man. Detective Moore can assist with locating the house. But she should go on her own. The old lady will probably be more comfortable chatting with a female."

CHAPTER 17

DC Lashley, in unfamiliar territory, was pleased with herself for finding the way to Pie Corner so easily. Pie Corner. What had Crick said about St. Lucy's exotic names?

She stopped in front of the small green and yellow wooden bungalow. There was an old lady sitting in the small veranda, no doubt waiting for the policewoman who had called her to arrange an appointment.

Aunt Merle, in a pretty yellow dress, got up from her rocking chair and greeted DC Lashley nervously. "Girl, you look too young and slight to be a police," she said, laughing.

"I am old enough to handle myself. But they told me I would be meeting an old lady. You don't look so old to me," said Lashley, smiling.

Aunt Merle laughed even more. Lashley reached out and gave her a very firm handshake, as if to counter any notion that her slight appearance might suggest weakness.

Aunt Merle hadn't seen Jamar for some time.

"Look, he is my little sister son, but he is no blasted good. When you call me, I know you wanted to talk about my nephew. My sister carry him up to America as a little child. Her husband never really like the boy; he ain't the father, you know. My sister never call nobody name as father. The people say that the father is a overseer off the plantation. The boy had a good job in a bank but get in with all sort of bad company in America and end up in jail. She never take out citizenship for him, so when his sentence over, they send him back here. I went to meet him at the airport. I understand he come off the airplane in handcuffs with two men, one either side. When he walk out the airport he didn't know me. But he get in my house, on the phone all hours, sometimes he talking Spanish, I can't understand a word he saying."

"How long did he live with you?"

"Child, he only lived at me for a very short while, three months in fact. After his first month, I received a telephone bill for over two thousand dollars. My dead mother dream me one night and tell me to get him out of my house."

Aunt Merle said she asked him to pay the bill and leave, and he did. He came by from time to time. "He does just turn up, I never know when he coming. A couple of times lately he come with this American girl, she real pretty, you know. I don't know what she see in him with all them tattoos all over his body."

"What was her name?"

"Anna."

Lashley's face lit up. Anna could be short for Brianna, the missing American who put a false address on her landing card, she said to herself and hurriedly asked, "What was her last name? What did she look like? What colour was her hair?"

"She was a pretty girl with dark hair, but I never know her last name."

"Are you sure about the colour of her hair?"

"Oh, yes. I old, but I ain't blind, you know."

"When was the last time you saw her?"

"It was Christmas Eve day. He bring me a little something for Christmas. We sit down on this little veranda and had a drink of sorrel. The girl hug me up and call me auntie. She too sweet, have nice long hair. I wish I had hair like that, soft and long."

"What else can you tell me about her?"

Aunt Merle thought for a moment and then said, "She got a little accent. It ain't pure Yankee."

"What sort of an accent?"

"I don't know, really."

Lashley asked to be excused for a moment. She distanced herself from the old lady and phoned Crick. "Brianna Davis may be Jammer's girlfriend. But she is not a redhead."

Crick said that she was still a person of interest as she had misinformed Immigration of her intended address in Barbados and she was associated with a suspected drug dealer.

Lashley turned to Aunt Merle and said, "You have been so helpful. Oh, I almost forgot to ask you. Do you still have that phone bill?"

"No, he take the bill. He pay it and bring me back the receipt, but he keep the bill."

Lashley made a note in her notebook.

"You know, he never even tell me where he living."

"And you have no idea where he is living now?" said Lashley, wondering whether auntie was hoping to get this information from the police.

"He ain't tell me, you understand, but I hear he living here in St. Lucy in a place they call Northwood Park."

Northwood Park was a small housing development, built in the boom years of the Nineties and marketed to returnees, persons who had immigrated to Britain, the USA or Canada when they were young. Now retired, they had chosen to return to the land of their birth, some for the winter months only, others for most of the year. Some of the houses were purchased purely as investments and rented out. It was located near to the Apple Bay Hotel.

"What about a phone number?"

"He ain't give me, but he still call me sometimes, though. And he does ask if I need anything. But I don't need anything from him, you understand."

"Did any of his friends visit him while he lived with you?"

"Not visit here. But they used to pick him up in cars. They never come inside this house. But he got his own car, now."

"Did you recognise any of his friends?"

"No, not at all. I tell you that they didn't used to come in the house."

Detective Lashley thanked Aunt Merle and headed for her car. She phoned Crick with two more bits of information—a possible address for Brianna Davis and the need to initiate proceedings to get a transcript of Aunt Merle's telephone calls from the telephone company. "Jammer might have made a serious mistake by making those calls on her phone," she told Crick. The police could not only obtain numbers of his overseas contacts but also any cell phone numbers Jammer was now using. Crick agreed and said, "We have already alerted Immigration about Brianna Davis. It would be good if we could accompany their officers on this one. And once we have Jammer's contact numbers we can turn them over to the tappers."

The matter-of-fact way he said tappers made Lashley uneasy. She certainly understood the need at times for telephone surveillance, but in her opinion it ought not to be such a casual affair and should only happen when the appropriate warrant had been obtained. She hesitated and decided not to say anything else to Crick on her cell. Telephone surveillance was a big talking point after one very senior officer went public with an allegation that his phone calls had been bugged by his own police force. There were also rumours that the telephones of some very senior politicians had been bugged.

Back at the station, Lashley suggested to Crick that they should visit Jammer to see if Brianna Davis was there.

"The Chief says that this is an Immigration matter, an overstay, so we should leave it to them and not get sidetracked but maintain our focus on the murder case."

"But don't you think that there might possibly be a link between Jammer and the redhead woman?"

"It's a possibility, yes," replied Crick, "because of the cocaine. But I think that the man nearer to any dope transaction with this woman would be Arman. And you know what they say...when the fruit is too high, you shake the tree."

Lashley eyed Crick uncertainly. "Do you know Arman at all?"

"I've seen him around but never had any real dealings with him, but I expect that he would know me."

"Yep, and probably better than you know him."

"You and I will pay a little visit to Arman tomorrow morning. And, after Arman, it will be Jammer."

CHAPTER 18

Crick and Lashley drove out of the Holetown station and headed north to the Triple R Bar. Crick parked behind a Banks beer truck in front of the bar, on the wide pavement of hard-packed marl. The two detectives walked to the front of the wooden building, through the open door, and crossed paths with a man wheeling a trolley stacked with crates of empty beer bottles.

The bar was an old three-bedroom chattel house with a fresh coat of nearly white paint on the outside and an extended canvas-covered area at the side and to the front, with plastic tables and chairs. The interior was unpainted, with rafters exposed below a close-boarded ceiling. A partition had been removed to accommodate the bar counter, to create more space by combining what was once a bedroom with what some people still called the front-house, others, the living room—the choice of name an indicator of one's social status in Barbados. Some effort had gone into the selection of furnishings, but Crick couldn't help wondering why they hadn't painted the interior. The wooden floor had been stained and the wicker furniture with cushioned seats was a nice touch, except the decorator's efforts had been spoiled by the graffiti on the walls. Crick had never been to the Triple R. He considered it something of a tourist trap, not a real rum-shop, and he was a real expert on rum-shops, not like his sociologist brother who had studied and learned about rum-shops in classrooms and had invited Crick to come hear him deliver a talk on rum-shops to some group of tourists.

The man behind the bar glanced over his shoulder and saw them but continued with the task at hand. He lifted a bottle from the shelf, turned it on its side and measured it with his eyes. He put the bottle back on the shelf, turned around and wrote on the sheet of paper on the clipboard on the bar counter. Then he looked up from his paperwork and asked, "How can I help you?"

Crick began to say who he was.

"You don't need to introduce yourself, Sergeant Crick. You know me and I know you. But the lovely lady is new to me. I could use a bartender like you," said Arman, casting a searching eye over Lashley.

"Yes, you would use her if you could, alright."

"I don't like your insinuation, Sergeant. Why you want to bad-talk me in front of a stranger? Listen, can I offer you something to drink? The bar isn't open yet, but I can make an exception for such important people."

"We want to ask you a few questions."

"One question I could handle but not a few. You could give me five minutes? Let me finish taking stock. Have a seat."

"Sure, you finish taking your stock, no problem," said Crick.

Crick nodded to Lashley and the two detectives slowly walked around the room examining the graffiti-splattered walls.

"He speaks well," commented Lashley.

"When it suits him," said Crick.

"Just like you," said Lashley.

They both looked at each other and exchanged smiles then continued their slow walk around the room. They discovered that John and Judith from Dartmouth were there 11th April 2011, Jackie and Bob from New Jersey wrote how much they loved Barbados, Kilroy had been there, too, and under Kilroy's message someone had written something in an unrecognisable language.

The two mused over the indecipherable etching. "It's all Greek to me," said Crick.

"No, it could be Latin…. Very unusual, very interesting," said Lashley, aiming her camera phone at the bit of graffiti.

Crick nodded at Lashley to follow him down the corridor. They had walked a few steps when the voice from behind the bar spoke up.

"Alright, folks, I am ready to talk to you now," said Arman quickly as he came out from behind the bar. He was wearing a pair of smart olive-coloured shorts, loafers, a polo shirt with the name Arman inscribed on the left breast, a weighty looking gold chain and a smile to match. Crick looked for and noticed the outline of a faint letter *i* after *Arman*.

"Shall we sit outside?" asked Crick.

"Ah, no. Leh we sit down here."

They sat at a round table. Arman looked relaxed as he leaned back in his wicker chair.

Crick weighed straight in. "Pimping or, as we say, living off immoral earnings, is a crime in Barbados. Sex trafficking is a global crime...."

"Hold on. What you talking 'bout, man?"

"This escort agency racket you are involved in is criminal activity and you are under investigation."

Arman raised a hand. "Sergeant, you are mistaken. We arrange companions. That is all we do, nothing else. If the persons involved decide to take their relationship further, that is nothing to do with me. They are consenting adults. The escort business is a global business." He spread his arms outward, palms up, and raised his shoulders, his brow raised, too, and eyes opened wide.

"You are a sex trafficker, Ronald, and one of your girls has turned up dead."

Crick and Lashley kept their eyes focused on Arman, reading every line in his face, every twitch and every movement of body. A perplexed frown rapidly formed on Arman's face. "What you talking 'bout, man?"

"You know what I am talking about, the redhead lady."

"Whoa, whoa, whoa, —whoa—hold on." He stretched out both arms, palms up again. Crick glanced at Lashley and knew she could also see the cogs turning in Arman's brain.

"All the redhead ladies I know *living*. Don't go no further, sir. I know exactly where you coming from. I ain't in nothing so," he continued very quickly in a raised voice. He smiled, somewhat nervously, and said, "I like my ladies hale and hearty, beautiful and bountiful." He made an air-sculpture of a female figure with his hands and laughed louder but still clearly nervous.

Lashley opened the thin case she was carrying, pulled out a photograph and laid it on the table. "Have you ever seen this?" she asked. She pointed at the photo of the red shoe with studs all over.

Arman stared, then his eyes shifted quickly back and forth before saying, "No, I never see that," in a tone of voice noticeably lower.

Crick responded immediately, leaning forward, looking directly into Arman's face and speaking in a controlled tone. "I hear what you say, Ronald. But your eyes tell me something else. You see these shoes before, right? What you know 'bout them?"

"Not me. Not me. I never see shoes like that."

"Well, you know what? The woman who wore it left her DNA in that shoe. We will soon be able to identify her," said Lashley.

Arman's face registered a very slight tremor, an involuntary minor movement of the muscles. Crick's face did not change even though he knew she was bluffing.

"You know what? I think we should go down to the station and talk about this," said Crick, sitting upright.

"You don't understand. I can't help you at all, at all."

"What I understand is what I see. You almost caught a fit when you saw the picture of that shoe. Tell me something. What happened to the other shoe and the bag and her jewellery?"

"What bag and jewellery? I tell you, I ain't know nothing 'bout no shoes and no friggin' bag. And you can keep me at the station for as long as you like."

Arman now seemed confident enough. Only the tiny droplets of perspiration that appeared on his nose countered the bravado in his voice and his face.

Crick smiled as he remembered something Lashley had said to him before they left the station. *"We must be sure to take a picture of the shoe with us and ask about the handbag. There must be a handbag to go with that outfit. We may not know who she is, but you don't dress like that to go unnoticed."*

"Look. I will come to the station as soon as my barman get here. You go 'long, I will come."

"How soon will the bartender be here?" asked Crick.

Arman looked at his Rolex. "Ten minutes."

"Where is your car?" asked Lashley.

"It park at the back, a red BMW. Do you want a lift in a classy machine? You have a choice, the BMW or I could give you a ride in my limousine."

"No, thank you. But you can be our guest for the ride. We'll wait," said Crick.

"I better call the barman to make sure he on the way," said Arman, getting up and heading toward the bar. He picked up the phone on the back bar-counter, glanced over his shoulder at Crick and Lashley, and started to speak softly.

Crick walked up to the bar. Arman paused, turned and looked him up and down scornfully. "Can I have a glass of ice water?" asked Crick. Arman raised his voice as he concluded his conversation with the words "Come quick. I have to accompany these two policemen to the Holetown Police Station.... Yeah, see you soon." He hung up, grabbed a goblet, lifted the handle of the post-mix dispenser and put it over the goblet. He pressed the water button.

"I will come to the station, but I can't help you. So there is really no point. I ain't got a thing else to say, man."

"Let's head down to the station anyway and we'll chat some more there. By the way, the picture you just saw will be on TV tonight and in the papers tomorrow," said Crick. He observed Arman closely again.

"You think them is the only pair of shoes like that in the whole world? Even if I did see a pair of shoes like them sometime, I couldn't tell you when or who was wearing them."

"Well, come down to the station with me and give the matter some more thought. You might remember the woman and maybe even who she was with," said Crick.

"No, not at all. All kinds of people come through here 'round Christmas time." Arman gulped back his words. But the pebble had left the gutter-perc. There was no recalling it. Crick's face took on a look of triumph.

"Ronald, we never mentioned Christmas or any other time. Why don't you want to help us? We would like to know what this woman looked like. We are asking for your cooperation. We are not accusing you of anything. We would like to sit you with an artist to produce a drawing. I'd like you to accompany us to the station," said Crick, "that's all. We'll give you a lift...and bring you back."

"I can't help you, officer. I can't remember the people."

"You know, a long time ago I discovered that proximity to a police cell improves memory. It is an amazing fact."

The barman walked through the door. Arman said that he had something to show him and led him into the back room. They remained there for five or six minutes. Crick phoned SIO Thomas. Lashley was beginning to think he may have sneaked off when Arman reappeared. He strolled slowly between the detectives to their car and sat in the back seat. No one spoke on the way to Holetown. They parked outside of the front of the station and started to walk in the direction of the entrance. Arman walked very slowly, as if he were shackled at the ankles, and kept looking over his shoulder.

SIO Thomas was waiting at the entrance to the police station. He watched as Arman shuffled in, constantly looking back over his shoulder.

Thomas called out, "Hey, Arman, are you some kind of a Sankofa?"

Arman stopped in front him. "What the hell is a Sankofa?"

The SIO frowned. "Perhaps you should look it up. Let's go, man."

Arman looked over his shoulder once again and smiled as he saw a green SUV swing into the station's car park. The car park was full and the driver of the SUV waved two fingers at Arman as he guided the vehicle out the other end of the car park, past the post office, and turned right toward the beach.

"I see you gone and got yourself a lawyer. Lawyers in Barbados can take ages to do a simple task, but you can get one to come to you in less than half an hour. You are a big shot now," said Crick.

Arman stared at Crick. "Bigger than you will ever be, Crick."

"Tell me, then. Why do you think you need a lawyer?" asked SIO Thomas, putting an arm gently around Arman's shoulder to look him in the eye. The Chief smiled. Arman was surprised by the gesture and ducked out of the embrace immediately. He looked around to see who might be watching this public display of friendship. Thomas placed his arm on Arman's shoulder again.

Arman threw off Thomas' arm and turned to face the SIO. "Now let me tell you something, Mr. Policeman, me and you ain't no fucking friends," he shouted, his face contorted and an index finger inches from the SIO's face.

"Uh-oh. Indecent language in a public place?"

Some passers-by stopped on the sidewalk and in the car park, and gawked, curiosity outweighing the urgency of their planned tasks.

"Indecent language? Whuh, you ain't hear *nutten* yet, yuh *igrunt*, short-me-crutch idiot. You doan know who you messing wid," Arman yelled.

"Oh? That sounds like an insult *and* a threat to me. Sergeant, please take this man inside and charge him. Be sure to add insulting and threatening an officer of the Royal Barbados Police Force to the charge, and make sure to fingerprint him."

The SIO was a picture of calm, like a teacher talking to a student, giving friendly advice. Crick had seen him employ this tactic on similar occasions and had used it himself many times before. The minute a suspect started cursing, he'd immediately inform him of his arrest for indecent language. Once done, the suspect would then go all the way, with more cursing as if to say, "If you are going to charge me with using indecent language, let me make it *really* nasty." The thing was to stay calm; this irked the suspect even more, leading to escalated cursing and threats.

More passers-by stopped and moved closer to the scene. They looked and listened, seemingly eager to follow what was happening; two other policemen came out of the station. The driver of the green SUV walked briskly toward Arman and the SIO.

"What's going on?"

"And who are you?" asked SIO Thomas.

"You know who I am, Superintendent, you've seen me in and around the courts quite a few times," said the man who had waved at Arman as he drove past moments before.

"We have never been introduced. Who are you?"

"I am his lawyer."

"And does his lawyer have a name?"

The young lawyer stared directly into the SIO's eyes. "My name is Corey Greene."

"Well, Mr. Greene, your client is about to be charged with a couple of offences."

"I wish to speak with my client privately."

"After we have charged him, he is all yours. We don't plan to hold him, unless he gives us cause to change our mind, of course."

"Bad things happen to people like you, Thomas," said Arman.

"Be sure to write that down as well, Sergeant."

"Ronald, control yourself," said the lawyer with some acidity in his tone.

Crick noticed that Lashley looked as if she was intrigued by the exchanges taking place.

The SIO turned smartly. He followed Crick and Arman as they entered the arched entrance of the police station, Corey Greene behind them.

Arman turned his head and said to his lawyer, "This is bare foolishness. You got to get rid of this."

"Sankofa," said the SIO without breaking stride. He then sped up, overtook the two in front and headed toward his office.

Arman shouted after the departing SIO, "You know whuh you can do, Thomas...?"

"Ronald, Ronald, no more talking. Just shut up, man," said the lawyer.

"He call me a sankofa. Wha' that?" Arman asked, looking back at his lawyer.

"Some kind of a bird."

"So he think I going sing. He can think again."

"No, the sankofa looks back as it goes forward. It flies while looking back. So turn around."

"Talking about looking back, I have a question for you, Arman," said Crick. "Why does a man with no criminal record have a criminal lawyer on his speed dial?"

"Do not answer that or any more questions," said Corey Greene.

"And why did they only send a junior to represent you?"

"You see you, Crick, God blind you...," menaced Arman.

"Ronald, shut up!" said Corey Greene.

"That's right, shut up, little boy," Crick sneered.

The words stung, and Arman swung like a tightly coiled spring unravelling, his balled right fist speeding in the direction of Crick's face. Crick swayed backward, surprised not by the attack but the speed of it. Arman's fist caught Crick's nose. Crick's head jerked backward. He was still off balance when he saw Lashley fall to her left. Her right leg flashed upward in an arc and the heel of her shoe crashed into Arman's ribcage. There was a sharp crack. Arman yelped, tumbled, holding on to his sides, and yelped again. The other two policemen fell on him, pinning him down. Exclamations, chatter, mocking laughter erupted among the handful of onlookers in the car park and on the sidewalk. Arman whined and winced.

"Cheese-on-bread, you see that girl? She like a ninja woman!"

"Oh, Lord, man, that woman policeman just lick up Arman!"

"Blummah, he get kick real hard, yeah."

Crick wiped a hand across his bloody nose and turned to Corey Greene. "We are holding him, *now*."

Arman spluttered, wheezed and grimaced. Lashley kept her eyes on him, pumped and steely, ready for any other sudden moves. More passers-by paused, some on the sidewalk; others drew nearer.

Corey Greene faced Crick. "Clear case of provocation by both Superintendent Thomas and you, Sergeant. My client is injured and in need of medical attention."

"I am injured, too," said Crick, holding his nose. "I guess we better call an ambulance."

"No, I'll take him across the road to the Sandy Crest Medical Centre. You may send an officer to maintain custody."

"He is in our custody. He will leave here in an ambulance," called out the returning SIO in a voice whose authority was not to be questioned.

Arman moaned loudly.

"My client needs immediate medical attention. Do you know how long it may take to get an ambulance here?" asked Corey Greene.

"Your client is alert and making a lot of noise. He is in pain, yes, but not seriously injured," said the SIO.

"So you are a medical doctor, now, Superintendent? I will hold you personally responsible. This matter will be reported," said Corey Greene. His voice was loud and angry.

"I am not a doctor, but I have seen seriously hurt people before and I know enough that we should not move him. We should leave that to professionals. The constable on desk duty is trying to get hold of the nearest available doctor." The SIO turned to one of the officers and said, "Bring two glasses of water, one for Mr. Arman and the other for his lawyer."

"I don't want anything to drink from you, Superintendent Thomas, now or never. I will deal with you in court, you'll see," said Corey Greene. His face was as serious as a boar-cat at a christening, thought Crick, recalling one of his mother's favourite expressions. He never understood whether the boar-cat was being christened or was simply a confounded witness to the ritual splashing of the child's head.

"I didn't say I wanted you to drink the water. You may want to pour it over your head to cool yourself down," said Thomas, calmly, but loud enough for the audience to hear. Laughter broke out among the onlookers. Corey Greene looked even more serious than a boar-cat at a christening.

"Let me make something clear, Superintendent. My client is not going all the way to Bridgetown to wait in a so-called emergency room for the rest of the day. He is going to the nearest private medical facility. He will pay for his treatment and will sue you and the police force."

"That's fine with me, but he is under arrest and will return to our custody. On his return from hospital, whenever that is, he will be charged and held," said the SIO.

Recent arrivals, whatever business they had planned in Holetown now put on hold, were all enquiring about the goings-on. "That girl drive a kick in he ribs," somebody said. There was laughter. Arman's face contorted in pain and contempt. His eyes darted from Crick to Lashley.

"The doctor's here," announced a female voice as she made her way through the onlookers. "The ambulance will be here in another ten minutes. Let me have a look."

She knelt beside Arman and asked where he was injured. She proceeded to press his ribcage gently, causing him to wince and moan.

"Breathe easy, don't cough," said the doctor. She took his blood pressure and eventually declared that, in her opinion, he had two badly bruised ribs and even possibly a fracture.

The ambulance arrived and took Arman away. A police car, followed by Corey Greene, tailed the ambulance.

A late arrival enquired what had happened to the man in the ambulance. "The police beat he," someone said as the ambulance sped away.

The SIO pulled Crick and Lashley aside. "What happened here?" he asked in a low voice.

"He attacked me, and Lashley put one of her capoeira moves on him. Jesus, Chief, you shoulda seen her, like lightning. Arman didn't know what was happening. He couldn't react, she was so fast." Crick turned to Lashley with undisguised pride. "Thanks, Mandi." Lashley smiled, and the tensions in her face, in her body, faded.

"You will have to submit reports. A man has been injured while in police custody. I am glad it happened outside the station, in front of witnesses. It would help if you could get some statements. Have a look at that crowd and select a couple persons. Crick, you know what to look for. I am heading back to the Triple R to talk to the barman while Arman is not there. We need the names of as many people as possible who were there around Christmas time. Sergeant, call your informant. He might be able to help as well. And get that blood off your face."

"I ain't see *nutten*" was the response of the first selected potential witness, a well-dressed young man. He walked away.

"I saw him hit you, Sergeant," said the second choice, an elderly woman. "Some of these young people frighten for their own shadow," she added.

An elderly man also volunteered. Witness statements and the writing of reports plus repeated interruptions from other officers wanting to talk about the incident took up much of Crick's and Lashley's time. The male officers all fussed over Lashley, repeatedly checking to see if she needed help with anything. It was as if they had found a new hero, someone with whom they wanted to associate more closely.

"I didn't know you were into karate," one fellow commented. She talked about her capoeira training and was surprised how little they knew about it.

"Can I bring you some lunch?" one officer asked. She accepted but insisted on paying and asked that they check with Sergeant Crick as well. "And *van-food* will do," she said.

"I am treating you today," insisted the young man. "I am getting you something from Zacchio's or Lemon Grass. Can I call you Mandi?"

"No, you can't."

———

It was early afternoon when Corey Greene returned to the police station with Arman and his police escort. The attorney requested a meeting with Crick, in his office. Crick came out and stood behind the counter.

"We can talk here," he said.

Corey Greene began to apologise on behalf of his client. "You know that Thomas was provoking the man all the time, and you join in, too. And too besides, he has already been punished. He should be home resting. He has a fractured rib. The doctor said he received a severe blow. The doctor didn't believe that a woman kicked him. Who is that female officer? Is she a trained martial artist? Because if she is, her response was excessive, and I will have to deal with that if the assault charge is not withdrawn."

Crick stared at the man for what seemed a long time before responding. "Corey Greene, your apology is not accepted. Arman get kick in his ribs, not his mouth. He can speak for himself. He don't need no voice box to make an apology on his behalf. And you know what I have to tell you to tell your client: tell him that he lucky that DC Lashley dealt with him, because if I had retaliated, he would still be in the hospital."

"Yes. I know what you would do to him, Crick. You think I don't know 'bout you and your old partner, that brute Nuffada Nicholls, who had to run away from Barbados."

"One of the problems with lawyers is that they believe whatever their clients tell them. But I am not going to get into any argument with a lawyer about right and wrong. One of my old school teachers told us a long time ago that lawyers have two opinions on every issue...they pull out whichever one suits the client they are representing at any time. Your client threatened one police officer and assaulted another today. Those are facts. As far as I am concerned, he is wrong and will have to face the consequences. He is under arrest and will be charged and placed on remand until the courts decide he may leave. Any further discussion on the matter, you have to talk to Superintendent Chet Thomas."

"I don't want to talk to Superintendent Thomas. I know exactly what he is going to say. He will very politely tell me to eff off. But you can tell him what I said to you."

"You can tell him yourself. The charge sheet is already written up," said Crick, raising his voice to make sure that Arman heard. "You can bring your boy inside now. We'll see you in court."

Crick watched as Corey Greene spoke to Arman, who was sitting on the bench under the window with two policemen standing next to him. Arman handed his wallet and cell phone to Corey Greene, all the while glancing in Crick's direction, and then he called out, "Every dog got he day, Crick. Every dog got he day."

"Wuff, wuff," Crick barked slowly, then said: "DC Lashley is going to fingerprint you. I think you met her already." Crick laughed mockingly.

"You are deliberately goading my client, Crick. This is not right. You have been working with Thomas too long. You getting just like him, now. When I explain the circumstances, the provocation, to the magistrate tomorrow, Ronald will be out in no time."

Crick motioned to the two officers accompanying Arman. "Take him through. DC Lashley is waiting on him. Bow, wow."

"God blind you, Crick. This ain't finish yet...," Arman snarled with a grimace. Corey Greene put an open hand in front of Arman's mouth. "Just ignore the taunts. They just trying, hoping for a response from you that will get you in trouble. Right now, they really ain't got no case against you, so be cool, be smart."

"Who let the dogs out?" Crick sang, waving his hands like a conductor. He was joined in a chorus of "Wuff, wuff, wuff...wuff, wuff" by the other police officers.

Two officers accompanied Arman to the fingerprinting process. DC Lashley was waiting in the room, just standing there, her eyes focused on Arman as he entered. Crick followed. Arman stared at Crick, speaking with his eyes, his face bursting with restrained anger. Crick liked it better when Arman spoke up, when he reacted. Arman's silence was more menacing than his words.

Fingerprinting over, the two officers took Arman away.

"I expect Arman will be out on bail tomorrow morning. This may be a good thing for us. We have to keep the pressure on him," said Crick to Lashley. "I plan to ask The Chief for some help monitoring his movements and to get the tappers to work on his phones."

As the detectives walked out of the room, Mason sidled over to Crick and said in a low voice: "They should let the two of us at him for one hour. One hour is all we would need. To get a full confession."

"Those days are over, now, Mason. We have scientists and policemen with degrees.... But you know what? I miss those days, sometimes."

"What are you two whispering about?" asked Lashley.

"My new girl," said Mason. "She is so sexy when she—"

"Stop, stop. I don't want to hear anymore," replied Lashley, waving her hands.

Mason laughed and shook his head.

CHAPTER 19

Crick drove out of the police station and headed for Tanya's apartment. He had not thought about it before calling her, he just picked up his phone and called. Perhaps after the day's events he wanted her company. He had been avoiding her because he had decided to end their relationship, but he kept putting it off.

Tanya opened the door. She was wearing a loose robe. Crick noticed that she had lost a little weight off her already trim figure and she noticed the little bruise on his face.

"What happened to you?" she asked, gently touching his face.

"Nothing, really. An idiot took a swing at me."

"He must be an idiot for true. But are you alright?

"I good. It ain't no big thing."

"I am not going to ask how he is."

"Oh, my partner, the girl I told you about, DC Lashley, dropped a kick in his ass, his ribs to be exact, and sent him to the hospital. He is in a cell for tonight. She is a martial artist."

"Oh. If I was there, I would have beaten him up. He would still be in hospital." She laughed, then smiled a strained smile and held him tightly; he barely held her back. They remained like that for a few moments, neither saying another word. He thought he should address the matter of their future together immediately but, looking at the sadness on her face, he couldn't do it. They moved over, sat on the sofa and small-talked for a bit. Crick said he had not been able to visit because he was under a lot of pressure to solve the murder of the woman found in Prickett's well. "You know how it is when I am on a big case," he said.

She relaxed a bit.

"How are things at your work?" he asked, immediately thinking it was the wrong thing to ask.

The muscles in her cheeks tightened. "Well, I've had to put up with some whispering and looks of amusement. I can imagine what they say behind my back. Those snickers would turn to outright laughter...I still don't understand why you didn't come to live here with me, AD, now that you are a free man."

Crick looked toward the door and said rather dryly. "I think we should end this relationship."

She looked at him, her mouth open, and she spoke in a raised voice. "You mean *you* want to end this relationship. You are a bastard, AD. You never really loved me, you know. I was humiliated by your wife in front of my neighbours."

In fact, her neighbours were quite sympathetic. They liked Crick. But that had not stopped them from spreading news of the incident.

He tried to console her. "I will always care for you, you know, and will always want to be your friend." Then, as if to blame her: "You always knew I was married."

She ignored his last remark, looked into his eyes, her tone softened, and she said, "If I can't have you, I want your child."

Crick raised a hand and covered his forehead. "*Oh, shite,*" he said to himself then aloud, "that would not be a good idea. Why would you want to do that?"

She did not answer. She stood and turned toward him, wriggled out of her robe and let it fall to the ground, displaying the naked body that he loved and loved making love to. "If I can't have you, I want your baby."

Crick certainly did not want a baby, but sitting on the low sofa he faced a dilemma. He shifted his gaze upward toward her face and pert breasts. He stood. She drew closer. He held her lightly then tightly, rocked her sideways. Like their first time, she rode him right there on the rug.

They lay on the rug after. She cried softly, her head on his shoulder. He stared at the ceiling, not speaking, either. He peeled himself away gently, got up and went to the bathroom, taking his clothes with him. When he returned to the living room, she was robed and sitting on the sofa. She looked at him with tumid eyes and a face full of sadness. She did not respond when he said, "I am leaving," and she didn't come to the door when he left.

CHAPTER 20

At home that evening, around midnight, Lashley had started to tire from reading. Her thoughts returned to the day's events at the station. She felt they were on the verge of a break in the case. It was evident that Arman knew about the shoe and there had to be a reason he lied about it. He had to be connected with the body in Prickett's well. Was the woman one of his escorts who stepped out of line? "Oh, I promised myself to check on escort services. I am too busy. Work, study, capoeira, and social media take up so much of my time."

She moved to her bed and sat cross-legged, hunched over her laptop. She quickly typed *barbados escorts* into her browser and up popped a list of links to several sites. There were YouTube videos of the famous Seventies Barbadian group *The Escorts*. She recognized them. They were a favourite band of her stepfather, and he would from time to time sing bits of one of their hits, like, *Who ain't looking good, good looking, Who ain't looking sweet, sweet looking, Who ain't looking nice in front, looking nice behind....* The memory brought a smile to her face. All the other YouTube links, however, touted female "companionship" for a fee.

Lashley clicked on the first site, then the second and third. All these sites promoted paid "companionship"; and in spite of an attempt at a denial of prostitution, they clearly insinuated that sex was available as part of the service. They were explicit in their detailing of services offered. The suggestion was that the purchaser paid for the companionship but the sex was free, or that the sex in "sex therapy" was simply health-giving or curative. She clicked on site after site, her jaw dropping from time to time reading about the "services" available. Then she read about Denise, who identified herself as European. According to her profile notes, she was beautiful, classy, fun loving, multilingual, loved to travel particularly the Caribbean islands, was very attracted to the lifestyle of the rich and famous, which she found to be "a great aphrodisiac," and was confident that she could satisfy any man's dreams. Then Lashley's jaw dropped again, and this time her mouth stayed open as she read the next line. This Denise had declared that she "loved Christian Louboutin shoes. I would say that I have a fetish for these shoes."

She sent the link to Sergeant Crick and to Inspector Thomas immediately, with a note—*look at her fetish*. She headlined the email "Urgent."

CHAPTER 21

Lashley's email created a buzz in the station next morning. The Chief had already set the ball rolling to trace this Denise who loved Christian Louboutin shoes. But soon it was time to go to court.

Arman had turned mute during his one night in custody, a sign of renewed determination or perhaps of abiding faith in his attorney. And true to his word, Corey Greene had Arman out on bail. The police had objected to bail on the grounds that not only had the accused threatened and assaulted a police officer, he was also a person of interest in a murder case.

Corey Greene denied that his client knew anything about any murder.

"Your Honour, the police have offered no evidence of substance to support their frivolous notion, just an allegation that my client may have seen a pair of shoes similar to those believed to belong to a victim. My client runs a bar and all kinds of people frequent his place."

He went on to explain to the court that his client had willingly accompanied the police to the station, where he was subjected to extreme taunting and abuse from senior police officers. His client had been assaulted with extreme force by a police martial arts expert, causing injury which required hospitalisation. The taunting and abuse had continued even after he returned from the hospital. "After this mistreatment, my client is now very afraid of the police and would continue to live in fear, especially if remanded further."

The magistrate agreed to bail and denied the request that the accused surrender his passport and report to the police station weekly. "If you find some real evidence, you can re-arrest him and bring him back to court," she said.

"I wish my comments on the conduct of the police to be a matter of record, Your Honour," requested Corey Greene.

Magistrate Rhonda Bishop responded that his comments had been noted and advised him that his client had a right to complain to the Police Complaints Authority. The matter was adjourned *sine die*.

As Arman and Corey Greene walked out of the courtroom, a voice from among a small, curious gathering shouted, "Hey, big man, I hear a woman put some licks in your ass." This prompted great laughter among the spectators. Arman looked over the gathering. He turned toward the heckler, opened his mouth to speak, but Corey Greene immediately poked him in the ribs, causing him to wince.

———

"Good work on the escort agencies. The Chief was excited. He is getting international help on it," said Crick to Lashley as they walked the short distance from the Holetown Magistrate's Court on the way back into the police station.

"Ah, Sergeant. You have your rum-shop and I have mine...online. My blogger buddies are sending me even more information. Denise will not be her real name, and the silhouette-photo may or may not be her."

"The Chief is enlisting the help of Interpol to identify her.... You look like you got something on your mind. What's up?"

"I am thinking about changing my career focus."

"You have my interest, Lashley. Why and in what way are you changing your 'career focus'?"

"There is a lost generation out there, on our streets, on the blocks. When we catch them breaking the law, we lock them up."

"Let's go into my office," said Crick.

Lashley closed the door and Crick sat behind his desk. "Tell me more," he said.

Lashley paused thoughtfully before replying.

"You know, in the week before I was seconded to the Northern Division, I was to give evidence in a case at a magistrate's court back in the Bridgetown division. Memories of that morning have stayed with me."

She had waved to a couple of familiar faces as she weaved her little Carat through the car park. She looked at the shabby exteriors of what would have been at one time a set of handsome coral-stone buildings. She found a parking spot and slotted the Carat neatly into place. She exchanged greetings with some more familiar faces as she made her way to the courtroom. She walked up the steps, entered and sat on the first bench on the right at the back of the courtroom. She looked around the room. It had been repainted since her last visit, in a dull reddish colour that she found quite restful. The interior was quite a contrast to the exterior. Air-handling units over three of the deep windows with hurricane shutters kept the room cool. The feel of classical Barbadian colonial architecture had been preserved.

"I was waiting to give evidence in what had been my first case of armed-robbery. The accused was already in jail on remand. I was given an estimated time of when my case would be likely called. But I went earlier because I still like to observe court cases. I find the whole thing fascinating, it's a drama which offers a panoramic and at the same time an intimate view of society. I see in court this place where the educated, the uneducated, the slick, the rich, the poor, the weird, the curious, the unlucky, the hard-done-by, the callous and the wicked all meet to play out a drama, sometimes a drama of life or death. Criminal courts are not happy places, even though they can be very humorous at times; they are a point along a road that started with someone's misery. And the journey doesn't end there whatever the outcome of a case, because in court there are always losers but not always winners."

She sat through four cases, two men up for non-payment of child support and two traffic cases, one ZR driver followed by one minibus driver. They all represented themselves. The first deadbeat father had no excuse for his conduct as he was a working man earning above average pay. He was given a deadline to come up with the arrears under threat of imprisonment. The second father was a rather meek-looking man who had been unemployed for the last two years. Magistrate Benjamin was unsympathetic. "You have a responsibility for the children you bring into this world. You live near the sea; you should consider taking up fishing." Lashley thought the magistrate was being a bit harsh.

The minibus driver pleaded not guilty because he claimed that as he had no standing passengers whatsoever when the policeman came to his bus, he had not broken the law. The policeman explained to the court that he met the bus and, as he rode past, he saw many standing passengers. He spun his motorbike around to pursue the bus. The driver stopped the bus, opened the door permitting the schoolchildren who were standing to flee the bus, and he shut the door again. The policeman counted the students as they ran off. The driver kept insisting that when the policeman came to his door there were no standing passengers, therefore he could not be guilty. The magistrate laughed along with the rest of the court.

The ZR driver represented himself with a level of aplomb, which spoke of his familiarity with the court, its procedures and customs. His questioning of the policeman who had arrested him was as good as any lawyer's. The policeman was unable to answer his question on whose responsibility it was to ensure that there was a fire extinguisher in the vehicle.

"Is it the driver's responsibility or is it the proprietor's responsibility?" he had asked.

The policeman seemed to think for a while before responding with some show of embarrassment, "I don't know."

"Well, I am putting it to you that it is the proprietor's responsibility, and I had discharged it and given it to him to refill."

In the end, both accused were convicted. Before sentencing, it was revealed that each of them had multiple prior convictions. Lashley went from being entertained by the drivers' crossing of the officers who had arrested them to utter disgust when they were simply fined and no further sanction imposed. They would be back on the road immediately and would continue their wild ways until maybe they killed someone. Then and only then might their apparent right to put the public at risk every day be revoked. The police had done their work but the system and the politicians had failed the public.

"I sat through a couple of cases until someone shook me by the shoulder and said, 'Your case coming up next. You need to go outside until you are called.' As I started to walk out of the courtroom a policeman approached the magistrate and spoke quietly to him. The magistrate asked that the courtroom be cleared. There was some hubbub coming from outside. I walked out the room and saw prison guards leading a manacled man from their vehicle. It was Braxy, the man I had been waiting on. The man I would testify against.

"You know him, Sergeant. This young dreadlocked man who looks as if he hasn't yet lost his mother's features. His hands and feet were bound by chains. He walked noisily, accompanied by two sturdy members of the Task Force in their blue jumpsuits, hands never far from their weapons and constantly looking around. The officer who had spoken to the magistrate now stood at the door and was telling those gathered—family members of Braxy, I presumed—that they could not enter the courtroom. Someone demanded to know why. His lawyer, Horace Corbin, dressed, as usual, in an immaculate suit and wearing those trademark rimless glasses explained, 'I am about to make a submission to the magistrate on Barrington's behalf.'

"Apart from the family, there was a curious little crowd outside the courtroom. Another young man arrived and hurriedly approached. The group at the doorway parted for him. He had similar facial features to Braxy and sported gold earrings in the shape of guns, gold chains around his neck, gold rings on almost every finger, and several tattoos.

"'I tell you not to wear them things when you come to court,' Horace Corbin barked.

"'All of these legal, man. All of these legal, Mr. Lawyerman,' the clearly irritated young fellow said.

"To me, the young man's response suggested that he had other jewellery which was not legal. I made a note that he should be investigated.

"The attorney steupsed and told the young man, 'You are to stay out of the courtroom even if they decide to let you in. Coming in here looking like some stupid gangster will not help your brother, understand?'

"Another uniformed officer arrived and quickly marshalled the spectators into a queue. He then proceeded to pat them down as they approached the entrance to the courtroom. 'Wunnuh got to wait to see if the judge will let you in.' The young man with the gun earrings hung back. The lawyer stared at him. The young man retreated, made his way to a spot under a tree across the yard and sat down on a thick root, a dejected look on his face. The lawyer entered the courtroom.

"I studied the figure under the tree. He was maybe seventeen years old—a part of my work yet so far from my world of educated young people, talented and ambitious, with a real future ahead of them. That jewellery, what was its value? Maybe three or four or even nine or ten thousand dollars. I couldn't really tell. But for him to override his brother's attorney's instructions and wear those, those atrocious accessories into the courtyard indicated they carried significance greater than their monetary value to him. He was making a statement. *I am a badass, I am a gangster, and I want the world to know it, so I am showing off some of my wealth.* Right there and then I decided I had to go and talk with the young man. It was an instinctive decision. I had no expectation of what talking to him might achieve. The young man looked at me suspiciously as I approached him.

"'What's the point of having a lawyer and not taking his advice?' I asked.

"The young man stared, looked me up and down, a scowl on his face. 'You is a lawyer, too?' he asked.

"'No,' I replied.

"'Let me tell you something. Not even no big-shot lawyer can tell me what to do, yaunstand? I does pay them so. They does work for me. I help to pay for that big house he live in and that big car he drivin'.' He emphasised each sentence with a thrusting hand and jerky head movements.

"I understood his message loud and clear. I looked at what he was wearing, this costume of the disaffected, imitation camouflage jacket and pants (both quite illegal to wear in Barbados), military style boots, the assorted jewellery and hair. Irony of ironies, it reminded me of those pictures I saw as a child of a golliwog, in this case an un-golliwog. But it wasn't the accoutrements of this soldier at war with the society that schooled and nurtured him that concerned me most; it was what was inside his head. His hero big brother inside the courtroom was facing a long jail sentence. It wouldn't be long before it was his turn, if he was lucky to survive. For me, this was a hill too steep to climb. I retreated and returned to where I was sitting before.

"I sat there for a couple of minutes and suddenly the young man rose lazily and ambled over to me.

"'You look like you is work in a bank or a office. What they charge you with?'

"'I am a witness in a case.'

"'You ever went in court before?'

"Before I could answer, there was a tap on her shoulder. 'DC Lashley, matter adjourned. They don't need you today,' the uniformed officer said.

"The young man's eyes narrowed. His face hardened.

"'Wait, so you is a police?!'

"'Yes,' said Lashley, thinking he was not very bright.

"'And that is why you come over to talk to me, to suss me out? You feel you smart?'

"'Not at all. I came to speak to you because I would like to understand you.'

"He stared at me, slack jawed. Neither one of us spoke for half a minute.

"'You want to understand me? Well, understand this, I hate the police.'

"'I am not threatening you in any way."

"'No, you trying to fuck with my mind instead. There are no good police. All of wunnuh is the same. Some will beat you with a stick and some will try to trick you into saying things you don't want to say. You is one of them tricksters.'

"'Tell me something. You really want to go to jail, to be locked away from the rest of the world?'

"'I went to jail already. I learn a lot in jail. I just come out, you know. I was in there for two years. Went in a boy, come out a man. I learn never to trust people like you and I don't want to hear *nuh* more o' your bullshit.'

"He trained his eyes on me with a venomous stare. 'So you was going in there to tell lies pon my brother. Well, next time we meet, it will be different.'

"'Youngster, I will ignore your threat. I can only encourage you to try and turn your life around. Prison was wasted on you. You didn't learn a single positive thing. It seems that you came out worse than you went in. I wish you well.'

"'And I wish you hell.'"

"He turned and strutted his way back to under his tree. Shortly after, as his brother trundled and jangled his way from the courtroom to the bus surrounded by his security detail, his attorney following closely behind, the young man attempted to walk alongside the procession, to talk to his brother. Two Task Force officers muscled him aside and treated him to a few choice words. I watched until they boarded the bus and it drove slowly away. I remained seated where I was. I watched the young brother join others, probably the same family members who were at the door, as they walked away. He looked over his shoulder, pointed at me, talking non-stop. His group's gaze followed his pointed finger. They glowered and spoke. I could only imagine what they were saying. The young man had two problems, in my estimation: one was his own limitations; the second was nobody to put him on a right path. Yes, we lock them up, and after a few years they are out as even harder criminals committing more serious crimes...."

"Well, we are only a part in the criminal justice system," said Crick at last, easing back in his chair, "and our part is to deliver good convictions and get the criminals locked up."

"Yes, Sergeant, and that is an important part of the system. But perhaps the more difficult and more important aspect of the system ought to be how to reduce recidivism and how to persuade these people not to get involved in criminal activity in the first place."

"Sounds like you want to take over their parents' roles, their schools' roles. I mean, aren't your parents supposed to teach you respect for fellow human beings? Aren't our schools supposed to reinforce moral teachings? We only come into it when homes and schools have failed. And perhaps they fail because some of these people are just wicked and evil. "

"But then we just lock them up. What happens to them in jail? Isn't that another failure? We can't school them, we can't parent them, but I think we are missing an opportunity when they are in prison, an opportunity to put them on a path of desistance. And that is where I want to place my focus. Now, is there a place for this kind of thinking in the RBPF? I don't know."

"I believe this kind of thinking has existed in the police force for some time, but I don't know what level of support it has. There is a lot of new thinking in the current leadership. SIO Thomas is very much a part of that new thinking. Me? I know my limitations. I will catch the criminals. The rest of you can work on them. You know, your task is bigger than you think, Lashley. There is some level of community support for these criminals, and then there is the pull of old friendships. When they leave jail and head back to their communities, they are no longer in rehabilitation. You are looking through a small window into a very large room. There is a lot going on in that room. And let me tell you something. These criminals don't give a shite about nobody. A cocaine dealer told a judge that if people were foolish enough to use cocaine, he was quite happy to sell it to them. Last year, there was a drive-by shooting one Saturday morning. These two fellows sprayed a group with a semi-automatic and went to a rum-shop and ate pudding and souse as if nothing had happened. As far as I am concerned, I just want to lock up these bastards, make our communities safer for the rest of us. They don't care 'bout me, and I don't care 'bout them. I care about the people they hurt. That is why I want to find the man who killed this young woman."

"I want to do that, too," said Lashley.

"I know, I know," replied Crick, "but the difference between you and me is that, after I catch him, I would like them to pop his neck or lock him up and throw away the key. You, you want to rehabilitate him and set him free. That is a very risky thing to do. And if he kills again, you share the responsibility."

"So you really believe that people cannot be rehabilitated?"

"You know, I believe that some people can be rehabilitated. But when you have spent as much time as me dealing with these criminals without any conscience, it influences your perspective."

Lashley was quiet for a moment, then she stood and said, "Thank you for the advice, Sergeant Crick. I have to get back online. The SIO wants me to continue with my enquiries."

CHAPTER 22

Crick woke early next morning and went downstairs to the den to work out before his granddaughter appeared. Sweet as she was, he didn't have time to spend with her this morning. She copied him as he loosened up with a few stretches and bends and twists. Her mother called out for her and she looked sad as she left turning at the door to say, "I have to go now, grandpa. Bye." Crick stepped on to the treadmill. He used it more than its owners, his daughter and her husband. He had spent time earlier reviewing the case of the redhead lady and pondering his next move. DNA and dental tests had not produced any positive results, nor had attempts to extract latent fingerprints of a suspect, nor checks on cash-for-gold shops. His team was still interviewing hotel and villa staff, beach vendors and beach security personnel, but these had produced no leads, so far. Some redheads recalled by hotel and villa staff were easily identified and had all left the island. The redhead in the well was still a mystery woman, and until she could be identified, the police were hoping for a miracle. He did not want to be distracted by this Brianna Davis, but two missing women could somehow be linked, and they knew who was linked to Brianna. He wondered if that was her real name. Brianna Davis was a typical Anglo-American name, but they now had reason to believe that she had an accent of some sort. Questioning Jammer was now a priority. Crick had stopped exercising while he thought. He started again and stepped up the pace. He was feeling energised. Not just from the exercise or the fact that Lashley may have discovered a clue to the identity of the redhead lady. He had spoken to Natalie the night before. She had mellowed somewhat. He agreed to counselling with her pastor and she agreed to have dinner with him. His phone rang again and he reached over and picked it up. This time it was SIO Thomas.

A drug boat had crashed in St. Lucy. The Drug Squad was on the way there. Speightstown and Crab Hill were already there but were too late to catch anyone. "I want you to head up there, see if there is any reason to link this with Jammer or Arman. That would be a stroke of luck. Sometimes when we chase them, they catch themselves."

Crick headed for the shower then dressed quickly and jumped into his car. He drove faster than he should downhill through the twists and turns of the St. Thomas roads, down through Rock Hall and on to Highway 2A. He sped all the way to St. Lucy Parish Church, took the second exit at the Theodore Brancker Roundabout. He was heading for Monk's Bay. It used to be a tiny fishing village below a bluff in St. Lucy, not far from the Arawak cement plant. It was now a community of mixed housing. The remaining old chattel houses of the original fishing families were in a cluster at the lower end near the beach. These houses were now overlooked by ostentatious new villas, higher up the slope, owned by a handful of locals and some expats and returnees, former immigrants to the USA, Canada and England.

The crashed boat had been hauled ashore. There were a number of curious onlookers but none volunteering information, according to Sergeant Clarke of the Drug Squad. He exchanged greetings with Crick. "Not a soul ain't see a number plate. But I handing out cards. I will hear later. Somebody called this in and they will call again."

Crick turned around, surveying the surroundings. He looked at the damaged boat and the collection of persons gathered, mostly men, from the neighbourhood. Others were content to follow the events from the windows of their homes. Then he expanded his survey to the houses further away. He saw over to his right an elegant new house on the very point of the hill overlooking the bay. There were two people on the balcony looking at the proceedings. He wondered how long they had been there and thought that if they had been there early enough, they would have had an excellent view of the events. He whispered to Sergeant Clarke, turned and went to his car. He drove back uphill and around to the newly constructed house overlooking the bay. He strolled to the portico and rang the bell. A tall, elderly and erect, white-haired gentleman came to the door. "And how may I help you?" he asked in an accent that was unmistakably Bajan but blended with American. Crick introduced himself and showed his ID. The old man said, "Please come in. I think I know why you are here."

The old man offered Crick a seat; his smiling, diminutive wife joined them and asked if he would like a cup of coffee. "No, thank you, but a glass of water would be fine," said Crick. It turned out that Crick's hunch was right. They had seen the whole thing from the balcony of what was their holiday home up on the hill overlooking the bay. They had heard the engines first then saw the blue and white speedboat as it headed for the reef.

"It was moving fast alright," said Mr. Mascoll.

"If it was high tide, they would have made it," said Mrs. Mascoll. "They would have driven right over the reef with no problem."

Mrs. Mascoll excused herself and went to the kitchen.

"Whoever was piloting the boat did not know the area. It was early in the morning; dawn was just breaking," said Mr. Mascoll. "The reef appeared when the waves receded and disappeared each time a wave came in and swept over it. In the dim early light, the boat's pilot would not have seen the flat dark mossy rock until he was very close to it.

"Three men and a woman rushed out of two SUVs parked on the grass amid the casuarinas and started waving and yelling. Their attempt to alert the crew to the danger fell on ears most likely deafened by the roar of the speedboat's four engines. By the time the driver sensed that the people waving on the beach weren't just saying, *We are here*, it was too late. He swerved and the boat skidded onto the reef, careened and shot into the air at an angle. It fell on its side, people and objects flying. Filmed, it would have made a spectacular slow-motion replay. The four from the SUVs ran to the water and waded in. They and the two men from the boat were all yelling at once. They chased after the packages, now strewn across the water. The two men from the boat did not appear to be injured. They were lucky they did not land on the rocks. The people from the cars seemed more interested in recovering the packages than the welfare of the crew.

"They recovered several of the packages, making trips to and from the two vehicles. There were still some packages drifting away with the tide when one of the men from the SUVs must have yelled because everyone turned in his direction and, once he had their attention, he pointed to his watch then made circular motions above his head with his hand. They piled into the two vehicles and drove away leaving the wrecked boat and the unrecovered packages drifting further out to sea. Somebody must have called the police as soon as the boat crashed," concluded the old man. Police units arrived about five minutes after the SUVs had disappeared, the Coast Guard about twenty minutes later. They recovered some drifting bales and towed the battered boat ashore."

"We were too far away to read the number plates on the SUVs. We are in our seventies, you know. Left Barbados nearly fifty years ago. Spend the entire winter back home, now. Go back up to Connecticut in May for the summer and our medical checks, and to see friends."

"Have you ever seen anything like this before, minus the crash, I mean?" asked Crick.

"No, but one of our neighbours told us these people have used the cement plant jetty at night," said Mrs. Mascoll, returning with a glass of water for Crick and two glasses of coloured liquid for her and her husband.

"They must have been off schedule last night so had to change the meeting point," said Crick.

"And whoever told them to come in here didn't think about low tide," said Mr. Mascoll.

The elderly couple looked at each other. Mrs. Mascoll nodded and Mr. Mascoll spoke. "Now, young man, we have some information which should be of use to you. We are willing to share this with you but on condition that we are not required to be witnesses in court and there is no disclosure that we were the source of this evidence. We know enough about these kinds of people back in America. You know, we just want to come back to our birthplace every year from November to May, for the rest of our time on this earth, and enjoy the sea, island life, family and old friends. We need assurances before we reveal our information. No court appearance and no revealing of us as the source."

Crick was thoughtful for a moment. "I really can't make any such promises. But if you tell me what information you have, I can discuss it with my superintendent. He would decide whether your information is critical for a conviction. But at least tell me what kind of information it is."

Mrs. Mascoll spoke. "Sergeant, we would need an absolute guarantee up front. Those people are not nice people. We want no exposure to them."

"I understand your concern. You know...." Crick thought a moment. "There is a police hotline you may call with information. You remain anonymous," Crick said.

"I know, but I don't trust it. I have my reasons," said Mr. Mascoll.

Crick handed over a card, thanked the old couple, got into his car and drove off. He immediately called the SIO and said he wanted to meet with him ASAP. The SIO said that he was on his way to the station.

Crick couldn't help wondering if there was a drug connection to his murder case and was happy that the Drug Squad had kept their promise to include them on any drug busts up north. He hadn't called Lashley. He knew she would have been up early studying and preparing for court in Bridgetown the following morning. She prepared; he simply went. She was young and still had the time.

He returned to the beach.

The boys from the Drug Squad now had vehicle numbers and were checking the owners' names and addresses. It didn't take them long to learn that one number plate was bogus: it belonged to a delivery truck owned by a Bridgetown firm, but the other was registered to a Mr. Frederick Wall whose address was the West Hills Golf Club.

Crick met the SIO at the station and recounted the conversation with the Mascolls. The SIO telephoned the Mascolls immediately. "This is Superintendent Cetshwayo Thomas, head of the Northern Division of the Royal Barbados Police Force. You may call me Chet. Everyone else does because they can't pronounce my name."

The SIO tried his best to reassure the Mascolls of the confidentiality of any information they shared. Mr. Mascoll would not budge. He and his wife had missed church that morning because of the goings-on, and he was not in a good mood. At the mention of church, the SIO said, "I have an idea. Mr. Mascoll, why don't you share the information with your priest, and he can tell us without ever disclosing his source? You don't even have to tell us who your priest is."

The SIO placed his hand over the mouthpiece of the telephone and spoke to Crick. "He says it is not a simple matter of telling his priest and asked me to hold on a moment. I expect he is consulting with his wife."

After a few seconds, Mr. Mascoll came back and explained the nature of his problem. He wanted desperately to see those people caught, but the information he had could be traced back to him. He had taken photographs while the people were chasing after the bales, and anyone with a bit of intelligence could tell where these photographs were taken from....

SIO Thomas interrupted him. "Mr. Mascoll, those photos are critical. We have to have them. I am sure that we can work out some way of protecting you as the source. We have to see those photos.... Look, look, look. If we see the photographs and can identify the people, we may be able to find the drugs and make arrests. In that case, we do not even need to mention the photos."

SIO Thomas paused, listened, nodding. "Yes, we can work with that. No problem."

He thanked Mr. Mascoll and the two continued to talk until the SIO told Mr. Mascoll that he had an urgent matter to attend to, right away.

"Wow, that man can talk and talk," said the SIO to Crick as soon as he hung up. "He agreed to let us have the pictures. He will upload them to his computer from his camera, print and give them to his priest."

"But Chief, if we don't find the drugs, we may still need the photos to get a conviction," said Crick.

"One step at a time, one step at a time. We'll cross that bridge if we come to it," responded the SIO.

CHAPTER 23

The big brown envelope that SIO Thomas returned to the office carrying was marked PRIVATE & CONFIDENTIAL in bold lettering. Bevaney Wood had knocked, then poked her head around the door. "There is a priest outside who says he has something for you, and he can only deliver it to you in person. I don't recognise him and he hasn't introduced himself. All he wants to be sure of is that the person who comes out to meet him will be Superintendent Cetshwayo Thomas. Well, there is only one Cetshwayo Thomas in the whole wide world, I told him."

The SIO opened the envelope as soon as he sat and a smile slowly spread over his face. He splayed the photos across his desk facing Crick and Lashley, whose Bridgetown court case had been adjourned again. Mr. Mascoll had not sent the full photographs. The pictures were cut-outs, presumably to obscure the point from which the photos were taken. The photos showed one woman and three men transporting bales from the sea and placing them into two vehicles.

"These may be subject to challenge in court. But we can clearly see who the people —are—and find them," said SIO Thomas.

Crick tapped a finger on one of the photos. "Wait, that is...?"

SIO Thomas completed Crick's sentence. "The barman from the Triple R. He is a cagey devil. I couldn't get a thing out of him that day when you brought in Arman. But we have him now. And he will lead us to Arman."

"And that is I-Want," said Crick, pointing at another head. "He is from the same district as Moore."

"The boys at the Drug Squad will be happy to see these," said Lashley.

"I'll get Moore to pick up I-Want for questioning," said Crick.

The SIO called Clarke at the Drug Squad.

———

According to Moore, I-Want was very easy to track down. They found him watching a game of dominoes under a mango tree in the village, his regular liming spot. More and Mason transported him to Holetown. Moore said that he had lived up to his reputation as not being too bright by claiming to know nothing before being asked any questions.

As a child in the village, he was often seen begging. "I want a dollar" was how he often greeted villagers. When he grew his dreadlocks, the nickname I-Want stuck. Those odd dollars went to support his early marijuana use and linked him with dealers who provided him with free substance and a little cash when doing errands, like helping to move product.

Crick discussed interview tactics with Moore. He believed they had found in the dim-witted I-Want a potential weak link in the group, so the plan was to go in heavy with the evidence against him, let him know how much trouble he was in and how he might help himself if he cooperated with the police.

Moore was joined in the interview room by two officers from the Drug Squad. "You in nuff trouble, Reggie. We got witnesses who see you off-loading dope at Monk's Bay Sunday morning."

"I does swim down there regular. Yesterday morning a boat crash and I went and help save the people."

"And you didn't touch the dope, Reggie?" asked one of the Drug Squad officers.

"Wha' dope you talking 'bout, skipper? I ain't see no dope."

Moore placed a photograph on the table and asked Reggie if he recognised the person carrying the bale of dope.

Reggie looked at the photo, his head drooping. He looked up at the officers.

Moore spoke first. "That was a lot of dope. We are charging you, and your bail going to be high. You looking at 'bout ten years, Reggie. How much money they pay you for this job? It worth ten years o' your life? I know you from small, Reggie. Don't do time for these people. Give us some information and we will go easy on you. I sure they pay you peanuts, while they pulling down big bucks. You would have to be a fool to take the fall for this, and Doris Prescott only boy child ain't no fool."

I-Want's eyes glazed over as he considered his options before speaking. "The boat come in from St. Vincent. I don't know where they take the two men but I hear that the girl take the drugs to a house in West Hills."

This information created some excitement among the detectives until I-Want explained further. This was not the original plan, but because of the crash they knew the police would be looking for them. The West Hills Villa was to be a safe house. The owners of the house were away and the housekeeper looked after the place in their absence. She was the girlfriend of one of the other fellows who met the boat and she drove one of the vans. "They had called her in because the other fellow who was supposed to do the pickup had a problem and couldn't make it."

I-Want didn't know the number or street of the house in West Hills, but Crick knew the chief of security at the gated community. The man, Roger Bowen, was most cooperative. He put a name to the suspect immediately. "I feel that is Shaniqua Harper. I see she driving 'bout the people SUV since they gone away. She don't drive it when they here. *And* she is not supposed to be at work on a Sunday. Let me call my gate and call you back."

Bowen called back within minutes, excited. It was not their practice to log the movement of villa owners' vehicles in and out of the property, but Shaniqua had reported for work two days before and there was no record of her leaving that evening.

"She was, however, seen driving the owner's SUV yesterday morning, so she must have been sleeping in the villa. She drove out early yesterday morning and came back in a couple hours later. She hasn't left since then."

The chief of security provided the number and street of the villa then added, "She got a child for a fellow who does work at the Triple R. I think he is one of the barmen there."

They planned the raids to occur simultaneously at the West Hills Villa and the home of the barman. It was a joint exercise, Drug Squad and Task Force along with detectives from the Northern Division. The raid at the villa produced three hefty fifty-pound bags of marijuana, the vehicle seen at the crash site, and a surprised Shaniqua Harper. Shaniqua was arrested and the SUV was impounded at the police station.

———

The Triple R bartender was in bed when he was aroused by the law enforcement officers. Einstein Skinner was remarkably calm, smiled a lot, displaying two protruding front teeth with a wide gap between them. He insisted on his innocence. "I ain't got a clue wha' wunnuh talking 'bout." That was until one of the officers discovered two five-pound packets of marijuana under the cellar of his house.

"Skins, these belong to you?" asked Crick, displaying the two packages."

"No. Where you get them from?"

"You know where we get them from, but you right—they don't belong to you. They belong to Arman, right? Wait till we tell him where we find them. Since the shipment capsized, you guess they wouldn't miss two packets, nuh?"

Einstein Skinner, a man better known by either of his two nicknames, Styne or Skins, smiled a weak smile, a pleading smile.

Crick spoke again. "But maybe, just maybe, your boss don't need to know about these."

"I want to talk to *your* boss," Skinner said.

———

As soon as Crick got to the Holetown station, SIO Thomas told him that he had just spoken to the inspector at the Drug Squad for the second time that day. "He informed me that he was considering dropping charges against Einstein Skinner if the information he gleaned from the barman on Arman turned out to be valuable."

"What was the information?" Crick asked.

"He does keep coke and guns at he grandmother house, in The Garden."

CHAPTER 24

The three police vehicles stopped on the road in front of the chattel house in The Garden. Men in dark blue jumpsuits, the word POLICE emblazoned in white across the backs just below shoulder height, jumped out and one of them knocked on Ursaline Grannum's door.

"Who that is knocking at my door so early in the morning?"

"Police. We got a warrant. Open the door now!"

Hurried footsteps neared the door. "I coming."

An old woman looked at the two very large, tough-looking men at her door and the man in plainclothes. She could see two others at opposite ends of her house. They were all armed. One at the door and the two at the opposite ends of the house had their weapons drawn.

"Lord *hav'is* mercy. What the police want with me?"

The policemen didn't answer. The one in front flashed a piece of paper in front of her face and stepped into the house followed by the other two. The others did not enter the house. Ursaline stepped aside and asked, "What you all want?"

"Ask your grandson," one of the officers replied.

"My grandson don't live here. I calling my pastor."

"You could call the Lord," one of the officers said.

The first policeman gave instructions to the others. The team separated and went toward different areas of the house. Ursaline picked up the telephone and started to press numbers. A policeman returned and took the phone out of her hand. "You can call after we leave."

The man in plainclothes returned and said, "Let her make her call." He took the phone from the other policeman, handed it back to Ursaline but remained where he was. Ursaline put the phone down. She didn't make the call. She looked Crick in the eyes and said, "I know you, yuh know. I know your mother and your father from up in Orange Hill."

"That won't stop me from doing my job, m'am."

"Something interesting here, Number One," a voice called out.

The policemen followed the direction of the voice and converged on the second bedroom. The officer kneeling by the side of the bed with a flashlight in his hand said, "Come and look at this."

Number One gripped the underside of the bed and lifted it on to its side. He immediately saw what he had been called to see. There were three clear rectangular spots in the dust and fresh drag marks.

"Bring her in," said Number One.

The expressionless old lady faced three unsmiling policemen in the pale light of a single low-watt incandescent bulb.

"My grandson is travelling; he came and picked up his suitcases." She answered the unasked question.

"When did he come?"

"Last night."

"Where is he going?"

"I don't know," she replied.

"I find that hard to believe."

The old lady's expression changed to one of deep thought before she said, "He don't live here and he is his own man. I don't ask him 'bout his business."

"So, he is going on a business trip, huh?"

"I didn't say so."

"Don't worry, we'll find out when we catch up with him." He turned to the others and nodded his head in the direction of the door. They filed out.

Crick watched Ursaline Grannum as she watched them approach their vehicles. They were joined by two more men in blue jumpsuits—the ones who had been at the back of the house.

The policemen huddled. "You know what this means," said one officer. "Yes, he's been friggin' well tipped off. This is a serious problem." "I can't believe it," Crick said.

———

The raid on Arman's grandmother's house was the talk of the Holetown station that morning. There was much speculation about the source of the leak. Then came the news that the forensic pathologists from Trinidad were so busy coping with their workload, a result of an upsurge in their already high number of murders rate, that it would be another two weeks before they could spare someone. The body from the well would remain on ice but the case wouldn't, decided Crick.

Mid-afternoon, a scanned letter of complaint from Corey Greene to the Commissioner of Police and copied to the Attorney-General arrived via email to the station. The letter stated that police harassment of his client Mr. Ronald Ricardo Russell had now been shamefully extended to Mr. Russell's grandmother, an aged pensioner living on her own whose only possible offence was that she had raised her grandson. The final line in the letter appealed to the commissioner to ensure that there was no further harassment of Mr. Russell or his family by members of the RBPF.

Crick walked out of the station and headed toward the beach. He stopped under the almond tree to light a cigarette. He walked a bit further, nodded gently to the young man renting out beach chairs, and stretched out on the nearest one. Inspector Thomas had warned that any further contact with Arman, without good probable cause, could do more harm than good. Einstein Skinner would be of critical assistance with the dope case, but could he connect Arman with the body in Prickett's well? Crick couldn't forget the look on Arman's face when he saw the photo of that red shoe. That photo must now be published, in newspapers and online. Let's see who else recognises it, he said to himself. Summa Dat had pointed them in the direction of Arman and Jammer. Crick had known Summa Dat was not telling them everything about Arman, or Jammer. In his experience, fellows like Summa Dat didn't like talking to the police, period. And if they considered it important for whatever reason, they didn't often unburden themselves totally but offered the minimum to point you in the right direction. It salved their conscience.

He flicked his cigarette butt into the sand, pulled out his cell phone and called the Doc. When he walked back into the station, he found Lashley and said, "You wanted to meet the Doc. I am going to see him tomorrow evening. Can you come?"

CHAPTER 25

SIO Thomas put down his mug of half-drunk coffee and pushed the photocopied web page of an article from that morning's edition of a British tabloid across his desk to Crick.

"Have you seen this yet?" he asked Crick, who had just sat down across from him. These early morning one-on-one sessions had become a part of their routine whenever Crick had a major case.

"No, but I heard about it," responded Crick.

The headline read, *Mystery of the redhead lady on paradise holiday isle.* Crick skimmed the article. It contained no new information about the body from the well. Its focus was criticism of the RBPF and the inadequacies of Barbados' criminal justice system. Specifically, it criticised the absence of a forensic pathologist, the lack of autosomal DNA testing, facial reconstruction, and the alleged refusal by the RBPF of an offer of help from Scotland Yard. It was as if, the article accused, "The Island's authorities wanted the case to go away for fear that it might damage its tourism." The paper made a comparison with the Natalie Holloway disappearance in Aruba, noting that in that case they knew who the victim was but not where she was. This case was the opposite.

"By tomorrow, this will be in our daily newspapers. It is already in the online publications, and fan-scattered turds are landing on desks everywhere. The AG's desk, the Minister of Tourism's, the Commissioner of Police's, and mine. This extra scrutiny is an additional reason we have to solve this case and solve it soon."

"How are we responding to the article?" Crick asked.

"I will leave that up to Horatio Barker. He sent me his draft response. Here, have a look at this." The SIO clicked on his keyboard then turned his monitor toward Crick to reveal a document emailed from Inspector Barker.

The ever so smooth police public relations officer had gone on to immediate counter-attack, accusing the tabloid of sloppy journalism, publishing outright falsehoods, and failing to respect a basic tenet of journalism, getting both sides of the story. He even questioned their apparent concern for the welfare of women when one of their principal marketing tools was the regular publication of photos of barely clad young women. He said that autosomal DNA had in fact been requested and they were expecting the results shortly. If that did not help with identification, then after the forensic pathologist had completed his work, the skull and face would be reconstructed so that the police artist could then do an artistic reconstruction. The conclusion to the response said, "What the reporter, and I use that word cautiously, does not seem to know is that if you give the same skull to six different facial reconstruction artists, you will end up with six different faces. It is not a precise science. It is an approximation. The case is still very much on the front burner and solving it is well within the capability of the RBPF. Indeed, we have made some headway and expect to make an announcement soon."

"Horatio seems to know things that we don't know," said Crick. "What is he going to announce soon?"

"Inspector Barker's response is very much for the attention of the murderer. I didn't know about the autosomal tests, though. I can only guess Culloden Road were waiting for the results before they informed us. But the pressure just went up a few notches, Sergeant."

Crick pushed his chair backward, rose and said, "One important thing before I go. Arman has disappeared."

"Well, I am not sure if he is hiding from you or from whoever's shipment he lost. He'll have to pay for that shipment. He is probably in negotiations to save his life," the SIO said.

Crick took his exit. Bevaney Wood ushered in a smartly dressed mature woman. Crick did not recognise her. He waved a finger at Bevaney Wood and walked out of the station.

———

"He has someone in with him right now," said Constable Bevaney Wood, guardian of the SIO's door, to DC Lashley. "He should be finished soon."

Wood went back to the task on her PC. "I here reviewing statements prepared by police officers," she said to Lashley without looking up from her monitor. "I vex, vex, vex. The Chief fed up with some of these officers' statements reaching his desk with spelling errors and poor grammar." She fumed as she made her corrections. She swore each time she encountered something that displeased her. In her fifteen-minute wait, Lashley counted three shites, two rassholes and a drawn out cheese-on-bread before Wood sat back, shook her head and sighed.

"You could believe this? Johnson wrote 'de man,' d-e, instead of t,h,e."

"I can believe it, but you should calm down a little, you know," said Lashley.

"And them is the ones that complaining when they don't get a promotion."

Lashley did not respond. Wood stopped typing, looked up from her monitor and said. "Listen, I have something to tell you, Shondette." She paused, her face taking on a look of concern. Lashley watched her, wondering what was coming next.

"Girl, I wanted to talk to you for some time," Wood continued.

"What about?" prompted Lashley.

Bevaney Wood rattled off her response in a low and intense tone. "You see the policemen and policewomen in this station? They get in here and talk your name. They call you Inspector Lashley behind your back. They say that you don't talk like a Bajan. One of them told Crick the other day that he training his next boss. They say you feel you better than everybody else and that Crick left his wife for you and it is he who bring you down here to work on this case. And that is why you kick Arman so hard, because he hit your man...."

"That is unbelievable. How stupid can these people be? Me and Crick?"

"I only telling you because I am a woman just like you and I don't like to see nobody getting stab in their back. But don't mind them, though. You don't have to worry. The Chief like you.... But some of these people 'bout here? They dangerous, so I want to warn you that they ain't got your back."

The SIO's door opened and the smartly dressed woman exited.

"You go in. We can talk another time," Wood whispered and smiled warmly, a smile that seemed to say, *We are friends, now.*"

DC Lashley sat across from a frowning SIO Thomas. He turned the photocopy of the UK newspaper article toward her. "Detective Constable Lashley, I want to make sure that the information in this article did not originate from my team. Some of the journalist's views appear similar to yours. You know that all our discussions in the briefings are confidential—"

Lashley interrupted him. "Excuse me, sir. I can assure you that I have not discussed matters from our briefings with anyone apart from my colleagues here and at Culloden Road."

"Who did you speak to at Culloden Road, Constable?"

"Olivia Boxhill, sir. But I am confident that she would not speak to the press." Lashley responded unhesitatingly.

"In this life, Constable, you can only speak for yourself."

"But sir, any visitor reading our local newspapers could have passed on the story."

"That might very well have started the enquiry. But there is detail in this article which must have come from us or our connections. I will speak with Miss Boxhill's superior."

Lashley paused thoughtfully and then asked, "Will that be all, sir?"

She exited the office, went directly out of the building and called Olivia.

Olivia admitted that she had "bounced things off" a former colleague at Nottingham Trent University in England. "She does the same with me. We chat via computer regularly." Her old friend now worked with the

Manchester police. "I wish we had some of the equipment that they have." Olivia didn't think her friend would talk to the press, though.

"You should ask her. The SIO thought I might be the source of a leak."

"Oh, Jesus, no."

"He is going to speak to your boss."

Lashley couldn't help wondering if she had been the only one spoken to and, if so, what others might be thinking. Her glum face reflected her thoughts as she clicked off the phone then immediately and instinctively moved to Crick's name in her contacts and touched it.

"Hey, what's up? I was looking for you on my way out, but I heard you were in with the SIO."

"Can we meet?"

"I am on my way to meet someone, but I can turn around. There is a rum- shop—"

"No, no rum-shop. Too many people know you there, too many interruptions. How about across the road at Relish in Limegrove?"

"I've been in the mall but never in Relish. I go to the open-air bar at the other end. But it's okay, if you paying."

"Okay. I'll head straight over."

"See you there."

———

The uniformed security guard lowered the chain that crossed the entrance to the northern end of the Limegrove car park to permit Crick's entry. He drove directly toward the far end, turned right, stopped and reversed up to a low wall. He got out of his car, looked over the wall at the cemented watercourse over which water flowed from the hills into the hole that was Holetown and into the sea beyond. It was quite dry. He headed into the mall and took the few steps to Relish Epicurea. He pulled the door open and spotted Lashley sitting at the far end. He took in his surrounding as he slowly walked in. It was a shop, a deli, a restaurant. He walked past glass food display cabinets on his right then glanced at the busy food-prep staff before he reached Lashley.

"So this is where you spend your spare time," he said as he pulled out a chair. He sat next to her so that they both faced the entrance.

"No, I don't, but welcome to the new Barbados. It's not like your rum-shops, is it? Everything is neat and tidy. Food is beautifully presented. Isn't the smell of fresh coffee better than stale beer? And there is no noise of dominoes slamming. Instead, there is gentle chatter and warm laughter, no loud drunken singing and arguing...."

"Hey, stop it. Stop sounding like some voice-over on a documentary. We have things to talk about. What you call me for?"

Lashley laughed. Then she became serious. She told him about the conversation with SIO Thomas and that Olivia might have been the un-witting source behind the UK press story. Crick didn't think she should worry about that. Then she spoke about the conversation with Bevaney Wood before she went into the meeting. Crick had an interesting take on Wood's comments.

"Well, if they see us here, it will add fuel to their rumours."

"I don't think they will see us in here, and this is better than us having a whispered conversation at the station."

"Let me tell you something. When they start talking about you like that, it means you are doing some things right. They think you are sepa-rating yourself from the herd, and they want to drag you back. You don't achieve at anything in this country without people bad-talking you. You ain't got a thing to worry 'bout. So don't let that foolish talk bother you. You are on this case because of the good work you have done so far."

Lashley's face relaxed.

"But I am glad you called me because we have to talk about this case. I spoke to the SIO this morning. The photos of the shoe and ankle bracelet have to be published. I don't understand why this hasn't been done. The forensic pathologist from Trinidad has been delayed. We need to do some more digging. I have a meeting with someone but it could be a waste of time. And we need to talk to Summa Dat again. Don't forget that you are coming with me to meet the Doc."

CHAPTER 26

The photos of the shoe and the ankle bracelet hit the papers next morning and produced a flurry of phone calls: a number from anonymous female staff members at Apple Bay and the Hilton Hotel, and some from Barbadian women who rang in the New Year at both hotels and, significantly for the detectives at the Northern Division, the Triple R Bar. But they all said the woman wearing the red shoes was not a redhead. Bridgetown would follow the Hilton lead, but Crick and Lashley would explore what came in on the Triple R and Apple Bay.

The Apple Bay Resort Hotel was the only new major development in St. Lucy since the Arawak Cement Factory was built back in the 1980's. Coming at the beginning of the global recession, it was a most welcome development, both by government and the people of St. Lucy who were happy to see much needed job opportunities in the far north.

It was located on what used to be called Manchineel Bay. The owners of the hotel, weary of the association of manchineel with Eve's poisonous apple, chose to simply call the hotel Apple Bay. In short time, only the locals were still calling the bay by its former name even though there was no official change of name. It was located between Mothers' Day Bay and Greshie Bay. Viewed from atop the bluff, the beach was shaped like a bird in flight with wings of sand and an outcropping of coral that formed its head and neck. The hotel's seventy-six rooms and suites were built in a horseshoe and tiered from the top of the bluff down to the beach.

At about eleven o'clock in the morning, Lashley's Carat stopped at the barrier to the entrance of the property. The security guard cast a wary eye over the two occupants and asked, "Can I help you?"

Crick hated these so-called security barriers at the entrance to a place of leisure. He thought they ran counter to what ought to be the very ethos of hospitality. They sent a message that they wanted to keep out people, not welcome them. And in his opinion they made no real difference from a security point of view.

"Yes, you can raise the bar," said Crick from the front passenger seat.

The security guard eyed Crick and repeated his question. Crick flashed his ID.

Lashley smiled and looked away. Straight ahead, an arrow pointed left to the **Car park**, another pointed right to **Villa Manzanilla**. Lashley turned left.

They entered the open lobby and looked straight out to sea. Standing there, one understood why Apple Bay became an instant hit with tourists from around the world. The bright breezy lobby was minimally but very attractively furnished. Centre stage, straight ahead of them at the far end of the lobby, sat a wide antique coffee table with a large ceramic vase at its centre displaying a beautiful arrangement of hibiscus, ginger lilies and anthurium lilies. Past it was the calm turquoise waters of the Caribbean Sea. It was a view that made a body go *hmmm* and left him feeling warm inside and appreciative of this marriage of nature and architecture. Lashley knelt on one knee, aimed her smartphone and took a photo with the floral arrangement dead centre, framed by stone columns with the shimmering waters as the backdrop. The reception desk was off to the left. Opposite, in front of a large mirror with an antique frame, was an elegantly carved antique-looking wooden desk with three matching chairs. A wooden sign with gold lettering bore the declaration *Guest Services Director*, but it was unmanned, or unwomanned as it turned out, at that moment.

An elegantly uniformed young lady emerged from a back office. She positioned herself at the reception desk and surveyed the lobby, eyes settling on the two police officers. Lashley went over, exchanged greetings and a few words. The Guest Services Director had not noticed the shoes and suggested they speak with the receptionist. The receptionist was off duty Old Year's Night, but her friend Monique was on. She would try to contact Monique. "But there are other people here I could speak to, bar and restaurant staff but particularly the bar manager." Crick asked that the general manager be notified of their presence.

The detectives descended the curved staircase, crossed the dance floor and strolled down to the beach. The number of bodies on the sand indicated that hotel occupancy was good. Guests were everywhere, in various stages of undress, stretched out on lounge chairs, apricating or sheltering in the shade of pink umbrellas, or swimming or at the bar. A jet ski sped by with a young boy in charge and seeming to be having the ride of his life. Two young women in bikinis jogged along the beach. A beach ranger relaxed on a plastic chair in the shade of a sea-grape tree. A man with a briefcase hurried over to the water sports shop at the far end of the beach and engaged the attendant there in seemingly urgent conversation but kept glancing in the direction of the two officers.

Crick and Lashley turned around and took in the property in its entirety. The landscape architect had done a brilliant job of making the white buildings look as if they really belonged there. Pathways wound their way gracefully between buildings. Picturesque gardens of bougainvillea, ixora, atria, frangipani, oleander, hibiscus and other tropical flora embraced buildings, edged pathways and lawns. It appeared as if they had been able to retain some of the original vegetation as well: tall coconut palms, mahoe, shack-shack, sea-grape, and of course manchineel (with a band of red paint at eye level circling the trunks to warn of the danger of the trees' toxicity; even the drops from the trees after it rained caused acid burns) looked like they had always been there. A sense of good taste, an appreciation of nature, pervaded. No wonder a travel writer called the place "a tropical wonder." At the top and to the left they could see a mansion with Grecian columns, very different from the architecture of the hotel. It smacked of a rich man's folly.

"Coloured," sometimes shortened to "Cully," was one of those tongue-in-cheek euphemisms of a Bajan nickname that described a person who was proper-black. In new bajelect writing, it was sometimes spelt "Kullard." It was friendly when used among friends, unlike "Blackard," which was denigratory when used by anyone. Jeffrey Burke was a smart-looking figure of a man. His very pronounced jaw muscles were an extra dimension to a handsome face, and with his ready smile, buffed physique, smooth coal-coloured skin and jovial personality, Lashley thought she understood why the receptionist had said, "Talk to Kullard if you want to find out anything about women in this hotel."

Jeffrey Burke invited Crick and Lashley into his tiny office behind the main bar in the hotel. "You might be undressed, but you got police write all over you. Better to talk in private," he said, smiling. There was a dimple in his right cheek.

Constable Lashley laughed at the use of the bajelect term undressed to describe plainclothes police.

Jeffrey Burke said he didn't recognise the shoe or jewellery, but he recognised Brianna's photograph instantly.

"Cute girl. I haven't seen her for a while. I know her as Anna. She and another girl used to hang out at the beach here." He smiled, the sinkhole in his right cheek appeared. He pushed the photo back across the table to Crick.

"She used to lime on this beach regular. She is Jammer's girlfriend. He came to the beach sometimes with her, and over Christmas with another girl, Kathy with a K, as she used to say. The three of them had dinner in our seafood restaurant one night. You people must know Jammer."

Jeffrey Burke stopped and Crick asked, "Why would we know Jammer?"

"Well, people say he is a drug dealer. I don't know, I stay clear of them kind of people. I into women, not drugs."

"Were you into her?" asked Crick.

"No, there was nothing between us, just a casual friendship. It's my job. I'm a professional friend." Smile and sinkhole reappeared. "No, man, we just used to talk."

"What did you talk about?" Lashley asked.

"What we talk 'bout? We talk 'bout the weather, New York, how much she loved Barbados."

"She have any other friends here?" Crick asked.

"She was friendly to everybody but was close to the water sports guy, Sollie, and she became very friendly with some people who were here Christmas, New Year's time on a big yacht, especially the girlfriend of the big man, Mr. Briggs. He owned the yacht. Anna, Kathy, and sometimes Anna boyfriend used to go on the yacht pretty regular, daytime, night-time. Sollie used to carry them out."

"What was Mr. Briggs' girlfriend's name?" asked Crick.

"What was the girlfriend's name? Tandy. I didn't know her last name."

"What colour was Tandy's hair?" asked Lashley.

"What colour was her hair? Tandy was a blond."

"Why do you repeat every question before answering?" asked Lashley.

"Why do I repeat....?" Kullard laughed.

———

The security chief's air-conditioned office was located at the back of the checkpoint at the entrance to the hotel. Contacted by radio, he agreed to meet the detectives there. The chief, Victor Applewhaite, was a former soldier, an ex- member of the Barbados Defence Force. He was a youthful-looking fifty with something of a flat-top, sides close-shaved. It was difficult to see his eyes behind his prescription sunglasses.

"Yes, I remember the girl, Anna. She is very friendly," he said. "If she see any of my guards in Speightstown, she always greet them. One of my fellows tell me she belong to the man called Jammer. One of our guards who live in Broomfield seems to know Jammer very well. He ain't here right now, he working nights this week. She was also friendly with Sollie, the water sports man."

"Is information on all vehicles entering the property logged?" asked Lashley.

"If they come through the gate, yes. We record the vehicle number as well as the name of the driver. But a lot of local people come to the beach through the woods to the south of the property. That land does not belong to the hotel."

"Can I have a look at your security log?" asked Crick.

The big blue dog-eared book looked out of place at the Apple Bay Hotel, where lawns and gardens were all so well managed and the front-desk staff could be models in a photo shoot. The search revealed no entries for Brianna Davis or Jamar Richards.

"Chief, let us have contact numbers for your security guard from Broomfield. I also need information on all of the guards who were on duty Old Year's Night," said Crick, looking over his shoulder as they exited. He turned to Lashley. "Let's talk to this water sports guy. His name keeps getting mentioned."

They headed back down the curved staircase under the gaze of beach-attired, or barely attired, hotel guests, perhaps curious at the sight of two fully clothed persons who were not in hotel uniform. They turned left along the beachfront pathway and headed for the water sports hut and asked the lone occupant for Sollie. The young man in the hut pointed to the swiftly moving, noisy, twin-engine speedboat dragging a female on one ski, a hundred meters offshore. The man with the briefcase spotted earlier from above fidgeted and looked out to sea.

"When Sollie come in, call me. We'll be at the bar," said Crick. He then looked the man with the briefcase up and down. "Excuse me. You have a license to sell on this beach?"

"You see me selling anybody anything? But look at my crosses today, though, nuh?"

"We don't want to look at your crosses, we want to see what is in the briefcase," said Lashley.

"That is none of your business, young lady. You have a warrant for this?"

A uniformed bellman interrupted. The receptionist wanted to have a word with them. She said it was important.

"We'll be right up," said Crick.

As he was leaving, he said to the man with the briefcase: "We will have to continue this discussion another time."

"I can't understand. Wunnuh ain't see me selling nothing to nobody. Why wunnuh don't go and look for who kill that redhead lady instead of harassing people who trying to make a little living? Wunnuh always want to make the small man life miserable. People getting kill, and you want to know what in my case. Lord have mercy."

The man with the briefcase smiled with his eyes as the two officers sped away.

"You handle yourself real good, Summa Dat," said the water sports attendant.

"I ain't frighten for them so, you know," replied Summa Dat, flinging off a dismissive hand and letting out a long steupse.

Crick and Lashley dashed along the pathway next to the beach, crossed the dance floor and ran up the stairs. The receptionist, a woman whose name tag said Gayle, called out to Lashley with some degree of excitement. Lashley and Crick went to her and learned through a whisper that she had spoken to her colleague, Monique, who not only recognised the shoe but also remembered the woman wearing them.

Gayle excitedly told them she had her colleague, Monique, who was on duty Old Year's Night, holding on the phone. They spoke to Monique, who told them that it was a girl called Anna. She was with a man called Jammer.

"We had a bit of a bassa-bassa down here Old Year's Night. I hear that she got slapped by her boyfriend down by the dance floor. All I know is that he came up the stairs dragging her, more or less, and she was sobbing. She said something to him, which I didn't hear, but I heard him say, 'Don't tell me no lies. I saw you.' And then she said, 'I told you I did not want to come here.' And he said, 'That is why I brought you.' And then they were out the door."

"Only problem, Sergeant, is that she is not a redhead. We may just have two women wearing similar shoes. We are no closer," said Lashley.

"Not necessarily. She could have made a gift of the shoes. Or, as you say, there were simply more than one woman with red shoes. But every time we seem to be finding our path, it branches off. We are still looking for a name for our body. But Immigration's missing woman is connected to Jammer."

Crick became broody for a moment.

"What's that nose of yours telling you, Sergeant?"

"Quite a lot. Kullard did not say a thing about the Old Year's Night incident with Anna. All the reports on sightings of the shoes have come from women. The only man we believe to have recognised the shoe is Arman. I think we should head back down to the beach and arrest Summa Dat."

"Dis is harassment," yelled Summa Dat as Crick demanded that he open his briefcase.

"Open it!"

Crick peeked into the briefcase, gripped Summa Dat's free arm and said out loud, "Come le' we go to Holetown."

Crick ushered Summa Dat into the back seat of Lashley's Carat, sat next to him, and as soon as the door was shut and Lashley drove off, said: "Thanks for telling us about Arman and Jammer, but we need to know more. What happened Old Year's Night?"

Summa Dat looked out of the car window. "I don't know. All I can tell you is that Jammer and he girl left the Triple R about eleven o'clock and come back two hours later, but they didn't come inside the bar. They got a bedroom at the back and they went in there. She friend, the one that they call Kathy, went in the bedroom and we hear screaming. We could hear some shouting, but with the music we couldn't make out what anybody was saying. A few minutes later, Jammer come out and get Arman and the two o' them went in the back. The party was hopping, so nobody ain't really pay them no mind. About half hour later, Jammer come back in the party, but every now and again he going back to the bedroom. We didn't see the two girls after that, nor Arman."

"You sure you ain't got nothing else to tell us?" asked Lashley.

"Well, Arman limousine drive out just before Jammer come back in the party."

"Who was in it, who was driving it?" asked Crick.

"I don't know. The windows dark, man. I just know that it left."

"Did you see Arman again?" asked Lashley.

Summa Dat hesitated then said, "I don't think so...."

Just then, Crick's phone jingled. It was DC Moore.

There had been a development. Einstein Skinner's dead body was discovered on a beach in St. Lucy.

The body had been spotted by neighbourhood kids on a morning ramble in the far north of the parish. The wooded cliff near to their homes was their normal play area. It was also a popular park for picnickers on public holidays or moonlit nights and anytime for lovers.

Crick decided to leave the scene to Moore and Mason so that he could continue questioning Summa Dat. "You can update me later," he told Moore.

He clicked off. "Einstein Skinner's body just washed ashore on a beach in St. Lucy with a bullet in his head," he announced.

"Lord hav'is mercy," said Summa Dat. "Styne is my good, good friend."

"You mean was your good friend. I am sorry. You really have to tell us everything, now. You wouldn't happen to know the last name of the other woman, Anna's friend Kathy?" asked Lashley, more urgently.

"No."

"You could remember when you first saw her?" asked Crick.

"I think I see she just before Christmas.... Styne gone, just so.... Lord hav'is mercy."

Crick picked up his cell phone and called Immigration. "I need to know if there was a Kathy somebody on the departure manifest of Mr. Briggs' yacht when it left Barbados on January First."

Lashley slowed as she turned into the Holetown Police Station car park and took a quick look over her shoulder at Crick.

Crick told whoever it was on the other end of the phone, "I only got a first name, man, Kathy with a K, could be plain Kathy, or Katherine or Katrina, Katerina...you get where I am going.... She arrived around Christmas and may have departed on the yacht.... Alright, do your best."

Crick hung up. "Who else was there that night?"

"Man, the place was ram pack with people."

"Who might have known what went on in that bedroom?" asked Lashley.

"The only body that went back there was Styne, the barman, my friend, but he didn't stay long. He come back pretty quick."

As they exited the vehicle, Summa Dat tapped Crick's arm. "Skipper, you could let me get away with this little bit a thing, you know. It ain't much."

"I ain't got a clue what you talking 'bout, man. But if I don't get some solid information out o' you when we get in the station, I will do a thorough inspection of that briefcase of yours."

"Well, we ain't got to go inside. The girl Anna that you looking for, I hear that she left on the big yacht New Year's Day."

The trio stopped walking. Crick's eyes and then Lashley's focused on Summa Dat standing between them.

"You sure 'bout that?" said Crick.

"I ain't see she. I only hear she went out on a speedboat early in the morning. Sollie, the water sports man, carry she out and mussee get some money to keep he mouth shut."

Crick turned to Lashley, who was staring at him, both knowing what the other was thinking.

"You got anything else to tell me, Summa Dat?" asked Crick.

"No, man. Not a thing else."

"Why didn't you tell us this before?" asked Lashley.

Summa Dat steupsed. "You is the detective, not me. I is a man just trying to make a lil' living off the beach. Do wunnuh work before more people get kill.... Styne gone, just so.... I can't believe it."

They let him go, and Lashley coughed up the bus fare he demanded to get him back to his place of work, as Summa Dat put it. They walked quickly into the station and headed for the SIO's office.

"We are looking for the wrong victim," said Crick before they sat in SIO Thomas' office. They brought The Chief up to date.

"You had better call your man at Immigration again, Sergeant. You get answers from there more quickly than I. We need to see who was on that passenger manifest the day that yacht departed. And we need to know the yacht's next port of call and who was on the manifest when it arrived.

I will have the American authorities contacted. You should get back up to Apple Bay, talk to hotel security and that water sports man."

"Sir, Einstein Skinner is dead because we cut him loose so that we could pretend that we had nothing on him. But somehow word must have gotten out that he was compromised. Remember that the raid on Arman's grandmother's house was leaked. If we go back to Apple Bay now, that could put my source in danger. I believe what he told me, we don't need confirmation from hotel security or the water sports man at this stage. The water sports man will simply deny any knowledge of the matter. I will call Immigration again, and if Kathy whatever-her-name was is on the yacht manifest, we should bring in Jammer for questioning, simple as dat."

SIO Thomas nodded. "Point taken, Sergeant. And I will try to find out where the yacht's next port of call was. There was no Kathy on our list of overstays. And why was she not missed?

"Sir, it seems likely that the body from the well is Kathy and that Brianna left on the Briggs yacht, using Kathy's passport and then switching back to Brianna after the next port of call," said Lashley.

"That is just what I am thinking. I will have Jammer picked up for questioning," said the SIO.

"Good," said Crick. "Sir, right now, I would like to get up to St. Lucy. Moore is already up there."

On the way out, Crick said to Lashley that, after Cove Bay, he wanted to go see the Doc. He and Lashley got into Crick's car and headed to St. Lucy. Once in the car, Crick explained further that, at critical times, he would call the Doc, who always helped him to understand situations, to clarify matters. "When I need to talk to a big brain, this is the man I talk to."

Crick pulled out his cell phone, made the call. "Artifus Crick here, sir. May I come and see you...? Yes, sir, in a couple hours."

CHAPTER 27

The beach below the cliff was small, and the surrounding rocks and flora made it picturesque and intimate. A concrete staircase had recently been added to improve access to and from the beach.

According to Moore, the youngest child had been the first to see the body and called out, "Looka' that man lying down on the beach." An older child interpreted the unnatural positioning of the body and declared, "He look dead." They all raced home.

Three men had accompanied the children back to the edge of the cliff. They looked around for signs of other persons or anything unusual and, seeing none, two of the men proceeded slowly down the newly built staircase. They walked around the body, not wanting to touch it but trying to see if they recognised the man who lay there. One man looked upward to the adult who had remained at the top with the children and signalled to him, rocking his hand back and forth, a little finger to his mouth and a thumb to his ear. The man on top pulled a cell phone out of his pocket and pressed some numbers.

It didn't take long for the police to arrive from the nearby Crab Hill station. They made their way through a throng of people from the surrounding areas and immediately directed all those on the beach to vacate and head topside.

The two officers inspected the body, turned it over to get a better look at the face. It was swollen and bruised, but to one of the officers still recognisable.

"Christ!" he said to his colleague.

He tried his radio but was unable to communicate from below the cliff. He ran up the stairs and tried his radio again. He reached Crab Hill.

"The body is a barman from the Triple R. He get shoot. There is a bullet hole over his left ear. He's been in the water, and nobody here heard any gunshots. Must have been shot somewhere else and dumped in the sea. He either get beat bad or the rocks out there mash him up. I could hardly recognise his face."

Moore had interviewed the first responders, the children who first saw the body and the adults who called it in. Mason had focused on the other people gathered.

Family members of Einstein Skinner arrived. The bartender's mother, to whom, according to one of the observers, he had never been close in life, now wept over him in death. A policeman tried to console her. Her wailing bounced off the rocks and echoed through the casuarinas on top of the cliff to be heard by people still in their houses in the nearby village. On the cliff top, heads bowed, mothers held their bellies, in a primeval show of empathy.

The Crime Scene Crew arrived, took lots of photos and agreed with the initial assessment that the body had washed ashore.

Just after Crick and Lashley arrived, a woman appeared with three friends. The police tried to stop them from descending the staircase. "I have to see him," one woman insisted, emphatic.

"And who are you?" asked Moore.

"I am Konjit, his princess. He is the father of my two children. He was my Negus."

They let her through but not her friends. She ran down the stairs, holding the hem of her long skirt with one hand, the other hand sliding along the top of the concrete safety rail, long dreadlocks bouncing behind her as she descended. The detectives followed. She embraced his mother then knelt by the body, lifted its head and spoke to the corpse as if it were a living being. "If it is war they want, it is war they will get. This is not the end, my sweet." She wept. "I will avenge your death, so help me, Jah."

The Three Sisters funeral home team waited patiently before removing the body. Princess Konjit and those who accompanied her started a chant as the body was brought up and placed in the hearse.

Lashley decided to have a word with Princess Konjit. "We overheard what you said and have to caution you not to do anything foolish. This is a matter for the police."

"Police? Wunnuh too busy looking for who kill the white woman in the well. I don't expect nothing from Babylon. I and I can take care of this."

She spun away and moved off, entourage in her wake.

After the body was taken away and family and friends of Einstein Skinner had left, Crick phoned SIO Thomas. Thomas said he would ask the Coastal Zone Management Unit to assist with a calculation of tidal movement to see if they could identify where the body was dropped into the water. In the meantime, he asked officers from both Crab Hill and Prickett's to question communities along the northern coast to see if anyone had heard or seen anything.

Crick told Mason and Moore to join the uniformed officers questioning the local communities. He and Lashley left for the Doc's house.

By the time they reached, they were getting feedback that uniformed officers had spoken to a resident near to Cluffs who said that he had heard what could have been a gunshot around 01:30 and that a vehicle had sped away from the area a short time after. He hadn't seen the vehicle, but it could have been an SUV from the heavy sound it made. "It was an automatic. I could tell from the gear change it was an automatic transmission."

On further investigation, others in that area corroborated the report. But if anyone had the curiosity to have a look at the speeding vehicle, they weren't saying.

"We have a probable crime scene for Einstein Skinner's murder," Crick said to Lashley, putting away his phone.

They walked up the front steps of the old bungalow where a frail-looking old man with a boyish smile sat in a rocking chair, gently rocking and waiting on them. He rose and welcomed the two detectives. "And who is this beautiful young lady?" he asked.

"She is Detective Constable Lashley. She is working with me on the case of the body from Prickett's well. I understand you were there that morning the redhead lady was discovered, and I trust your powers of observation more than those of the other witnesses, and even my own. We believe that we are about to identify the woman but have a problem with the colour of her hair. Is it possible that it is not really red?"

The old man thought for a moment then leaned over toward Lashley, his brow wrinkled a bit. "I saw red hair, too." He paused, as if mulling over his answer. "But there is possible explanation."

"What is that, sir?"

"Do you know that mummies have red hair?"

"No, I didn't. You mean collectively? Wouldn't that be a bit odd?"

"No, it's not odd at all. It's all to do with the two types of melanin in hair. In the damp conditions of that well, the eumelanin in her hair would have oxidized, leaving the pheomelanin, the red pigment. Two hundred feet down in a well in the tropics, her hair would have changed to a reddish colour. Egyptian mummies go through the same change."

"Are you serious?" asked Crick.

"Oh, very serious indeed."

"Oh, my, God," said Lashley. "Why didn't our analysts think of this? Please explain that to me again."

The Doc carefully repeated the explanation of the two types of melanin that make up the pigmentation of hair and what happens to them in certain conditions. "Down in that well, the change would have taken place quite quickly. Her hair would have faded to red."

Crick moved away from his teacher and made a call to Superintendent Thomas. Lashley was soon at his heels. After he hung up, he turned to her and said, "I wish we knew this from the beginning."

"Yes, but we were completely unaware of this Kathy woman. We would still have been looking for Brianna. Tell me something. We haven't heard anything from the tappers on information about Jammer's cell phone, have we?"

Crick noted that Lashley now had no qualms about the ethics of this practice. He would bring it up with her another time.

"No, but I can tell you that we will, by the time I meet with the chief tomorrow morning. He will also be working on getting a positive ID on the body and tracing the movements of Brianna after she left Barbados. My contact at Immigration confirmed that the immigration process for yacht passengers simply involved collecting the manifest and checking the passports. The passengers and crew were not individually processed. So Brianna could get on a private yacht here with some other person's passport. But she could not get on an airplane or re-enter the US with it. So she had to make the switch before the yacht entered a US port."

"One thing. It was Brianna who was wearing the red shoes at Apple Bay, Old Year's Night?"

"I was thinking about that, too. It will all come out in the wash, I am sure.... They could both have had red shoes. It's going to be a busy day tomorrow. It's been a long one already. You can head home after we get back to the station," said Crick.

"I am staying with you, if you don't mind," replied Lashley.

"Alright, then. The SIO is waiting for me back at the station."

————

"We haven't located Jammer yet. His residence is under observation. We will have a presence at Einstein Skinner's funeral, whenever it takes place," said the SIO. "We will put in some mourners of our own, take photos and listen in on conversations."

"These people will not talk around strangers, sir," said Crick.

"I know that. So we will have a very visible presence, which will serve to distract from our discreet presence," responded the SIO. "Our mourner must be someone with a legitimate reason to be there or accompany such a person."

"We need someone who grew up with Skinner, a childhood acquaintance, but one who is on the straight and narrow, obviously," said Crick.

Ever since there was a fusillade at a funeral in the parish of St. Thomas some years ago, the police kept an eye on gangster funerals. It was usually a visible presence, but this time they needed to be under the radar as well.

"We will team up with the Task Force. Have a van and a police car outside the cemetery. And we need to find at least one mourner for inside the church and at the graveside. I am betting that Arman will come to prove his loyalty to his childhood friend."

"Arman would be crazy to attend. He must know that we consider him a suspect, too," said Crick.

"That's an additional reason why he is hiding. But if he turns up, we need to be there to bring him in for questioning."

"Sir, can we discuss Brianna Davis and this Kathy?" asked Lashley.

Crick answered his jingling phone, listened, pulled out his notebook and wrote.

"That was my Immigration contact. Kathy with a K is a Kathy Drummond. Arrived here on December Seventeenth, by air, for a three-week stay, and left on the yacht *Giro Mondo* on January First. Or rather her name was on the manifest of passengers departing on that ship. The US authorities have been brought up to date and are investigating from their end. She had listed a south coast hotel as her intended address and not Jammer's residence."

"What was the next port of call for the yacht, sir?" asked Crick.

"I was just about to ask the same question," said Lashley.

"Antigua."

"Here is how it looks like it went down to me, Chief. Jammer beats up his woman, Brianna, then takes her to the Triple R. Her friend, this Kathy, gets into a fight with Jammer and gets killed. Then Arman puts her body in his limousine and dumps her in Prickett's well."

"But why didn't Jammer take Brianna home and clean her up there?" asked Lashley.

"He instinctively went to his friend for help," said the SIO.

"He probably didn't want her blood at his place, or it was a spur of the moment decision," said Crick.

"I wonder how he would have persuaded the person in charge of the yacht to take Brianna on board with someone else's passport?" asked Lashley.

"That is a good question," said Thomas.

"But if Jammer was supplying these people from the yacht with cocaine, that could give him some leverage," said Crick.

"Putting her on that yacht was very clever. It would mean that she could get off at another island and, using her own passport, go anywhere. She would be just another overstay here who we couldn't locate," said the SIO.

"And he might have succeeded, had not for that careless throw of the body," said Lashley.

"That time of New Year's morning, Arman was probably quite drunk.... I know I was," said Crick to some snickers.

"I wonder why he didn't kill Brianna as well and put them both in the well," said Lashley.

SIO Thomas' hand moved quickly to the ringing telephone on his desk. He picked it up, spoke briefly then hung up.

"Two bits of information. The forensic pathologist will be here day after tomorrow. And Einstein Skinner's common-law wife is requesting his body so that he can be buried by tomorrow in keeping with their religious faith, whatever that is."

"We have to move fast. That funeral is a priority, now. We'll move on Arman and Jammer after the funeral," said the SIO.

CHAPTER 28

The lady in black sat in the passenger seat of Randolph Turton's old car. Randolph was a cousin of detective Sergeant Steve Bryan from the Bridgetown division and grew up near to Einstein Skinner, his mother and siblings. They attended primary school together.

If Lashley was nervous, she didn't show it. She almost hadn't recognised herself in the mirror. The shoulder-length hair and makeup that the fussy stylist had so carefully added to her appearance worked well. When he placed on her head the wide-brim black hat with its downward curved rim and the veil plus the rather large pair of dark glasses, she agreed with him. "Girl, when I finish with you, you could fool your own mother."

The SIO had taken a lot of convincing that the woman who had taken down Arman in the police station should risk attending his barman's funeral. But the makeup artist had persuaded him that he could make her look like a different person, and he delivered.

There had been no newspaper or radio announcement of Skinner's funeral. The detectives came by the information from discreet enquiries until they located which of the six St. Lucy funeral homes had taken on the job.

They arrived at the little wooden church hall as planned, fifteen minutes before the service. On the way in, Randolph Turton spoke to a number of persons who recognised him. He introduced Lashley to one person as his cousin from America.

"How you all doin'?" asked Lashley in her best imitation of a New York accent. They moved on, and Lashley caught an oblique view of the person they had just spoken to addressing the ear of another person and pointing in her direction.

The casket was closed, so there was not the usual viewing. They found seating mid-church. The service got underway and, after some lusty gospel singing, the preacher paced up and down the platform, microphone in hand. "Matthew, Chapter Seven, Verse One. Judge not lest ye be judged," he shouted, voice straining.

Suddenly a woman in a long white robe, a huge wrap on her head containing her dreadlocks, made her way purposefully from the front row up to the platform and approached the preacher. Princess Konjit curled one hand around the wrist holding the microphone; with her other hand, she removed the mike from the preacher's grasp, leaving him not only mike-less but speechless, a look of total bemusement on his face.

"Comrades," she said, "one of our generals has fallen. But the struggle continues." She looked around at the congregation, waited for some murmuring to abate. "...We are not just fighting Babylon but also our own greedy, ignorant sons of bitches who want everything for themselves. They think that because they come from the big country, that they can rule over us small-island people. They are mistaken. The soldiers of Jah's army must rise up and deal with this threat. Our survival depends on it."

The congregation responded with a mixture of murmurs and yells. It was a shock and a revelation to DC Lashley, exposure to a type that she still had the greatest of difficulty understanding. Acerbity had enveloped the church hall. She was shaken. Nothing in her upbringing, in her Princess Royal College education or Police Training School, prepared her for the kind of nausea she felt. She thought of the young man at court in Bridgetown and worried about her island. As she left the church hall holding on to Randolph Turton's arm, people assuming her demeanour indicated distress offered her their sympathy. Among the mourners, she did not recognise the face she had memorised from the photo back at the station, Jammer.

They drove slowly to the graveyard at the St. Andrew Parish Church and parked on the sidewalk behind a queue of other cars. The graveyard sloped upward away from the road and was bordered on the far side by a wooded area. The grave was located at the upper end near the woods.

Several mourners were taking photos with their cell phones. Lashley joined them. Some stared at her, wondering who she was, it seemed to Lashley. When she noticed this, she would lean a bit closer to Randolph Turton, the local man.

They opened the casket for a final farewell, and a group of mourners clustered around, all women. The woman who had spoken in the church was at the head of the casket. She pressed fingers to her lips, parted them and inserted the fingers. She then wiped her hand across his mouth, back and forth, leaving a layer of moisture on the dead man's lips. The queen completed her ritual with a gentle lingering kiss on his lips. Her demeanour had completely changed from the rabid demagogue in the church, threatening revenge on her partner's murderer, to that of grieving widow. She stepped back, and the undertaker moved in to close the casket.

Lashley looked toward the police car on the outside; the two blue-suited Task Force officers were checking the road in both directions. She missed the raised hand that held the undertaker back from closing the casket. There was a little hum and heads turned toward a figure making loping strides over the short distance to the graveside. The women parted to permit the man to approach the casket. The man leaned over the corpse and spoke to it, then turned and ran back up the slope and into the woods.

The two large blue-suited policemen from the van across the road vaulted over the graveyard wall and sprinted in among graves toward the woods on the far side. They heard a motorcycle, a scrambler from the sound, start up and roar off. The two policemen turned and ran back to their Jeep. One tripped and fell on top of a grave. He got right up to jeers from the funeral goers. The lead officer jumped into the Suzuki and the engine sprang to life. He felt the weight on the steering wheel as soon as he accelerated. "Jesus Christ, this ain't no time for a blasted flat tyre."

The unmarked police vehicle sped past them.

The second officer was in front of the vehicle now looking down. "Not one flat tyre, two," he shouted. He heard laughter behind him and turned around. The laughter stopped. He walked over to the small gathering. People started to disperse. One man stood his ground, a big man.

"So you think it funny," said the officer. "Empty yuh pockets."

The man stared at the officer, the two of them squared off like two prized cocks sizing up each other.

"You think because you got a gun I frighten for you?"

"Empty your pockets or I will hold you up by your ankles and shake the knife out of your pocket," the officer said slowly, his face intent.

"You see me with a knife?" asked the man with contempt.

The other officer came alongside. The man looked at the two officers, glanced quickly behind him, then stuck his hands in his pockets and pulled them out. They were empty. He smiled, turned and walked away.

"Arman was here, but he got away, Sergeant," said Lashley into her cell phone as soon as she sat in the car. "What happened? Well, he was better prepared than we were. He watched the funeral from the woods. He was there the whole time. He had a scrambler stashed in the woods, just beyond the graveyard. There was no way the boys could catch him, even if he hadn't had someone slash their front tyres. Randolph says that there are dirt tracks through the woods. I have to admit, this man is slick, Sergeant. But I did my job. I have pictures for you. I will send them to you shortly."

CHAPTER 29

The call from SIO Thomas to Crick was short. "This crap would not have happened if you were there and in charge." He criticised every aspect of the operation. "Were there enough men to do the job? Did they really think that this man would have driven up the main road and walked through the cemetery gates? What did they mean by the police keeping a respectful distance?" Even after his phone call to Crick, SIO Thomas was still in a rage at his meeting with Crick the next morning.

"Sergeant Crick, the commissioner is not happy with us. Arman made us look like amateurs. We have just raised his stock in the eyes of the criminal community and their sympathisers. His name is ringing throughout the blocks. We have created a hero and at the same time managed to make us a laughing stock. On Facebook, there are pictures of our Task Force officers running through the graveyard and one flat out on top of a grave. Arman is now our Number One priority. He is about to find out something about this police force. We can take any amount of criticism. But we will not be made fun of. Find the bastard. Turn the north of this island upside down if you have to. Search the caves, the bays, the halls; use all your informants and stake out all the known drug dealers. Follow them wherever they go. *Do not let them sell an ounce.* See how long they will hold out."

Policemen on foot, policemen on bicycles, on motorcycles, in their Suzuki Jeeps, and in unmarked cars headed north. There were uniformed policemen, plainclothes policemen, Task Force officers, even island constables were roped into the occupation of St. Lucy. From Paul's point to

North Point to Clinketts, they were everywhere. They were in Free Hill, Hope, Content and Friendship, and in Spring Hall, Coconut Hall, Rock Hall, Checker Hall, Bright Hall, Friendly Hall and Chance Hall, in Pie Corner, Mount Gay, Fustic, Ragged Point, Cuckold's Point, Great Head, Blackbird Rock, Half Moon Fort, Cowpen, Blacksage Alley, Graveyard and Pico Tenerife. They even pulled Jammer's surveillance to assist with finding Arman.

Coast Guard vessels patrolled the St. Lucy peninsula. Drug smugglers in the north were spoiled for landing options because there were so many bays up there. There was River Bay, Granny's Bay, Nan's Bay, Abbotts Bay, Hangman's Bay, Gent's Bay, Little Bay, Mothers Day Bay, Ladders Bay, Goat House Bay, Laycock's Bay, Kings Bay, Apple Bay, and more.

It wasn't long before the police hotline was buzzing with tips on the whereabouts of Arman. The first three proved fruitless and Crick surmised, "He is the source of these tips. He is sending us on a wild goose chase."

"I don't think he is anywhere in the north," opined Lashley.

———

Prints of Lashley's photos and those of the officer in the unmarked car taken at the funeral lay scattered across the table in Station Sergeant Derwen Griffith's office. Lashley and Crick were at the Greenfield Police Station surrounded by officers who were examining photos and calling out names. Bridgetown had already identified some of the funeral attendees with criminal records.

Sergeant Griffith tapped on a number of the photographs. "Shekira Broomes...Zoriah Griffith, no family to me...Delbert Alleyne.... But hey, looka' Raj, also known as Packa. He is a Guyanese. Here legally, came in early on in the construction boom. I can't remember his last name right now, but I won't forget his nickname."

"Why?" asked Lashley.

"Could be after Kerry Packer who started World Series Cricket," said Crick.

Sergeant Griffith looked at the men then at Lashley. "Close your ears, miss." He turned to Crick. "His job back in Georgetown was packing cocaine into condoms and stuffing them into girls' pussies, the mules."

Lashley's eyes widened for a moment. "Gosh, the poor, silly souls who take on these risks. What drives them, greed or need, or not understanding the difference?"

"If you didn't understand that difference, you were truly desperate," said Crick.

"We were asked by the Drug Squad to keep an eye on him after they heard about him from the Guyana police and from a mule at Dodds who was caught at the airport. Apparently, his uncle is a big man in Guyana, a serious criminal, even suspected of murders. He tried to rope him into the business, but Packa couldn't handle the violence. His heart was never in it and in the end he fled Guyana."

"His heart wasn't in it. Only his hand," said Mason, snickering.

In the late 1990's, Barbados experienced a building boom and with it a shortage of skilled construction workers. The void was filled by imported contract workers, primarily Guyanese, economic refugees fleeing a country that still had not recovered from the devastation of two decades of Forbes Burnham's autocratic regime. The former president took the most resource-rich country in the Caribbean Commonwealth, a potential breadbasket, and made it into a basket case. Many Guyanese fled to wherever in the world they could find acceptance, taking their skills and talents. Those remaining lived in survival mode and in fear of their own government.

"Packa is a first-class tiler, a subcontractor for big construction companies," said Station Sergeant Griffith. "He does a lot of work in luxury villas. He did all of the bathrooms when they were building Apple Bay Hotel. My young nephew works with him sometimes. He is my sister son, down in Bright Hall. As far as I was aware, he had no known association with the drug trade here… until now. I mean, he has a legitimate job and I hear he makes good money."

Sergeant Griffith seemed puzzled.

"Sarge, you don't resign from organised crime," said Crick.

"I know, I know that, but this is a hard-working man. I know he has been trying to stay on the straight and narrow. He lives in Bourbon."

The station sergeant went to a filing cabinet, pulled out a file and held it up.

"Packa real name is…Raj…endra…Karam…chand."

The station sergeant had no idea where Mr. Karamchand was working. "But it wouldn't be difficult to find out. I will ask my sister to ask her son."

"I want to talk to your sister son," said Crick.

"That won't be no problem. I will get his mother to call him and tell him to call you."

———

After a lengthy phone conversation about Raj Karamchand with Station Sergeant Griffith's nephew, Crick and Lashley headed to Prickett's Plantation, where, they had been informed, Raj Karamchand was putting the finishing touches to the renovation of the old great house, which had been purchased by an expat millionaire. They paused near the entrance of the plantation yard then pulled over and parked in the shade of a fine example of a bearded fig tree. There were two other shade trees nearby, a flamboyant and a large Bajan cherry tree.

They took in the surroundings. The bare, rounded wall of an old windmill, looking like a giant cone with its top sawed off, was on the mound over to the left, perfectly positioned to catch the wind. It was scaffolded right up to the top. Not far from the mill wall was the old boiling house built of thick rubble walls, different-sized coral-stones carefully set on top each other and bound with the strongest mortar available at the time of its construction. The thick walls had withstood many a hurricane. Judging from its whitish colour and blade marks, the stonework had obviously been recently exposed, its plaster removed to show off its original beauty and to set it back into its time period. Over and at some distance to his right was a building Crick thought must have been the overseer's quarters and directly ahead at the end of a driveway lined with statuesque palms was the great house. Crick left the vehicle in the shade of the bearded fig and the two detectives walked toward the great house.

"Somebody must have paid big bucks for this," said Lashley.

"There is no real money in sugar anymore. Plantations have to use their other assets to generate income, and there are people from over and away who will pay incredible amounts to come live in Barbados," replied Crick.

"I wonder what they are going to do with the mill," said Lashley.

"Hm. I don't know, but they are going to start pretty soon. I imagine they will do something with the overseer's quarters as well. They could end up with a great upscale community, here. Now listen to me: I will bring Raj outside for a private chat. I want you to go on the opposite side of the house and record the conversation of those in the house."

"Sergeant, that would be illegal and not useable in court," observed Lashley.

"You hear me say anything about court? I want to know what his workmen say when Raj is out of the room. You may take out your notebook and write out their conversation in long hand if you choose. But I —want—no, this police force *wants* to have that information."

Lashley did not reply. Nearing the great house they could better see the impressive entrance with its balustered staircase and wide veranda. They walked in the direction of the voices of men, mixed with light hammering, coming from the ground floor of the great house. Lashley walked around to the right side of the building and Crick entered through the open door opposite. On his right was an elegant mahogany staircase, brand new, judging from its light colouring. There were three men working in the room.

The workers stopped tapping tiles with their rubber mallets and looked up at the man who had just entered.

"I am looking for Raj Kar-ma-chand," said Crick, directly addressing the only East Indian man in the room.

The East Indian stared at Crick. He uncrouched slowly, inspected Crick from head to toe to head, and slowly said, "Karamchand, Karamchand." The other two men in the room stopped work and they, too, inspected Crick.

"I would like to have a word with you, in private," said Crick.

"And who are you and what you want to talk to me 'bout?" asked Raj Karamchand.

"I am a policeman. My name is Sergeant Crick. If you would prefer to speak in front of these men, that's cool with me." Classic Chet Thomas response. It produced the desired result.

Raj straightened. "Leh we go outside, man." And in a louder voice as he walked out, still wearing his kneepads, "I got my papers, man, I legal."

Raj continued walking until he was well out of earshot of the two workmen. He stopped next to a royal palm tree.

"What you want me for, officer?" he asked.

"You been to any funerals lately, Raj?" Crick asked.

Raj took time to think about his answer and to study the man asking the question.

"I guess you wouldn't ask me that question if you didn't already know the answer. Yes, I went to Styne funeral. I used to drink at the Triple R and get to know him. He was a friendly fellow. So when he get kill, I decide to go and pay my last respects, nothing wrong with that."

Crick looked out over the cane-fields, at the canes bending with the light breeze. "Apart from friendly chats in the bar, did you talk about anything else?"

"Not really, maybe a bit about life in Guyana."

"Did you ever tell him why you left Guyana?" Crick looked back at Raj as he asked the question. He waited for an answer and was about to speak when Raj said:

"I come here to work 'cause that is where the work was."

"That don't really answer my question, so let me ask you another one. He didn't even ask you to do any packing for his boss?"

Raj's eyes narrowed. He was silent for a moment. He raised his voice.

"I don't get involve in nothing so in Barbados, man. I come here to get away from that kind of thing. Don't try and put me in nothing so, man."

"So you met a bartender, had a few casual discussions with him, and you felt obliged to go to his funeral. You never had any discussions about anything else?"

"No, Officer."

"What about his boss, Arman, did you talk to him, too?"

"Occasionally, just about this, that and the other. Man talk, you know?"

"So I guess he didn't want you to work on the house that he is planning to build."

The narrowed eyes returned and focused on Crick's face. Crick saw a pensive Raj searching for a response.

"I think he did mention something, but it was nothing concrete. You know what I mean?" He shrugged his shoulders.

"It was concrete enough for you to visit the site with him, though. Did he ever visit you here at Prickett's?"

Raj fidgeted, scratched his head and looked away. "Let me tell you something, Sergeant. I am a legal resident of Barbados. I ain't commit no crime, and I don't have to answer your questions. Please let me go back and do my work."

Raj didn't wait for the permission he sought. He started to walk away slowly.

Crick let him walk a few steps then called after him. "Packa, if you don't intend to cooperate, there is no point me asking you any more questions. But let me tell you something. We know you hook up with Jammer."

It was a test.

Raj stopped, turned and said: "You wrong, man. I barely know Jammer. I meet him near my work one day and then I see him a couple times in the Triple R. That is all."

"So you just butt up pun Jammer, just so?

"Look, when we was working on Apple Bay, my men used to take their lunch on the beach. One day I was working in a ground-floor room. I don't take no lunch break. All of a sudden, I hear this Yankee voice swearing loud, loud and threatening my men so I rush on to the beach.... It was Jammer. First time I ever see he. I step in and pacify the situation. Next time I see he was in the Triple R."

"What had Jammer so angry that day?"

Raj chuckled. "Jammer had a woman with him. They ran up and down the beach for some time, then they started to do some warm-down exercises. The woman had on a little bikini and at some point she bend over to touch she toes. The fellows had a rear view and started out whistling and shouting. Jammer went for them and blow he top. You know, he is a powerful-looking man and he was ready to take on three men. I stop a serious fight that day, because my fellows was ready to do battle."

Raj seemed to relax somewhat as he looked at Crick. He then turned, walked off quickly and entered the building. Crick leaned casually against the palm tree and waited for Lashley. He remained there for a little while, taking in the surroundings, thoughts churning through his mind. Lashley appeared at the corner of the great house. Crick held up his hand. She stopped in her tracks. Raj reappeared at the door, saw Crick and turned back into the building. Shortly after, the tapping of rubber mallets resumed and Crick suddenly realised that sound had been absent ever since he entered the building and called Raj's name. He made a call on his cell phone. He was still on the phone when Constable Lashley rounded the corner and headed toward him, a look of excitement on her face. She pointed to her iPhone and said, "I've got Raj on tape!"

"What about the workmen?"

"Yes, I got them, too, but you will be particularly interested in Raj."

The two officers walked to their vehicle, drove off and continued their conversation.

"He made two phone calls when he got back into the building. He was just on the other side of the wall, away from the men. I could hear everything he said. I think one call was to Jammer. He told him the police had connected the two of them. He said he wanted nothing more to do with him. *'I give you contacts in Guyana and I finish.'*"

"What about the other call?"

"It may have been to someone in Guyana or to another Guyanese. His accent became more pronounced. He spoke quickly, and I didn't understand everything he was saying. But I gathered that he was telling them what had just taken place and how it had him *aaffset*."

Crick laughed at her attempted Guyanese pronunciation of offset.

"The person's name sounded like Byer. He kept telling him to listen and he kept referring to some 'mudda skunt policeman.' My Guyanese dialect is limited, but I guessed he was referring to you, Sergeant."

"Byer could be a name or nickname, but he could have been talking to his buyer," said Crick. "We'll put the tappers on him and he will find out about this mudda skunt policeman."

Lashley played the taped conversation for Crick.

"This guy knows Prickett's Plantation, he knows Apple Bay Hotel. He's got to be a person of interest," she said "While you were talking to Raj outside, the two men in the building were speculating on the nature of the discussion. They didn't buy Raj's attempt to imply that the police visit was an Immigration matter. The Guyanese man said it probably had to do with Raj's family in Guyana who were big in the business but that Raj don't deal with them.... Station Sergeant Griffith's relative may have Raj's cell phone number."

"Call Griffith and ask him," said Crick. "We'll also see if we can get a search warrant for Packa's house."

———

"He is not talking to his buyer or anyone called Byer. He is talking to his *baiya*, his brother. It's an Indo-Guyanese dialect word of Hindi origin," said Charley Rampersaud, a Guyanese native, Economics lecturer at the Cave Hill campus of the University of the West Indies, and neighbour to

Crick's brother in Paradise Heights, where many Cave Hill teachers lived. Charley Rampersaud had just listened to the recording played to him on the telephone by Crick. "He is severing all relationship with his brother. He wants nothing more to do with him."

"I understood that part of the conversation. I just wanted to know who this *baiya* might be. Thanks."

Sounds like this guy really wants to make a break, thought Crick as he left Charley's home.

CHAPTER 30

Crick was right about it being a busy day. Crick and Lashley met with SIO Thomas, who had plenty of news for them. "Dr. Sharma, the forensic pathologist, arrived on the early Caribbean Airways flight from Trinidad and has set to work immediately. I have secured search warrants for the residences of Arman and Jammer and the Triple R Bar. A forensic team and the Drug Squad will be a part of the operation. The raids will be simultaneous, at a time to be confirmed."

By midday, there was confirmation that Brianna Davis had arrived in New York on January Eighth on a flight from Antigua and that the US authorities were now trying to locate her.

Mason brought in Solomon Isaiah Branch, better known as Sollie, the water sports operator from Apple Bay. Two policemen from the Crab Hill station brought in Charles Chase, the security guard from Apple Bay who was on beach patrol in the early hours of the morning of January First. Moore had interviewed the security guard's neighbours, who revealed that in early January he had given up his day job, started to dress fashionably, and he had bought a motorcycle. Crick and Lashley interviewed Charles Chase first.

"How much you pay for them sneakers, Charles?" asked Crick.

Charles Chase did not answer.

"And how much did you pay for the motorcycle?" asked Lashley.

Charles Chase did not respond.

"New Year's morning, early, early, Sollie carry out the woman you know as Anna to the big yacht. You were there. You saw them. How much did they pay you not to do your job and enter it into the security log and not tell anyone about it, like you trying to do right now?" asked Crick.

Charles Chase looked out the window, either trying to pretend that the two detectives were not there or looking for a suitable response from somewhere out there.

Lashley rose from her seat, walked around, and positioned herself between Chase and the window. She leaned over and locked eyes with him. "I am going to ask you another question. If the answer to my question is yes, do not answer." She paused then asked, "Do you understand?"

Charles Chase's eyes narrowed, his jaw muscles tightened. He stared at Lashley and said nothing.

"Very good, you understood me, so that is a yes."

Charles Chase frowned.

"Did you see Sollie early in the morning of January First?"

Charles Chase just stared at Lashley.

"Good, that's a yes. We are making progress here. Did you see him take a woman in his speedboat out to the big yacht?"

Charles Chase looked away from Lashley.

Crick joined in and asked: "Now, can we tell Jammer that you told us you saw Sollie take a woman out to the yacht New Year's morning?"

Charles Chase finally reacted. He waved a pointed finger from Crick to Lashley and back again. He shook his head from side to side and said, "The two o' wunnuh mad as shite, yuh know."

"I glad you know. Cause before you leave here, Jammer will know everything you told us, unless you do some real talking."

"And I know you would do that, too, Crick. I hear 'bout you already.... New Year's morning, I see two cars coming through the woods and stop near the water sports shop. I approach to find out wha' goin' on. They did not enter the hotel property, so I didn't see why I should make an entry in the security log book."

"OK. But did you see who the people were and where they went?" asked Lashley.

"Yes, but since they were not on the hotel property, the beach is public, you know...."

Crick grabbed Chase's chair, chucked him on to the ground and stood over him, the chair raised in both hands. "Listen, asshole. We want to know who the fuck was in those cars and where they went."

Lashley visibly tensed, ready to move if the chair started to descend, but Chase raised both his hands and spoke hurriedly. "It was Jammer, the girl Anna, and Sollie, the water sports man. They went out to the yacht."

The chair came down slowly. "And how much Jammer pay you to keep your mouth shut?" demanded Crick.

"Jammer shove some money in my hand and tell me get from 'bout here, and don't ever let he hear that I see he down here, so I disappear."

"Did you see anything else, anyone else?" asked Lashley quietly.

"No. I just see Sollie and Jammer. There was somebody else in Jammer car, but I ain't got a clue who it was. I left from 'bout there. I hear when the speedboat pull off, but I couldn't see nothing."

"How much money did Jammer pay you? Enough for you to buy a motorcycle, some new clothes and do some partying, right?" Crick asked.

"I was saving for that motorcycle every sence...when I left the beach, I went straight and check the money. It was two thousand US dollars."

"That is a lot of money. Is that about two months pay for you?" Lashley did not wait for an answer, she continued: "You must have known that something big was happening."

"I have nothing more to say, nothing, you understand? And you could answer me or you could don't answer me...."

He got up from the ground and headed for the door, looking over his shoulder sheepishly.

Lashley glanced at Crick, who nodded and said, "Let him go."

When the door was closed, she asked, "Would you really have hit him with that chair?"

"Oh, no...it would have left marks."

Lashley studied Crick's face. Crick smiled and walked toward the door. "I am going to get Sollie," he said.

Ahead of Crick, Sollie strolled in, bowlegged, hair turned reddish by overexposure to sun and sea. Lashley picked up the chair, invited him to sit, and he did.

"Welcome to the forget-room, Sollie," said Crick. "I call it the forget-room because when people come in here and you ask them a question, all of a sudden they just can't remember a thing. What you had for breakfast this morning, Sollie?"

Sollie smiled.

"I had some conch fritters and bakes. What you had, Crick?"

"I can't remember. I guess I been in this room too long. But you just come in, so you can remember everything. Right?"

Sollie laughed.

Lashley took over. "Early morning of New Year's Day, you took a certain young lady out to a big yacht. We would like you to confirm who she was and how much Jammer paid you to take her."

Sollie leaned back in his chair, closed his eyes, massaged the back of his head with his left hand, and played a bit of piano on the desk with the fingers of his right hand. He opened his eyes. "It was nothing unusual. I take people out to yachts all the time."

"But we only want to know who you took out New Year's morning," said Crick.

"It was Anna. It wasn't the first time I took her out to that yacht.... She used to go on that yacht regular. She and she friend Kathy spend a lot of time with people from that yacht...and Jammer didn't have to pay me, this was a normal thing."

SIO Thomas appeared and signalled to Crick and Lashley. They followed him until he turned and spoke.

"Thought you would like to know. There is a little DNA evidence in the boot of Arman's limo. If the blood matches the girl's from the well, we have him."

"We just have to find him," remarked Lashley.

"Anything on Jammer, sir?"

"Nothing. He has disappeared. But I expect that Arman will want to do a deal."

CHAPTER 31

Early next morning, Crick was wide awake, lying in bed, thinking, in the comfort of his daughter's house. That part of St. Thomas was a quiet, middle- and upper-income neighbourhood of attractively designed houses, mostly old-fashioned Barbadian-style bungalows, so-called wall-houses, with little patios occupying part, or in some cases the entire length, of the front portion of the house. The original inhabitants, old money and lighter skinned, lived at the top, the far end of the cul-de-sac, with views looking all the way to Bridgetown and out to sea. The newer residents, new money and darker skinned, lived either side of the entrance near the main road. The neighbours all knew each other and were respectful friends. They greeted each other whenever their paths crossed, but their neighbourliness didn't extend to home visits between the old and new residents, at least among the adults.

Crick's daughter and her accountant husband lived near the main road. It was just after four o'clock in the morning when a burst of gunfire erupted, raking the front of the house with bullets from end to end. The rapid gunfire followed by the screech of protesting tyres tearing at tarmac penetrated the night and completely awoke the neighbourhood. Dogs barked, lights came on, curtains slid aside, and people peeked. The sound of breaking glass and falling objects in the house were reduced to tinkles and bumps in the night by the confusion outside.

Crick rolled out of bed and grabbed his Glock 17 from under his pillow. He raced barefoot out of his room and into the corridor.

He heard the door to Joycelyn's bedroom open behind him, and he heard screams coming from his granddaughter's room. They all headed in her direction.

"Don't worry," shouted Crick. "She couldn't make that much noise if she was hurt bad."

Tassa's door opened and she came out running. Her father pushed Crick aside and scooped her up in his arms. Her mother wept.

"They will pay for this," said Crick, throwing his arms around all three of them. He spoke the words with frightening calm.

They looked outward through broken windows and saw that lights were on in houses across the street. The phone rang. Joycelyn picked up and told the caller that they were fine. She quickly ended the conversation, said it was a neighbour.

Crick dashed back in the bedroom, picked up his cell phone and called Superintendent Thomas. He quickly yet coolly recounted the events that had just occurred and asked for protection to be sent to his wife and children. He called his wife.

"Yes, I know what time it is. Listen, it's important. A police detail is on the way to you. Somebody come and shoot up Joycelyn's house a short time ago. Nobody hurt, though. You and the boys know what to do. I will be there soon."

The sound of sirens rent the air soon after as a quick response unit arrived. Some neighbours came over. Other police vehicles rolled in. Within a short time, the neighbourhood and household were saturated with police activity. Forensics were busy collecting shells, digging bullets out of walls, taking photos, neighbours were being interviewed. Some officers were just there for solidarity.

Crick felt that murder was not the objective of the attack but could have easily been the result if he or Joycelyn and her family happened to be on their feet at that time of the morning. The criminal mind focused on two things, one being the task at hand, the other, getting away with the crime; it never thinks of the wider consequences of its actions. Crick intended to make sure there were consequences. *Take me on, but don't threaten my family.*

Lashley called.

"They are just trying to scare me, girl. But they don't know who they dealing with. They will find out, though. They could have killed me or my daughter or grandchild. And you think you can rehabilitate these callous animals? You will learn. Things 'bout to get rough, now, but don't worry, don't worry...."

He paused for a few moments while Lashley told him that they would bring the perpetrators to justice, then said, "I got to cut you short. Right now, my concern is about my family. I got to go and look after them."

Crick walked briskly back to his bedroom. He placed a chair in front of the wardrobe, stood on the chair, and reached into the cupboard at the top. He grabbed the handle of the cricket bat protruding from the bag of cricket gear and drew down the bag. He placed the bag on the bed, pulled out the pair of cricket pads, pulled apart the Velcro ties that held the pads together, and picked up the Kel-Tec KSG shotgun nestled there. He turned the shotgun over, examined it, then placed it back between the pads and into the cricket bag. The shotgun was Crick's personal weapon. He, like some other detectives, felt the need for extra fire power as a response to increased gun crime. Unlike Mason, Crick brought out his shotgun only in times of perceived great danger. Mason never left home without his.

Crick dressed and exited the bedroom, carrying the bag. He was confronted by Gary, his hands raised.

"We have to talk, AD. I think you should leave. We can't be safe with you here."

"I sorry, man, I real sorry 'bout this...I have to hurry off now. I'll come back later. We can talk then. I sorry, man."

"Are you going to play cricket today, granddad?" asked Tassa, coming out of the kitchen with a plastic cup in her hand with some pinkish liquid in it and on her lips. A still terrified-looking Joycelyn stood behind the girl.

"Yes," said Crick, looking down at Tassa.

"Are you going to hit some sixes?"

"Oh, —yes—oh, yes."

"You are leaving, aren't you?" said Joycelyn.

"How do you know?" asked Crick.

"You have your cricket gear," she replied.

Crick embraced Joycelyn. "I am sorry. I will come back for my things later."

"Daddy, you are so cool, it frightens me."

Crick did not respond. He headed for the door. He opened his car boot and deposited his gear. He drove out of the neighbourhood and once he was in open countryside he pulled over to the side of the road and cut the engine. He stared at nothing for a moment then his right hand rose up then came crashing down on the steering wheel. He yelled at the top of his voice. "*God blind wunnuh. God blind wunnuh.*" He sat back in his seat, cracked knuckles on one hand then the other. His phone rang. It was Mason. He was fired up and told Crick not to worry. "We will bring justice to these bastards."

Crick started his engine and headed to West Terrace. When he turned into his old avenue, he saw two police cars and he recognised his brother-in-law's car. He spoke to the four policemen, briefly thanking them. Neighbours were there, in and outside his house. They greeted Crick on his way in and parted the way for him to greet his wife and children. He hugged Natalie and the boys. He asked Natalie to come with him to the bedroom; they needed to talk.

"I am moving back home. Now, if you don't want me in your bed, I understand. The boys can move in together and free up a bedroom for me. But I will be here. I will protect you and the boys."

She held on tight, squeezed him hard. Tears ran down her cheeks. "Come home, my husband. We have a lot to talk about, but this is where you should be."

CHAPTER 32

The Force rallied around Crick with repeated assurances. "We will catch these bastards. You don't worry." The consensus was that the attack on his home was the work of either Arman or Jammer or both. The two were advertised in the newspapers as wanted men.

SIO Thomas started to speak, "The commissioner is putting all available resources into finding whoever shot up your house last night. Tips are beginning to come in...," when his phone rang. Crick watched Thomas' face as it responded to whatever he was hearing. Thomas hung up and said, "A car has been discovered at the bottom of a gully in St. Lucy by some off-road enthusiasts on one of their weekend adventures. It was Jammer's car."

"Was he in it?"

"No, just the car. Forensics will give it a going over."

"I have some calls to make, sir."

Crick went to his desk and phoned Summa Dat. "What's the word out there?"

Summa Dat disclosed that Arman was hiding from Jammer. The two had fallen out big time. That is all he knew.

Crick was about to make another call when his cell phone rang. He answered, listened and then said, "Now, Bobby, the last time you gave me a tip it was a complete waste of time. You sure you ain't trying to stir up trouble for somebody whose woman you want.... Look, if you waste police time on this, there will be consequences, you understand?"

They heard the motor of the boat splutter then roar, then idle and then slowly accelerate as it eased away from its berth in the careenage. The fishing yacht, *Lion of the sea*, rocked as it rode the waves into deeper waters. There was an exchange of radio communication. Two Barbados Coast Guard Boston Whalers rapidly roared in from opposite directions and cut across the bow of the *Lion of the sea*. The combined noise of the engines of the three boats drowned out the instructions broadcast from one of the Boston Whalers. The captain of the *Lion of the sea*, his boat hemmed in, had no choice but to rapidly slow down and bring his craft to a stop. He stretched his hands upward and outward when he saw the weaponry pointed in his direction.

A third coast guard boat arrived, a bigger boat, a Damen Stan patrol vessel, with more men on board, including Task Force officers. They boarded the *Lion of the sea*. The captain raised three fingers then inverted his hand pointing downward.

"Come out with your hands up, Arman," an officer bellowed. He came out, arms raised. Two other men followed him. Crick watched from the third boat. He had pleaded with SIO Thomas to be on this mission. Thomas had finally agreed but restricted Crick to the role of witness and if only absolutely necessary could he become a participant.

———

Arman Arrested ran the headline in the *Daily Standard*. According to the report, "Two Barbados Coast Guard Boston Whalers intercepted the fishing boat *Lion of the Sea* as it exited the careenage just after 11 last night. Task Force Officers with weapons drawn rapidly boarded the deep-sea fishing boat, where they discovered Ronald Russell, a.k.a. Arman. Russell, wanted in connection with the murder of Einstein Skinner, was arrested. According to the police, a suitcase with two guns, a quantity of cocaine and over one hundred thousand dollars in cash were recovered. Two other men on the boat were also arrested."

Crick folded the newspaper and reflected on the call he had from Bobby telling him that a friend who had a deep-sea fishing boat in the careenage informed him of another boat doing a private charter to St. Lucia the following night. Somebody was paying over the top for the trip. He owed Bobby a drink and the details of Arman's capture.

Crick took the newspaper with him to the interview room, where Arman was sitting in contemplative isolation.

"We got a lot to talk about, Arman. First thing I want to know. You shoot up my daughter house? You threaten the lives of my child and my grandchild?"

"Not me, Crick. I ain't into that kind 'o thing, man, not me, not me."

"You know, I believe you. I don't think you would have the fucking balls to try that with me."

The door opened and SIO Thomas appeared. He beckoned to Crick. "My directive to you is that you ask no questions about the attack on your house," he whispered. "We do that investigation. This is a precondition for you to continue questioning this man. If you go down this road again, I will pull you out, understand?"

Crick and Thomas locked eyes. Crick nodded, said, "Understood, sir," and returned to Arman. He threw the newspaper on the desk.

"You made the front page, Arman. You famous, now...."

Arman looked at the newspaper then raised his head and said, "I ain't kill Styne, not me. You got the wrong man."

"Who is the right man, then?"

"I ain't know. Styne was my buddy, my boyhood friend. I risk my life to go to his funeral, man."

"We got a couple other things to talk about. Leh we start with why you kill Kathy Drummond"

Arman looked perplexed. "Kathy who?"

"The woman you threw in Prickett's well, New Year's morning."

"Huh. I ain't got a clue what you talking 'bout, man."

"Well, let me lay things out for you. A bunch of people saw Kathy Drummond at the Triple R on Old Year's Night. At some point, she went to the bedroom at the back. People heard her scream. Witnesses saw you drive out the limo soon after. Kathy Drummond was not seen again until her body was recovered from Prickett's well. And her DNA is in the boot of the limo. How would you explain that?"

"I don't have to explain nothing to you, Crick. I want my lawyer."

"I don't blame you, because if I was caught red-handed with guns and dope and facing two murder charges...."

"I ain't kill nobody, man. Who you think I kill?"

"Your barman who rat on you, tell us where you keep your dope and guns."

"You telling lies. Styne was my friend from the time we was little boys. We went to primary school together. He wouldn't rat on me. And I didn't kill him."

"And I suppose you going tell me that you didn't kill Kathy Drummond."

"I tell you I ain't kill nobody, man," Arman shouted.

"Well, whoever dropped her in that well killed her. She wasn't dead yet," shouted Crick.

Arman's head dropped and he supported it with his hands clapped over his ears.

"You hear me, man. She was not dead when you dropped her in that well."

Lashley entered the room. Arman's head popped up and he stared at Lashley, trying his best to say with a look, "I ain't frighten for you, you know."

Lashley stared back at him, placed both hands on the desk and leaned over. "Ronald, is it that you love this person so much, or are you so afraid of him that you are willing to spend the next thirty years in jail?"

"I have nothing to say. I just want to call my lawyer."

"In that case, I won't ask you any more questions...but let me recap the situation for you. Kathy's DNA is in the boot of your limo, which you were seen driving away from the Triple R New Year's morning. You would have a hell of a time convincing a jury that you didn't kill Kathy. Your lawyer can only try to get you some sort of a deal. But it won't be as good a deal as you will get if you tell us the truth right now."

Arman looked from Crick to Lashley and back again. "What deal you talking 'bout?"

"It's either murder or a lesser charge. You get to choose. If you want to convince us that we are wrong about you killing Kathy, then tell us why you put her in the boot of your car and dumped her body," said Crick.

Long tears slowly rolled down Arman's face. He placed his arms on the table, lowered his head and rested it on them. He stayed like that for a couple of minutes then looked up and spoke. "I only drive her to the well and drop her in, but I ain't kill she, man."

"Then who was it who struck her on the side of her head?" said Lashley.

"*That was Jammer....* When Kathy see the blood on Anna face, she start screaming and turn and attack Jammer. He pick up a lamp off the table and swing it. She try to duck away, but he was swingin' down too fast. The bottom of the lamp was heavy, and Jammer is a powerful man, real strong. She collapse, drop dead on the spot. We was panicking, and then Jammer come up with a plan. If we could make Kathy body disappear, he could talk the man from the yacht into letting Anna use Kathy passport to exit the island. He say that the Immigration people only check the passports but not the people on yachts. Anna would get off in Antigua, destroy Kathy passport and spend a week there to recover before going back to the US using her real passport. This way they would not be looking for Kathy in Barbados, they would be looking for her in Antigua...and she would never be found. Anna wasn't as bad as she looked. But, man, she was real, real upset about Kathy. Before we took Kathy body to the car, Anna take off them red shoes and put them on Kathy feet. She say Kathy did love those shoes."

"Tell me something. Why would Mr. Briggs cooperate with Jammer on this?" asked Lashley.

Arman thought about his response. "The two of them know each other from New York and have friends in common. Jammer is a man know some real big-up people."

"Another question. Why was no one looking for Kathy?" Lashley asked.

"I ain't sure. She was an escort, travelled the world. But she took Christmas off to spend with Anna. She joked that her clients spend Christmas with their families I don't know anything about her. I guess Anna could invent some story for Kathy friends. But anyway, they would be looking in Antigua, not here."

"Why wouldn't Anna tell the police in the US what happened to her good friend?" asked Lashley.

"You serious? You don't know Jammer. He got contacts back in the States would rub her out. All it would take is a single phone call."

"And where is Jammer?" asked Crick.

"He left 'bout here, man."

"Where did he go?" asked Lashley.

"I don't know. He must be somewhere in South or Central America by now. He could be in Mexico, Colombia, Venezuela...or Brazil. If you find him, let me know, 'cause I in all this trouble because of him. He panic when he hear 'bout the shoe and he blame me for that. I had to tell he that it is he who kill she, not me. He get real vex and tell me if this thing reach him, I would pay, big time. I know exactly what he mean. He was threatening me."

"So what would you do if we found him?" asked Lashley.

"I would catspraddle his ass—that's what.... But I in jail. I can't do he nothing, now."

"I can understand your feelings, Ronald. In addition to the charges for possession of firearms, ammunition, drugs and money laundering, we are going to charge you with being an accessory to murder and that could be upgraded to murder when the forensic pathologist submits his report. That is a lot of trouble in truth," said Crick.

Crick and Lashley left the interview room. SIO Thomas said, "Good job. Let's go into my office."

They sat and Lashley said, "If he hadn't run, I am not sure that we would have been able to get a conviction for the drugs at Monk's Bay with Einstein Skinner dead. His lawyers would have challenged Skinner's signed statement and, since Arman was not at the bay himself, I-Want's testimony could not connect him. So he needn't have run."

"His lawyers would have had to make a convincing case that Skinner's statement was coerced," said SIO Thomas.

"They would just have to muddy the water enough to create doubt in the jury's mind," said Crick.

"Well, perhaps we'll find out that he had another reason to run," said Lashley.

"Perhaps," said the SIO. "In my experience, some murder cases can take you in many different directions before you nail a culprit. And this is one of those cases."

CHAPTER 33

Crick was having breakfast at home with Natalie and the boys when his cell phone rang. He glanced at the screen and saw that it was Lashley. He answered immediately. "You are up early," he said. He listened for a while then said, "You want to take me for a ride in the country but don't want to say why because I would think you are crazy? That architect fellow who running you down ain't got *your* head kafuffle, I hope."

"God, man. How you know about that?"

"Ah, what I know would surprise you."

An hour later, the two detectives were in Lashley's car heading north.

"When you goin' tell me where we are going and why?"

"We have exhausted our search for the possible means of Jammer sailing out of Barbados. We have checked on the movements of yachts, catamarans, fishing boats, and have come up empty handed. Last night I had a crazy thought. This crazy thought kept bugging me all night, so I just had to call you this morning. You know Arman has been on remand for two weeks, now, and you told me that our prison contacts have said how much he hates Jammer because he insists it was Jammer who killed Einstein Skinner and it was Jammer who messed up his life. Do you remember, when we were questioning him, he said that he would like to catspraddle Jammer?"

"Yes."

"Did you notice the look on his face when he said that? There was a sneer, which I hadn't seen before. And when he added Brazil as a possible place where Jammer might be, for the briefest moment during a time when he had been rather sheepish, he showed a glimpse of cockiness. It came back to me last night. And I thought that had to mean something. Also, on reflection, he gave up Jammer too easily when we questioned him, which meant that he was no longer afraid of a man he knew could have him blown away with just one phone call. And then I thought, Jammer speaks Spanish, not Portuguese. Why would he go to Brazil with all those Spanish-speaking options at his disposal? And I remembered you talking about Millie down in the well."

"So how many wells you planning to search?"

"Just one."

Crick looked away quickly, out the window, thinking, and then said, "This is one hell of a long shot, Lashley."

Lashley glanced over at Crick. He turned and gave her the lizard look, that cocked gaze of curiosity.

"So when might Arman have killed Jammer?"

"He may not have done it himself. At Einstein Skinner's funeral, he delivered a message to Princess Konjit who had sworn revenge on the person who killed her Styne."

"Why you think he in *this* well?"

"Before I called you this morning, I recalled my conversation with Jammer's aunt. So I called her and asked a question: Did she know who Jammer's father was? You know what she told me? 'Jamar father was an overseer at Prickett's Plantation. He is dead, now. Died about ten years ago....' I thought that was very interesting. If Arman knew this, he would have thought that well was the perfect place to dispose of Jammer and he would do it right this time, leave no careless evidence outside the well. It would also be some sort of poetic justice. What have we got to lose, Sergeant? If there is nothing there, we would have had a nice drive in the country."

They turned into the cart-road and bumped along the rocky surface. They made a left at the four-cross intersection and stopped in line with the well. They mashed trash up to the well, Lashley with an impressive-looking flashlight in hand. They both leaned over the stone top and Lashley pointed the beam into the well.

"I see something," they both said simultaneously.

Then Lashley said, "What's the betting that is Jammer?"

"Son of a bitch," said Crick, "son of a bitch."

"But my money would be on Princess Konjit's associates. She called his shot at Einstein's funeral. Looks like you have another case," said Lashley.

"Looks like *we* have another case," said Crick.

Three hours later, a body was pulled out of Prickett's well. It was later confirmed to be that of Jamar Bentham, alias Jammer.

End

ACKNOWLEDGEMENTS

I wish to thank my first-reading crew of Gaga, Fuzz, Mickey and Cripps for their due diligence. Thanks also to Dr. Corin Bailey, criminologist. To Robert Edison Sandiford, my editor, teacher, mentor, supporter, friend, a big thank you. To my colleagues at Writers Ink for their encouragement, I thank you. Thanks also to friends and those readers of my first book, *Facing North—Tales from Bathsheba*, who encouraged me to write a second book.

For cover design, a big thank you to Russell Watson.

Finally, I must thank a few members of the police fraternity, current and former, whose passion for their work and their desire to see the RBPF become an example of a fine modern police force influenced some of the characteristics of this story. I hope that my effort helps their cause, which is our cause.

Made in the USA
Columbia, SC
14 January 2020